THE BOOK OF BRENDAN

THE BOOK OF BRENDAN

Ann Curry

HOLIDAY HOUSE / NEW YORK

© *1989 by Ann Curry*

Originally published in Great Britain by Macmillan Children's Books

First American publication 1990 by Holiday House, Inc.

Printed in the United States of America

Library of Congress Cataloging-in-Publication Data

Curry, Ann.
    The book of Brendan / written by Ann Curry.
        p.   cm.
    Summary: When the evil magician Myrddin appears, determined to sub-
due the monks of Holybury Abbey and the surrounding villages, Father Brendan and his young friends must rely on magical beasts and the help of Arthur,
Guinevere, and Merlin, summoned from their sleep on the Isles of Truth.
    ISBN 0-8234-0803-5
    1. Arthurian romances. [1. Arthur, King—Fiction.   2. Merlin (Legendary
character)—Fiction.   3. Knights and knighthood—Fiction.]   I. Title.
PZ7.C9358Bo   1990   89-36010   CIP   AC
[Fic]—dc20

THE BOOK OF BRENDAN

Chapter One

Elric stood at the top of the gently sloping path which led down to the beach and the Bay of Woden. It was early morning and a heat haze hung over land and sea, making all their colours blend into a mist. It was a Friday in May in the year 725, and Elric had sprinted the short distance from Holybury Abbey to look at the sea and enjoy his freedom before lessons began for the day at the monastery school.

Tall and well-built for his twelve years, Elric had the fair hair and colouring of his Saxon father, and his mother's deep brown Celtic eyes.

As he stood watching the gulls bobbing at the edge of the water, the sun broke through the morning mistiness. Suddenly, he saw a flash of red-gold near a cluster of birds further along the beach. Straining his eyes, he could see a small figure standing among the birds. He ran down the path, but dodged quickly behind some low rocks to have a closer look without being seen. The figure was a small girl, quite alone, and the red-gold was her waist-length hair. He stayed hidden, not wanting to disturb her.

She was standing on the sand with the birds clustering around her feet. As Elric watched, she bent and stroked one of them gently. The others jostled for her attention, and she laughed, touching

1

as many of them as she could. All the while she was murmuring to them in a low voice. Then she started singing sweetly in the same low voice. Her song grew louder, and she quickened the rhythm. Elric watched in amazement, feeling a slight twinge of fear, for the gulls swayed in time to her song. Some of them rose, beating their wings rhythmically, circling around her as though dancing in the air. The song ended and she called to the birds, "Away you go now, I shall come again soon."

She began to walk towards Elric's hiding place. Not wanting to startle her, he slid quickly out of sight to a place where he could climb easily to the top of the low cliffs. Then he made his way back to a point not far from the top of the pathway, where he stood in full view of her as she reached the top. She was small and slight, which made her look a lot younger than Elric. She was dressed in a blue robe and short overmantle. Round her neck was a golden torc, and she had several golden bracelets on her arms. Elric realised that she must be from a nobleman's family.

He bent his head slightly in a formal greeting.

"Good day to you. I am Elric, son of Eadfrid, scribe at the King's court. I am at school with the monks of the Abbey of Holybury."

"Good day. I am Bridget. Avaric, the Thegn of Wodenswood and his lady Ethelburga are my guardians. I must go home now, or my mother, for I call her Mother, will be angry with me."

Thinking of his own young sister and how she never left their home on her own, Elric said, "I had better go with you. You should not be out alone like this."

Bridget stared at him coldly, then angrily tossed her head, saying, "Don't be silly! I came on my pony and I can easily ride home. There is no danger for me." She turned and called in a high-pitched voice, "Here! Bertha! Bertha . . . a . . . a!"

A sleek pony trotted up the coarse grassy slope towards her. She ran to meet it and jumped on to its back, sitting astride like a boy in spite of her long skirt. Elric raised his hand in farewell, feeling a bit cross about the way she had spoken to him.

But she didn't ride away at once. Curiosity about the boy and the school made Bridget ask, "What do you do in school?"

Elric was glad she had not gone. He smiled at her, pleased to tell someone, especially a girl, about the things he was learning.

"We learn to read and write in Latin of course," he boasted. "It is very hard, for we have to study the Scriptures, and Latin poetry. We study History too, and now I am beginning to learn the Greek language."

Bridget was impressed. "I wish I could go to school," she said. Perhaps I shall later. I could go to the nuns and, when I am grown up, I could be a great abbess. I can read Latin, and I can write. My mother teaches me. She and I are Christians, but my father, for I call him Father, Avaric . . . is not."

As Bridget paused, Elric saw that she suddenly looked upset. She bit her lip and sat staring straight ahead, almost as though she might begin to cry. He wondered why. Then he remembered what he had heard from his friend, Chad, who lived in the village close to the abbey. Chad had told him how he had heard his parents talking about the way the people on Avaric's estates were being treated nowadays. They were punished if they were late with payment of their rent, and some had been sold into slavery. This cruel treatment had only begun in the past few months since an important visitor had arrived, and then stayed to live at Avaric's hall.

Elric changed the subject, so that Bridget need not continue to talk about Avaric. "I watched you with the birds. I heard you singing. I have never seen anything like it before! Do they understand you?" He stood beside the pony, looking eagerly at her.

"I don't know," she said thoughtfully, "I love birds, especially the gulls. I've always called to them and played with them. Even when I was small, if I sang they all came to me."

Elric could not help laughing at the way she said, "when I was small", for he thought her very small now. "And aren't you small any more?" he asked, teasing her.

Immediately, he wished he had not said it, for she looked furious. Without another word, she turned Bertha's head and rode away as fast as she could.

"I'm sorry!" he shouted, but the blue figure with flying red-gold hair disappeared into the woods nearby.

*

4

"That was stupid of me," he thought, "for she is nice, and funny! And I wanted to find out more about her way with the birds. Perhaps I might also have heard about this stranger at her guardian's, whose coming has changed things so much."

Standing staring at the spot where she had entered the woods, Elric suddenly realised that he would be late for school. He ran at top speed down the slope, away from the woods towards the back of the abbey. He leaped across the flat stepping stones which formed a path through an area of marshy ground, and hurtled across Long Meadow behind the abbey church, startling the peaceful cows. The church bell began to ring, and Elric remembered with relief that it was St Brendan's Day. There was a service first, before lessons. He slipped into his place and, apart from a frown from Brother Alban, no one noticed him.

Chapter Two

There were twenty boys at the Abbey School. Brother Alban was like their housemaster, keeping an eye on them when they were not in lessons. It wasn't a very strict eye, which was why Elric had been able to slip away to the shore that morning. He had been at the school for a year and was quite happy. Though there were long church services and hard work to be done, there were also games and free time. He had made a good friend, Chad, and he had his own horse, Thunder, which he had brought from home. A few of the boys lived in the village of Holybury, and came to school each day, but most of them, like Elric, were boarders. At Christmas and Easter they went home for quite long visits. At school, they slept in a large wooden dormitory with a thatched roof, and ate their meals with the monks in the main hall.

All the abbey buildings were wooden except for the church, which was made of stone. The monks were very proud of it. It had been a gift from their king, Ini of Wessex, in the early days of his reign. Stonemasons had come from Gaul to supervise the building, and they had brought other craftsmen with them who made stained glass windows. Abbot Benedict had been to Rome and had brought back beautiful altar vessels, books for the school, and many other treasures. There were paintings of scenes from thhe Bible on the walls, and rich embroidered hangings around the sanctuary where the altar stood. The king was getting old now, and there was talk of his giving up the throne to a younger man. Elric knew the king, for his father was in great favour with him. King Ini had consulted Eadfrid in the making of a book of laws for Wessex.

Kneeling beside Chad, Elric could not keep his mind on the singing and the prayers for thinking about the strange scene on the beach. He wondered whether he should tell Chad about it afterwards, but could not decide. Chad would probably say that it was the early morning mist which had made it seem as though the gulls were dancing to the girl's song and that girls always pretended that they could do magical things. By the time the service endeeed and Chad had to nudge him to stand up, Elric was beginning to think that he might have imagined it anyway.

He did not tell Chad, for he spent the rest of the morning with six other boys, struggling with the beginnings of Greek and his friend was a year older in a higher class. By mid-day he had decided not to, for he was told that after the meal he could go and work with Father Brendan, his favourite teacher. Old Father Brendan would be a much better person to tell if he told anyone.

The old monk was known as Brendan the Healer, for he had a special knowledge of the healing powers of herbs and spices. He had cultivated a beautiful herb garden at the monastery, and he made medicines. People from all the surrounding villages came to him when they were ill, or sent for his help.

That afternoon, Father Brendan was in his small writing room in the abbey. He was putting the finishing touches to the final picture of a book. He had been making the book for many years. It contained all he knew about curing illnesses, and his recipes for medicines. He had spent long hours writing with goose-feather quills on the pages made from calfskin. He had decorated the capital letters with wonderful designs. The pages were bordered with flowers and leaves, strange creatures and birds.

Elric loved the Book of Brendan though Father Brendan said that it should not have his name in the title. Elric's father had taught him to write very well before he came to school, and Father Brendan had allowed him to do a little of the writing at the end of the book. Now he stood by the old priest's writing stand and watched him gild the feathers of a bird on the last page. The book had already been stitched together, but Father Brendan was adding a last piece of decoration. The bird was the creamy white of the page. Now Father Brendan gave it a golden beak, gold-tipped wings, and a gilded crest on its head. It was rather like the gulls which wheeled around the abbey, following the ploughs in spring. In the picture it was poised in flight on a background of azure blue, with a border of herbs around it. In its beak was a sprig of rue, which is known as the Herb of Grace.

"That's a strange bird, Father. I remember how you drew it so quickly as though you could see it, though it isn't a real bird. Tell me, please, why you put it at the end of the book? You would not tell me when I asked you before."

The old man sat thinking quietly. Thin and wrinkled, his coarse woollen habit hung loosely on him nowadays, but his brown eyes were still bright, he was brisk and active, and his mind was as alert as ever. After a moment he spoke.

"I have told you, Elric, some of the story of my ancestor Brendan, who was a very holy monk, and who sailed away from Ireland with a group of his monks. As you know, it was no ordinary voyage, for they were guided to the Isles of Truth which lie in the Sea of Faith. They were allowed the privilege of visiting those Isles, which many people say are only legend. Their boat was a curragh made of hides, and do you remember my telling you how they camped on the back of Jasconius, the great sea monster, thinking it was an island? How frightened they were! But St Brendan stayed calm, led them back to their boat, and they sailed away safely."

Elric had heard a lot about St Brendan's voyage from Father Brendan since he came to school, but he never tired of hearing about it again. The old priest would suddenly remember another bit of the story told to him as a boy in Ireland and say that someone ought to write it down. Now Elric wondered what the story had to do with the question he had asked

9

about the bird, so he waited for Father Brendan to continue.

"Now, Elric, here is another part of the story which I have never told you before. St Brendan and his monks came to another island called the Paradise of Birds. As they neared the shore they saw white birds clustered on a tree like thick blossom. They were singing the psalms in praise of the Lord. They sang a great deal better than our abbey choir, my boy . . . so beautifully you might think you were in Heaven. To continue . . . the monks landed, and when the singing ended, one of the birds came to the saint and spoke to him. It told him that the birds were spirits, angels, who had begun to rebel against the Lord before time began. They had not followed the proudest angel, Lucifer, into open rebellion, but had repented before it was too late. They were sent into exile on their island and must remain there until the end of time. Only on Sundays and Feast Days are they given the form of birds."

As he listened to Father Brendan's dreamy voice, Elric gazed at the picture of the bird. Father Brendan looked at it now in a rather puzzled fashion, saying, "A white bird at the end of my book is a remembrance of my St Brendan, I suppose." He gave himself a little shake and said, "Today is St Brendan's Day and the book is finished. It has made me talkative. Old men like me either talk too much or too little. Come, Elric, we must go for our evening meal."

Elric did not answer and, looking at him, the monk realised the boy was staring fixedly at the picture with his eyes wide open. He seemed quite unaware that he had been spoken to.

Father Brendan said, rather sharply, "Elric, what is it, child?" Since he still did not move or answer, the priest gave his shoulder a shake and spoke almost into his ear. "Elric! Do you hear me?" The boy trembled suddenly and turned his head. He then spoke quickly in an excited voice.

"It was fluttering its wings! I could see it as if it were flying! The light was wonderful!"

The old man shut the book. "Enough!" he said harshly. "Come." He got down hurriedly from his stool, and went to the doorway. Elric leaped in front of him, and stood still.

"Please! Please wait, Father! You . . . you understand, don't you? I know you do. You have seen the bird, haven't you, Father? That's why you could draw it. It wasn't just imagination was it? . . . my seeing it I mean?"

Father Brendan looked at him, thoughtfully. Then he spoke. "No, I do not think it was just imagination. At present I do not know what it was, what may be happening, or . . . going to happen." He walked back to the reading stand, opened the book again, and looked at the picture.

"I have not seen it, Elric, as you say you did. I know not how, but when I came to this final page my mind and hand were guided to draw the bird, and even to add the sprig of rue in his beak. You know, my boy, I am a Celt, and I love and believe in the old tales, the legends of my people, but I should not encourage you to do so."

"But I'm half Celtic," Elric said excitedly, "and descended from King Arthur on my mother's side. She has told me stories and taught me your language too, from when I was small. I *want* to believe the old legends."

Father Brendan smiled at him. "We shall see then. For the present it is best not to dwell too much on such things. I do not know what Father Abbot would say!"

He closed the book and they made their way to the main hall, where the whole community gathered for the evening meal before the day boys went home.

In the small room, the Book of Brendan stood on its stand. On the cover a little baboon with a cheeky grin on its face clambered among the stems of flowering herbs. A small two-winged dragon sat on the opposite side of the cover picture, its tail twined among stalks of green ginger. Pennyroyal, coltsfoot, angelica and eyebright were all pictured there, and in the centre was rue, the Herb of Grace. It was believed to act as a defence against witchcraft and to give the gift of sharp-sightedness. Now the sunlight began to fade from the room, but as it did so, instead of the colours on the cover growing dim, they glowed brighter. The book gave off faint gleams of light into the darkening room.

Chapter Three

When Father Brendan and Elric entered the main hall, they separated, for Elric went to sit at the long table set aside for the boys. The monk went to sit at the abbot's table. As Elric sat down beside Chad, he was so silent that his friend asked him, "What is wrong? Have you been in trouble?"

Elric did not hear him. He had not recovered from the wonderful feeling he had had when he was looking at the picture of the bird. He had sensed the blue sky widening and had felt as though he were looking, not at a picture, but through an opening in a wall of darkness. Beyond, all was summer light, and there was the gold-crested bird, trembling and alive. It was coming towards him out of the sky. The spell had been broken when Father Brendan shook him and he had felt a terrible sense of loss in missing the chance to meet the bird.

"You haven't eaten anything, Elric. Are you sick?" Chad's voice broke through his thoughts.

"I'm sorry Chad. No, I'm well. I'd better eat or I will be in trouble." He could not tell Chad what had happened, at least, not yet. He did not understand it anyway. It had been such a strange day. First the girl on the beach with the gulls. Then the bird in the book. Birds! The white bird was rather like a gull. There must be a link. Elric's thoughts began to go round in circles, his supper left untasted until Brother Alban told him sharply not to sit day-dreaming.

Elric ate a bowl of broth and a piece of bread. After this the boys had small flat cakes sweetened with honey, and milk to drink. In the large hall there were two long tables where the monks sat, with an empty table at the end of the hall near the doorway, in case guests or travellers arrived, and the abbot's table facing everyone across the top of the hall. All was quiet apart from the voice of the monk who stood at the lectern reading from the Gospel of St John. Since the weather had been very warm, there was no fire burning on the stone hearth in the centre. It would be lit if the weather turned cold. Then the hall would be smoky, for not all the wood smoke escaped through the hole high in the roof.

Suddenly there was the sound of horsemen outside. Everyone looked up, and Brother Ethelbert stopped reading. There was a loud knocking at the huge doors. Chad whispered, "Do you think they are raiders?"

"Of course not," said Elric. "They've come through the village. Besides, the abbey has the king's protection. No one would dare to raid it."

Father Benedict, the abbot, rose. He was a big man, always quiet in his speech, unless roused by anything he thought to be wrong or unjust. Now he looked a little angry, for the knocking continued very loudly. He strode down the hall and called out in a mighty voice. "Who wishes to enter?"

An equally loud voice answered, "Avaric, Thegn of Wodenswood. I come in peace bringing a sick child who needs medicine."

Hearing this, the abbot swung the heavy wooden bar upwards and opened one of the doors. At the mention of the sick child, Father Brendan had come from the table and now stood beside the abbot. Two men came into the hall together. The broad-shouldered man with the reddish beard was obviously the Thegn. He wore a rich purple cloak fastened with a large golden brooch. The other man was thin and tall. He wore a sober grey cloak with a hood hiding most of his face. Elric felt cold fear as he looked at him. He started to tremble.

"What is it, Elric?" Chad asked him. "I'm sure you must be ill. You are so strange tonight."

Elric controlled himself, and whispered, "Who is that man, Chad?"

"That must be Myrddin," Chad whispered back. "He is very mysterious. Lots of people say he is descended from the great Merlin, and that he is a powerful magician."

The boys dared not say more. Avaric was speaking and everyone was listening. "I have a sick child outside. She is in a fever. Myrddin, my adviser, could cure her I am sure, but my wife wished her to be brought to Brendan the Healer. Where is the man?"

"I am he," said Father Brendan, stepping forward. "The child must be taken inside at once. I will open the infirmary." He hurried out to see that his patient was taken to a smaller separate building which was used as a hospital.

15

Avaric continued to speak. "My wife, as you know, is a Christian, like yourselves. Myrddin and I do not follow your practices. The child, Bridget, is ten years old. She is not our daughter. She is a Briton, but her parents died of the plague when she was small. Her mother was my wife's close friend."

Abbot Benedict had met Avaric at Court, when the king held councils for all the landowners, but the Thegn had never visited the abbey before. Father Benedict had never seen Myrddin until now. He had heard of the gossip about him, but had not listened to it. Now he replied in his usual friendly tone. "All are welcome here, both Christians and non-Christians. We are glad to be of service to our neighbour. Let us hope the little one will soon be well. Your wife is with her of course?"

"Yes, and if you can accommodate them, they had better stay until Bridget is better."

"Certainly. We shall see that they are comfortable in the infirmary. Now, you must have some refreshment. We drink only water, but mead can be brought for our guests."

The abbot led Avaric and Myrddin to his own table. One of the brothers went outside, returning with a dozen men who had come with Avaric. They were given the guest table at the end of the hall. At the boys' table, Elric sat motionless, watching the visitors. He had been amazed to hear that it was Bridget who was so sick. He had seen her only that morning. Still, he knew that fevers could strike quickly, and he felt sorry for her. He was not surprised that Avaric's wife did not trust Myrddin to

16

make her well. Although he knew that there should be no reason to be afraid, ever since Myrddin had entered the hall, it seemed to Elric that the peaceful atmosphere had gone.

But the monastery was a safe place. Wessex was peaceful now. Long ago, Arthur, the great leader of the Britons, had made his last stand against the Saxons at the Battle of Camlann and been mortally wounded. But that was over two hundred years ago, and things were settled now. Elric felt Chad tugging at his sleeve. He turned to him and Chad pointed to the doorway. Father Brendan was beckoning him. Elric said quietly to Brother Alban, "Father Brendan wants me. May I go?"

Brother Alban nodded. Elric glanced towards Myrddin. He had kept his hood up even though he was in company and sat silent as Avaric talked to the abbot. Somehow, Elric thought it would be better to try to slip away unnoticed. Quickly and silently, he faded into the shadows by the side wall and went out by the side door. He ran swiftly to the hospital.

Elric stopped in the doorway to peer through the hangings which covered the inner entrance. He saw Bridget, sitting up on a low couch. Father Brendan and a rather tall, stately lady were standing beside her.

"But she's not sick!" he thought to himself. "Surely Father Brendan can't have cured her already." Elric stepped into the room and Father Brendan called him over. The lady, Avaric's wife, Ethelburga, had a kind face, but she looked very

17

anxious. Her hair was brown and braided, and she wore a gold circlet across her forehead. She wore a fine red cloak. Elric looked at Bridget. She was watching him and she pulled a face. She certainly didn't look ill! They all sat down on the couch next to Bridget.

"Who is this boy?" Ethelburga asked.

"Elric, son of Eadfrid. His father is scribe at the King's Court. Speak freely, my lady, for he can be trusted to tell no one what he hears." Looking at Father Brendan's face, Elric was puzzled, and excited, for the priest looked so serious.

Ethleburga began to speak, clearly, but quickly, afraid that they might be interrupted.

"As you can see, Bridget is not ill, but I wanted an excuse to come here. For months now, my husband has been under the influence of Myrddin, and it is an evil influence. Perhaps you have heard that Myrddin is supposed to be a descendant of Merlin, Arthur's teacher. I do not know if that is true. He appeared at our hall one evening when the men were feasting. He said he was a travelling minstrel. He entertained the company with songs of the old Saxon heroes, and performed clever magical tricks. My husband was fascinated by him. They talked together for most of the night. Since then it is as though Avaric cannot think for himself. He talks to me about increasing his power and his lands. He tells me that one day he will be ruler of all the seven kingdoms. It is madness. We have a good estate and plenty of wealth. Times are peaceful now. These ideas will cause fighting, killing and much misery. Since Myrddin came to our home, our people are miserable. They are afraid of him and Avaric allows him to give all the orders. Now I fear that something terrible is going to happen, and I had to warn you." The others did not take their eyes off her face as she continued, "I overheard Myrddin telling Avaric that the time had come to make their first moves, and his plan is to begin by taking over this abbey and its rich lands!"

Father Brendan gasped in disbelief. "What! But that is impossible. They could not do it. We have the special protection of the king."

Ethelburga shook her head. "Did you not know that King Ini has left to go on a pilgrimage to Rome? He is old and the journey is long and dangerous. He may never return. Oh, Father Brendan, I should not have come here bringing Myrddin and my husband with me! When I pretended that Bridget needed to come here, I thought they would not trouble to come with me, but send me with one or two of the men. It is only a short distance. But Myrddin insisted that they come, and brought a dozen men. Now I am afraid that I may have placed you all in great danger tonight."

"Fear not, my lady," Father Brendan comforted her. "Nothing will happen tonight. Myrddin merely took the chance to see the abbey for himself, I suppose." He turned to Elric. "We must organise our defences. I shall speak to Father Abbot tonight, and we must send messengers to your father at Court . . . "

Elric, bursting with excitement, interrupted, "The bird! The bird will help us, I know!"

Bridget and Ethelburga looked at him as though he were mad. They were even more bewildered when Father Brendan cried, "Of course! It must have been a sign! Go quickly, Elric, and bring me the book!"

Chapter Four

When Elric went outside, the moon was shining brightly. Staying in the shadows cast by the abbey buildings, Elric went quickly to one of the side doors. This led to a passage which ran alongside the dining hall and the church. Opening on to it were small study rooms. Father Brendan's writing room was one of these. Once in the passage, Elric noticed the silence. He stopped. He did not know what hour it was but realised that the bell had not been rung for night prayers.

"What about the visitors?" he thought. Surely the whole community had not gone to bed without someone coming to the hospital. Had Avaric and Myrddin and their men gone?

Opposite him was a side entrance to the dining hall. Elric peered through the hangings which covered the doorway. He could hardly believe what he saw.

The hall was in semi-darkness, lit only by moonlight. All the monks and boys were lying sprawled across the tables.

Frozen with fear, Elric was unable to move, thinking wildly that they must all be dead. He leaned against the doorpost, and when his legs stopped shaking, he crept into the hall. Standing still, he heard with relief the steady breathing of sleepers.

Not understanding why they should be sleeping, he tiptoed to the abbot's table. There was no sign of Avaric, Myrddin or Avaric's men. Elric moved to where the abbot slept soundly, his head resting on his arms.

"Father Abbot! Father Abbot!" Elric spoke close to his ear, shaking his shoulder at the same time. Again and again he tried to wake him. Frightened in case Avaric or Myrddin should appear, he decided that he had better find Brendan's Book quickly and return to the infirmary.

Elric ran to the writing room. As he went in, he thought that the moonlight seemed very bright. Then he stopped and stared at the book. A gentle glow poured from it into the room adding to the moonlight which was streaming through the small window. It was a golden light which made the room feel warm. Elric was afraid to touch the book, but he knew that he must take it to Father Brendan.

Just at that moment he heard footsteps. Snatching the book in his arms, holding it close to his chest, he leaped into the darkest corner of the room, squeezing himself between a tall cupboard and the wall. Just in time he pushed the book inside his loose-fitting black school tunic, to hide its light.

Myrddin appeared in the doorway and stepped into the room. His hood was thrown back and at last Elric saw his face. It was not an ugly face, but thin and long, made even longer by a pointed grey beard. He had no moustache, only the beard on the end of his chin. His lips formed a thin line; Elric imagined his smile would be a cruel one. But it was his eyes which were really frightening. They glittered, cold ice-blue, and were so piercing that Elric felt that Myrddin must be able to see him. He almost stepped forward, for Myrddin's eyes were willing him to move. He clutched the book tighter, making himself stand still. Then Myrddin spoke in a deep compelling voice.

"Come forward!" Elric struggled against the command. If he had not been squeezed so tightly between the cupboard and the wall, he would have staggered out into the room. The awkwardness of his hiding place gave him the chance to think and he thought about the white bird inside the book. He fixed his mind on the picture, remembering the lovely feeling of freedom it had given him. He closed his eyes so that they would not be drawn to Myrddin's face, fighting hard to hold on to the image of the bird, to blot out the cold blue eyes of the magician. Elric realised now that he *was* a magician, and a powerful one. Today was no ordinary day. Everything was changing. Father Brendan had been mistaken to think that nothing would happen tonight. It *had* happened! Somehow, Myrddin had taken over the abbey. The monks were helpless. He wished he could open the book, but he could not. He held it tighter still, begging the white bird to help him, as Myrddin stepped towards his hiding place.

There was a rushing sound as the magician reached the corner, then the steady beat of wings. Myrddin whirled round, snatching at the air, for there was

23

nothing to be seen. The noise of wings grew louder, and Myrddin twisted and turned, beating at the empty air, lashing out with his arms, spinning frantically. Taking his chance, Elric wrenched himself out of his corner, dodged past the magician, and did not stop running until he reached the infirmary.

He arrived breathless and shaken, but blurted out the story of what had happened as quickly as he could. Bridget and Ethelburga now knew about Elric's strange experience with the picture of the bird, and were waiting to see it. There was no time to talk and make plans. Hurriedly, Father Brendan told them, "Elric and I must go into hiding at once. You are both wonderfully brave. Take care. Try not to be afraid, and we shall contact you as soon as possible."

The boy and the monk, with Elric still clutching the precious book inside his tunic, slipped out into the night. As they did so, they saw figures coming out of the hall. Just in time they slid along the wall and round to the back of the building. Father Brendan led Elric into the shelter of some bushes. Still under cover, they moved slowly and cautiously round to the back of the abbey church, arriving at last before a narrow door. The monk took a key from his leather belt, unlocked the door and took Elric inside. They were in the room where the vestments were kept for the services, behind the main altar.

Father Brendan whispered, "We are safe here for a few moments only, for we must get out of the abbey. Myrddin will be searching for us. Hold on tightly to the book, and follow me." Father Brendan opened the enormous chest where the vestments were neatly laid away. Inside were the rich robes, purple, red, green, embroidered with silks. Telling Elric to hold the lid of the chest, the old priest pushed the robes aside. He reached into the bottom of the chest, feeling around with his fingers. Part of the bottom slid away, revealing a flight of stone steps. "Quickly! Down you go. There are ten steps, then you are on firm ground."

In a daze, Elric stepped into the chest, and down the steps. He went backwards counting to himself. Soon he stood at the bottom in darkness. Father Brendan, surprisingly agile for his age, followed him quickly.

"One moment Elric, and I will make a light. There is a tinder box and a torch below the steps." He was about to search for these, but Elric stopped him.

"We don't need anything, Father, except the book. See!" He pulled it out from beneath his tunic and its gentle golden gleams showed Elric that they were in a tunnel.

With a gasp, Father Brendan crossed himself. "Ah, Elric, strange and wonderful things are happening! You told me of the light, but I did not realise!"

Elric gave him the book and, carrying it as though it were made of glass, Father Brendan led the way.

The tunnel was lined with rough stone and its roof was supported with stout timbers. They walked at first in a straight line, then the tunnel sloped gradually upwards. Suddenly, it opened out into quite a large circular room, with a low ceiling. In the centre was a wooden table and two benches. There was a pile of torches neatly stacked by the wall, made from stout branches, their ends wrapped in animal wool which had been soaked in fat. There was a pile of sheepskins to sleep on and two iron brackets embedded in the walls to hold the torches. They did not need to light one, for when Father Brendan placed the book on the table, the room was filled with a soft light.

Elric stood looking around him in amazement, and the old man was delighted by his surprise. "This is a good hiding place is it not, Elric?"

"It's wonderful, Father, but where are we?"

"We are at the foot of Holybury Tor. You know where you can see an overgrown burial mound at the base of the steep side of the hill? Well, it isn't a real barrow. Don't worry, there are no dead bodies here! It is a secret chamber known only to the senior members of the brethren. It was made long ago, in Arthur's time. He is supposed to have hidden here himself for several days. See, there is also a way out on to the hillside." He pointed to a low round opening, blocked by a boulder.

"We couldn't move that, Father," Elric said. Father Brendan gave a delighted laugh. Then, taking Elric to the doorway, he showed him an iron lever and pushed it downwards, causing the boulder to swing inwards just enough to let one person at a time through the opening. The door of the barrow was concealed, being close against the almost vertical grassy slope of Holybury Tor. It was good to know that they could get out of the cave-like room; to see the moonlight and smell the fresh night air.

Still inside the room, Father Brendan opened a small wooden chest to show Elric a large water jar, cups, bread wrapped in a cloth, honey and dried meat. He gave Elric a drink and a piece of bread and honey. They sat facing each other at the table, the book between them, and Father Brendan spoke very seriously.

"Elric, we now know that Lady Ethelburga's fears were real. Myrddin and Avaric have taken over the abbey. Myrddin must have great powers for he has placed all the brethren and the other boys under some kind of spell. He seized this chance of a supposedly friendly visit to catch them off guard, for they suspected nothing. You and I must stay free if we are to have any hope of defeating him and rescuing the others. We are in danger, for perhaps Myrddin may find this place by magical means. I do not know. I feel that our only chance is to ask the bird for help. Do you agree?"

"Yes, Father. I know the bird will help us." Elric spoke just as seriously. Father Brendan solemnly opened the book, so that Elric was once again gazing at the picture of the white bird.

Chapter Five

Elric sat on the wooden bench with his head in his hands. Instead of being in the room under the hill, it was as though he were in the picture under the bluest of blue skies watching the white bird. He began to hear the beat of wings. Then he saw the bird above him, its white feathers ruffled by a warm breeze, which he could feel through his hair and on his face. Filled with excitement, he stretched out his arm. The beautiful white bird landed gracefully on his wrist. It was exactly as Father Brendan had drawn it, but as large as a gull. It resembled the gulls but was more delicately formed and Elric could not feel any weight on his arm. As in the picture, its feathers were of the purest white, with gleaming gold tips. On top of its head was the fan of gold-tipped feathers, like a halo, and in its beak was the sprig of rue.

Father Brendan had kept very still and quiet, so that he would not disturb Elric's concentration. He had seen a bright core of light form above the picture, while Elric stared into the centre of it. He had closed his own eyes for it was too intense for him to bear. Then he too had felt a delicious warm breeze, stirring the air in the underground room. When he opened his eyes, there was the bird! Elric was still seated at the table, his arm outstretched

28

across the book; the white bird perched upon his wrist.

Elric was only aware of the bird. He waited, knowing that it would speak to him in some way. It hopped off his wrist on to the table, bent its head to place the sprig of rue on the book, then fixed its pale gold eyes upon Elric's face. It opened its beak as if to sing, but instead of birdsong, came speech, strange and musical.

"Listen carefully, Elric. I am called from the Paradise of the Birds, one of the Isles of Truth in the Sea of Faith. You will call me Avis, which simply means the bird, in the Latin tongue. I will help you in this fight against Myrddin, whose magic is the Magic of Lies. For the Magic of Truth to win this fight, you will need faith and courage. You will also need more power and help than I can give you, but I will show you where to find it. I cannot tell you more at present for I can only appear on Feast Days and Sundays. This feast of St Brendan is almost over. Here are your first instructions.

"In the magical hour just before dawn, go to the herb garden with Father Brendan. Take the water jar with you and this sprig of holy rue. Dip the sprig of rue into the water. You shall carry the water and Father Brendan, using the sprig of rue, must sprinkle the whole of the garden as he sprinkles the people with blessed water in the church. In this way, the garden will be protected. When you have done this, return here to wait until midnight tomorrow. At that time come to the shore in Woden's Bay. Bring with you the book and the sprig of rue. Act with courage and keep your faith in the Truth."

As Elric watched, the bird became blurred, and seemed to be dissolving into light. He wanted to cry out "Wait!" because there were so many questions he needed to ask, but the light grew dimmer, disappeared, and Avis was gone. Elric dropped his head on to the open book, and fell asleep.

Father Brendan had heard everything. He did not disturb Elric, but sat down beside him to think about what had happened. Although Elric was sprawled across the book, he could see enough of the picture to be quite certain that there was only a blank space where the bird had been.

"No, I am not dreaming. This is the strangest day of my whole life, and I am an old man of seventy years. My brethren are trapped in a spell cast upon them by an evil and powerful magician. If he takes over the kingdom there will be terrible times for all the people. But my book must somehow be filled with good magic. It is not *my* power as a poor old monk. The legends are true, and the power must have come down to the book through me from St Brendan. He went to the Paradise of the Birds long ago. He must have seen this same white bird and talked with it. This boy must have inherited some special gift from King Arthur's family. Many people believe the old tale that Arthur is not dead but sleeps somewhere and can return if he is needed . . . "

Father Brendan was lost in his thoughts and he realised that he had been sitting thinking for a long time. Quickly he stepped to the lever and opened the door. He could see by the changing light that it was time to go. He took the water jar from the chest, and shook Elric gently. "It is time to go to the garden."

Elric woke immediately and felt perfectly fresh. He was anxious for them to be on their way, once he knew that Father Brendan had also heard the instructions. They both felt stronger for seeing Avis and knowing that there was something to be done.

Father Brendan picked up the rue and Elric the water jar. They opened the door and slipped outside. Then, Father Brendan showed Elric how to close the boulder. It was a very clever doorway. On the outside the huge stone was covered with moss and trailing ivy. To the left of it, hidden by ivy, was the end of the iron lever, disguised with a funny knobbly gargoyle. By pushing this down to close the door and up to open it, they could enter and leave the burial mound.

It was the hour before dawn so they went quickly down the slope of the hill back towards the abbey. Going to the right, they were able to stay among trees before crossing the roadway a short distance from the abbey gates. Once across, they skirted the boundary wall until they came to the herb garden. Here there was a rough stile near the corner of the garden where Father Brendan had a beehive-shaped hut. He kept some tools there and often liked to sit there and read, or pray quietly, by himself. They slipped into the hut to rest for a few moments and to make sure there was no one about. Elric took the stopper out of the jar and put it into his tunic pocket.

"Are you ready, Father?" he whispered. "It will not be long before it is dawn. Look at the sky." Sure enough the moonlight was fading, giving way to that grey promise of daylight before sunrise.

Father Brendan nodded. He was just about to step out of the hut when Elric caught hold of his arm and pointed. They both stepped back into the deep shadow of the hut, for Elric had seen a tall figure entering the garden through the gateway on the opposite side. The thin hooded figure was unmistakable . . . Myrddin. They watched, not daring to move or make any sound as Myrddin strode to the centre of the garden. He took off his grey hooded cloak and placed it on the path.

There he stood dressed in his true magician's black robe with its wide sweeping sleeves. His robe was covered in silver symbols which glittered eerily in the fading moonlight. Motionless, and hardly daring to breathe, the boy and the monk watched from the little hut. Myrddin did not move for a few moments, but began to chant in an expressionless tone. Then, slowly, he took hold of the front edge of his long robe, lifting it as though it were an apron. His chanting grew louder and more mournful. His robe seemed to grow wider and longer, billowing over the whole garden. But it was no longer made of cloth, for it had become rolling clouds of black vapour. These clouds stayed at ground level, not rising higher than Myrddin's knees. He continued to chant, keeping his arms stretched forward. Then his chanting began to die away. He dropped the robe and stood perfectly still, waiting. The black vapour began to dissolve as the first light of dawn touched the garden. By the time the blackness had completely disappeared there was light enough to see its effect. The garden was dead. The carefully tended beds of herbs were shrivelled and blackened and an evil smell began to rise from the rotting vegetation.

Before Elric had time to think or move, poor Father Brendan staggered through the doorway of the hut, crying out to Myrddin in a terrible voice, "Wicked and evil spirit that you must be to blight and destroy my lovely growing things! . . . "

Myrddin, seeing Father Brendan, turned towards the gate. "Seize him! Bring him to the hall," he roared. Then he put on his cloak and without a backward glance, strode from the garden.

Elric, about to dart forward to help Father Brendan, drew back out of sight. At Myrddin's command, two of Avaric's men ran into the garden and led the poor old monk away. He did not resist but walked from his ruined garden with his head bowed. Elric stood trembling with rage and fear, still holding the water jar. He had not been seen, but the garden was dead, Father Brendan was captured, and he was alone.

Chapter Six

When Bridget and Ethelburga were left alone in the abbey infirmary, they had sat wondering anxiously if Father Brendan and Elric had managed to escape. Suddenly heavy footsteps sounded beyond the curtained doorway.

"Quickly, Bridget, be asleep," Ethelburga told her. Bridget lay down and closed her eyes as Avaric strode into the room. Ethelburga stood up and arranged the covers over Bridget to hide her own nervousness. She must not show that she knew what had happened.

"Where is the priest?" Avaric asked his wife.

"I do not know," she answered truthfully. "He left when Bridget seemed better. She is sleeping peacefully now and should be much recovered in the morning."

Avaric looked at his wife searchingly for a moment. Then, satisfied, he did not look at Bridget. "You had better stay here tonight. I shall have you taken home tomorrow, if she is well enough."

"Are you staying tonight, Avaric?" asked Ethelburga quietly.

"Yes. I have business here. I have much to discuss with Myrddin. I may not come home tomorrow. Get some rest now with the child. Oh . . . did one of the boys come in here when the priest was here?"

Ethelburga hated to tell a lie, but knew she must. Father Brendan and Elric were her only hope. She looked at Avaric sadly. They had been a happy family before Myrddin's arrival. "I'm not sure. I was attending to Bridget." Avaric did not question her any more. He went out quickly.

After a moment, she whispered to Bridget, "Did you hear all that, child?"

Bridget sat up. "Yes, Mother. You were quite right, you know. We must not betray Father Brendan and Elric. You do believe that Myrddin is a magician, don't you?"

"I must, I'm afraid. There seem to be strange and evil forces working here. But see how it spreads, Bridget, for now I have started to tell lies. Myrddin deals in lies and deceit. It is like a poison, child, for honest people are forced into lying in order to protect themselves and their friends. Myrddin is breaking up our family. I thought all the old superstitions and witchcraft were ending, but I see now that they will continue until the end of time."

Ethelburga sounded so sad and hopeless that Bridget hugged her and said, "It will come right in the end, Mother. See how good magic is starting to help us against Myrddin. The white bird saved Elric when he went to get the book. Lie down and rest now. I'm sure they will get in touch with us soon."

Ethelburga lay down on the couch next to Bridget. Covering herself with a rug, she fell into an uneasy sleep. Bridget felt somehow too excited to sleep, as though something were going to happen. She settled down, pushing her long red hair out of her eyes, and fingering the golden coil which was always around her neck. It was a torc, an open-ended necklet. It was made of intricately plaited gold wires. Its ends were made of little golden knobs engraved with tiny Celtic crosses. Ethelburga had told her that it had belonged to her own mother and that she must always wear it. Now, as she touched it, she began to drift into a pleasant sleep and a strange dream.

A tall and very beautiful lady with long red-gold hair, like her own, stood smiling at her in her dream. The lady was richly dressed in a robe of silky green, embroidered with golden flowers. On her head was a golden circlet in the shape of a delicate crown and round her neck was Bridget's torc! Or it was one exactly like it. The lady was standing in a garden with carefully arranged beds of flowering herbs, and a little stone cell in the corner. Bridget realised that the garden was familiar to her. She had seen it once before when she visited the abbey. It was Father Brendan's herb garden. The lady did not speak, but beckoned to Bridget several times. Then the dream faded and Bridget was wide awake.

She looked around the infirmary, and sat up. Ethelburga sat up at the same time. They stared at one another.

"I was dreaming", said Bridget, "of a beautiful lady, a queen I think. She was in the herb garden. I must go there. There may be a message."

"I dreamed of her too! Yes, I think you must go, but it is very important that you do not take off the golden torc. It must be very special. She pointed to it over and over again. I know she must have meant that it will protect you."

They both got up and Bridget put on her cloak and sandals. Together they went to the outer doorway. Ethelburga looked out. There was still enough moonlight to see that there was no one around.

"Go now, child. Come back when you have found out what is in the garden. Father Brendan may be there. Take care. Remember the torc."

The infirmary building was just inside the main gate of the abbey, on the right hand side. The walled herb garden was on the left, immediately opposite. Bridget had only to slip quickly across to the gate in the stone wall and in a moment she was in the garden. She thought there was no one there, but at that very moment, Father Brendan and Elric were in the little hut, and Elric was removing the stopper from the water jar. They did not see Bridget, for she did not like to walk out into the middle of the garden. She crept around the side of the wall to make her way to the hut. She saw Myrddin enter just as she reached the stile. Quick as thought, she slipped over it. From behind the wall on the far side of the garden, she too watched Myrddin destroy the herbs and capture Father Brendan.

Bridget stood frozen with horror, peering over the wall. Dawn was breaking and in its grey light she could see the terrible destruction as the last of the black vapour settled. She could not move or think. Suddenly a figure loomed up in front of her on the other side of the stile. She gave a low cry and turned to run, but slipped on the grass which was wet with dew. As she fell, she recognised Elric as he half-tumbled over the stile, for he was holding the water jar.

Bridget struggled to her feet and faced him. "You! You were there too! Why weren't you captured? Why didn't you try to help him?"

"Hush!" Elric hissed at her. "Follow me. We can't talk here. We must get away." Before she could answer, he set off, diving into the trees, leading Bridget away from the abbey. She had to follow in order to find a way back to the infirmary now that she was outside the abbey grounds. Continuing through the trees Elric reached a point on the roadway where they would have to cross. Pausing only to check that there was no one on the roadway, they hurried across and into the trees on the opposite side.

Elric did not slacken his pace until they reached the foot of Holybury Tor. Bearing left, he led Bridget round the base of the hill to the burial mound. There he stopped at last.

Bridget was breathless from hurrying to keep up with him. "Why have we come here?" she asked.

"Watch," Elric felt for the gargoyle head, pushing it in the right direction. The huge stone swung inwards and Elric stood aside, motioning Bridget to go in.

She shook her head angrily. "I'm not going in there unless I can get through into the infirmary. I have to tell Mother what has happened."

Elric, tired and desperately worried that someone

might find them at any moment, snapped at her. "If you come in at least I can explain. Then I'll take you to the infirmary."

"I'm not coming in. You didn't even try to help Father Brendan— "

He interrupted her angrily. "It's no use you telling me what I ought to have done. What could I have done? Flung myself on Myrddin I suppose! I was single-handed against a powerful magician and two armed men. Then I'd have been caught and no one would be free. You don't know what has happened since we left you."

Bridget flung back at him. "Better to be captured trying to help your friend than be a coward and stay free!"

They stood facing each other. Elric, white-faced and biting his lip, Bridget, flushed and upset, but not allowing herself to cry. He turned from her and closed the boulder door, then said, "If you were a boy, you would not dare to call me a coward." His voice was low and angry. Before she could answer, he went on, "If you follow the slope down to the right from here, you will come to the abbey wall. There's a large hole. If you climb through you'll be behind the infirmary. You'll have to watch for a chance to slip inside." Without another word, Bridget ran down the slope and out of sight.

Despite his anger, Elric followed Bridget to make sure that she was safe. He saw her small figure disappear through the gap in the wall. It was much lighter now and much more dangerous. He leaned through the hole as far as he could and watched her creep along the side of the building. Then she was gone. Elric waited for a few moments, but all was quiet. He turned away and went wearily back to the barrow.

Chapter Seven

When Elric reached the barrow he let himself in quickly and closed the door. The room was filled with a gentle glowing light from the book which lay on the table. Elric sighed and went to the chest in the corner. Then he remembered that the sprig of rue was inside the water jar. He had found it on the floor of the hut and pushed it there to keep it safe. He took it out now, glistening and dripping, and laid it on the table near the book. He drank some water and ate a piece of bread and honey. Then he sat down at the table and opened the book.

Elric felt a little better by now and realised that he would have to make the best of things. He decided he would wait in the barrow until dawn on Sunday. It would be a long wait, all day and most of the night, but there was some food left, and he was reasonably safe. Then he would take the book and the sprig of rue to Woden's Bay to meet Avis. Beside the book, the rue seemed to add to the light in the barrow. Ordinary rue has a strong unpleasant smell, but these evergreen leaves and yellow flowers gave off a beautiful perfume. Elric began to look through Father Brendan's well-loved book. He had read it all before, but now it was alive with magic. Even as he turned the pages, he could feel a tingling sensation in his fingers. The colours of the richly-decorated capitals glowed and the curling stems, flowers and leaves in the borders looked as though they were actually growing. He read some of Father Brendan's recipes again. He had always thought that some sounded magical. For example, wormwood or green ginger was useful for curing sea-dragon bites!

Elric began to feel tired. Before closing the book he looked at the blank space where the picture of Avis had been, wishing there wasn't such a long time to wait before he would have the bird to help him again.

As he closed the book, Elric stared hard at the cover, wondering if there was something wrong with his eyes. The cheeky little baboon and the two-winged dragon were missing from the cover picture. He rubbed his eyes and looked again, expecting to find that he had made a mistake, but there were two spaces where they had clambered among the flowering herbs. He sat staring at the book in the quiet cave-like room. All at once he lifted his head and listened carefully. There were faint scuffling noises coming from the passage which led back to the vestment room. Quickly he picked up the book and the herb, glancing round desperately. There was nowhere to hide! The barrow was a simple round room. He was caught!

The noises came nearer, not footsteps, but scrapings, rustlings, scratchings. Thinking it was better to risk going outside, Elric leaped for the lever. As he reached it a tongue of flame shot past his head, narrowly missing him. He dropped to the ground as something landed on the table and slithered to a stop. Then there was a slight thump. Elric had bumped his head and lay with his eyes closed trying to recover.

"Don't send out any more flames until you know what you're doing. You've singed my fur once," grumbled a squeaky voice, "and now look what you've done."

"Alas! I have killed the human child who holds the book. He lies dead upon the ground." This time the voice was low and booming. Elric opened his eyes.

Peering down at him over the edge of the table were the faces of the baboon and the dragon from the cover of the book. He sat up. At once the dragon swooped down and almost landed on top of him. The baboon, with a graceful leap, landed neatly.

"You will have to excuse Wyvern. He's a clumsy fellow, you know. Dragons are, because they are not really fish, flesh, or fowl, but sort of all three."

"You, Babwyn, are an insulting fellow," interrupted the dragon. "But I am so happy you are not dead, child. What are you called? This is Babwyn, the baboon, and I am Wyvern, the two-winged dragon."

Elric was quickly getting used to the world of magic, so he said politely, "I'm Elric. I'm at school with the monks in the abbey, or I was until this terrible trouble started yesterday."

They cocked their heads sideways, listening, as he told them all that had happened so far. When he had finished, Babwyn said, "Ah! The whole thing

43

is clear to me. Magical powers stay in families you know. Father Brendan has some, but not as strong as yours. That's why he was guided to draw the bird, so that you could contact Avis. It all fits, you see. But you will have to prove yourself. You won't be helped by good magic unless you are faithful and brave." He nodded knowingly.

"How did you come out of the book?" asked Elric. "Avis can only appear on Feast days and Sundays."

Wyvern puffed some small clouds of blue smoke, which made Elric cough. "Try not to do that, old fellow," Babwyn said.

"I must breathe out or I'll burst. Let me talk to the child now. You can't talk all the time. You never stop once you've started."

"All right. Explain to him some of the magic of the book. He won't mind my saying that he's a very ignorant boy – can't help it of course – too much Latin and Greek in school and no lessons in magic."

"Now, child," said Wyvern kindly. Elric thought he was a bit like one of the old monks when he spoke like that. "Father Brendan is a good man, descended from St Brendan, who was allowed to journey to the Isles of Truth long ago. You know *that* story, I think. People who have inherited magical powers can sometimes have those powers awakened. They can use them for good or evil. Perhaps you know that you are descended from King Arthur's family, from Patricius his brother, on your mother's side of the family?"

44

"My mother told me I was," Elric said quietly.

"So", Wyvern continued, "the powers inherited by Father Brendan and yourself came together when great danger from evil magic arose with Myrddin. He has twisted the good magic he had from the great Merlin. He has turned to the Magic of Lies. But the Magic of Truth is stronger and has filled the Book of Brendan. It will stay in the book until the end of time. Now the book cannot burn or rot away. If it were torn into pieces, and it would need great power to do that, the fragments would each be magical. But it must stay in the hands of those who will use it to do good. Myrddin would use it for his own evil ends. We must make sure he does not get hold of it." Wyvern sighed and shook his heavy head.

Babwyn hopped up and down impatiently. "You didn't answer his question, you know. We were released, Elric, when the light of true magic worked its way through the book. We are different from Avis. He will never return to his picture unless he needs to be called again at some future time, but when we have helped you we must return to the book. If we need to, we can go back. Watch!"

He hopped on to the cover, into the glow of light. He closed his eyes and shrank quickly to the size of his image in the picture. The light gleamed stronger for a second and there was Babwyn, back in his place. Wyvern was troubled and puffed out a few red sparks. The book was still on Elric's knees and Wyvern told him to place it on the floor. Then Babwyn began to emerge from the cover again. It was wonderful to watch him. He sat on the book,

45

growing before Elric's eyes. But Wyvern kept giving angry little puffs.

When Babwyn was his own size again, he danced around the room jumping on and off the table, but stopped when Wyvern said to him, "Foolish monkey! You must not play tricks with the magic of the book or perhaps the good Lord will recall you and not release you from there ever again."

All this time, Elric had been sitting on the floor, so fascinated by the two creatures that he had not noticed how stiff he was. He stood up now and stretched. Babwyn and Wyvern watched him, looking up from the floor, for Elric was quite tall. Babwyn was only small and Elric could easily have picked him up and carried him. His fur was greyish-brown. He had long arms and legs and a long tail. Wyvern was about the size of a small dog, but he had a bigger head and clawed feet. His wingspan was about three feet.

Elric felt very solemn as he thought of the seriousness of all that was happening. This battle was not just about the abbey lands. It was about good and evil, truth and lies. Not little lies, but monstrous lies which could lead people into misery. Myrddin had deceived Avaric. He would not have been able to deceive the monks, so he had pretended friendliness, a simple visit, and caught them unawares. Elric felt sure that Myrddin would probably kill the monks eventually, unless he meant to keep them asleep for a very long time. Elric sat down at the table and put his head in his hands. Babwyn and Wyvern watched him sadly. They got on to the table, and Elric felt

46

the dragon's warm breath blow gently on to his hands and the baboon's hand patting his shoulder.

He must not give in. He uncovered his face, straightened up and said, "We must act. We can't sit here. We must rescue Father Brendan first. Now I have your help, we can plan a rescue, can't we?"

"That's good! You have courage and you will become stronger and stronger," said Wyvern.

Babwyn gave a leap, somersaulting on to the floor, calling cheerfully, "To the rescue!"

Then the three of them froze as the boulder door swung open. Elric stared as Bridget came quickly into the room and, working the lever efficiently, closed the door. Babwyn and Wyvern gazed at her, then Babwyn said, "She wears the golden torc of Gunamara!"

They bowed low before Bridget who was now dressed in a simple brown cloak, carrying a large basket. As always, the coiled golden necklet gleamed at her throat.

Chapter Eight

The little girl stood proudly in her coarse cloak, its hood fallen back from her gleaming copper-red hair. Elric looked at her, thinking to himself. "It's very like magic the way this girl appears. I wonder how she's managed it this time? I wish we hadn't quarrelled. It's all too serious to quarrel between ourselves about anything. There isn't time! . . . But she did call me a coward!"

He was looking at her while he was thinking and suddenly realised that she was smiling at him. He stepped towards her and held out his hand. Before he could speak, she said, "I'm sorry I called you a coward. You're not."

Elric grinned and shook her hand. "I'm sorry too. Let's forget about it."

The two small creatures looked at Elric, surprised by the way he had spoken to Bridget. Then they looked at each other and nodded wisely as if in agreement that humans were very odd creatures. Elric introduced them to Bridget and she shook Babwyn's hand and stroked Wyvern's scaly head. Elric could see that they both loved her immediately.

She behaved as though she met baboons and dragons quite often. Then Elric rememberd the gulls on the beach, and reminded himself that she was no more an ordinary girl than he was an ordinary boy.

Bridget emptied the basket on to the table. There was fresh bread, meat, an earthenware jar of milk, some pieces of cheese and some apples. The four of them had an early Saturday lunch, safely hidden in the burial mound, while all around them was danger. They talked, for there was a lot to tell. Bridget heard all about Avis and the power of the book, of how Babwyn and Wyvern had appeared, and of the seriousness of the battle which lay before them. Then it was her turn to tell of her dream and Ethelburga's dream, which had made her go to the garden.

When Wyvern and Babwyn heard this, Wyvern said, "Your lady of the dream was Gunamara, Arthur's queen. Your golden torc belonged to her. She always wore one, that is why we bowed to you, for we recognised you as being of her family. You must be the child who is descended from Gunamara's sister, Mabwen. Did you not know?"

"No, for I never knew my real parents. My second mother, Ethelburga, must not have known either, but I know that this torc was my real mother's most treasured possession. She told Ethelburga to place it around my neck as soon as I was old enough and that I must always wear it. I have worn it every day since then."

"It will protect you from evil," continued the dragon. "It must have done so, for Myrddin has lived in your home for many months."

"Please, Bridget," asked Elric, "have you any

news of Father Brendan?" He was very anxious to find some way of rescuing the old monk as soon as possible. He thought that they could not make a move in daylight, but must work out a plan in time for nightfall. So Bridget told them the latest news from the abbey.

"When I left you, Elric, I slipped into the infirmary without any trouble. My mother was alone and no one had been in while I was away. I told Mother about the destruction of the garden and Father Brendan being captured. She was so upset that she wanted to speak to Avaric at once and try, again, to persuade him that Myrddin is evil, but she has tried many times and he will not listen. As we were talking a lady came in with some breakfast. Mother knew she was from the village, so she asked her what she knew. She told us that she was Winfred, Chad's mother. When Chad, one of the school boys, did not go home last night, his father had been to ask after him. He was told there were some special visitors and all the boys were staying. Since that sometimes happens, Chad's father suspected nothing. But this morning when the abbey bell did not ring for service, a group of the villagers came to see if anything was wrong. They saw no one except one of Avaric's men. She said there were quite a lot about, so more must have arrived last night. The other villagers were sent home, but she, her husband, and his brother were asked to stay. She was sent in with our food. The three of them were told that the abbot wanted them to take Mother and me home later in the morning."

"Oh, so you have no idea where Father Brendan might be?" asked Elric.

"No, for my father came in then and sent Winfred away. He told us we were being sent home soon, since I was so much better. Poor Father, he is so kind and so fond of me, but he did not bother to speak to me."

Bridget hung her head and looked so sad that Babwyn took her hand. "We will rescue Avaric too in the end, for he is the only father you know."

Bridget smiled at him, and continued, "We left soon afterwards. Instead of going straight home, we went to the village, to their house. Mother told Oswy, Chad's father, that Myrddin had taken over the abbey. Chad's mother was very frightened. The men wanted to gather a force and storm the abbey, but Mother begged them to wait, until stronger help could be found. They listened to her and Oswy decided that they would wait to see what happened. He said that he would keep in touch with Mother. Mother let me slip away to bring you some food for she knows now that the torc will protect me. I have arranged to send her a signal if Father Brendan is rescued and we are safe. I can stay and help or go back to Oswy and he will take me home."

Elric did not say that Bridget should go home. He realised now that she was someone special and he would need her help. "Stay if you can, Bridget. We need you. First of all we must find out where Father Brendan is being held. I'll slip into the abbey through the vestment chest as soon as dusk falls. From there perhaps I can scout around and find out where he is.

51

If I can get him out, I will. If I can't manage it, I'll come back and we'll all go to the shore at dawn to meet Avis without him."

"No," Babwyn said quickly. "You are a brave boy, but I must go. I can scout where no one else can. I can climb and swing out of reach of any man. I can curl up and hide in any corner."

"That is the best plan," Wyvern agreed. "We must wait now until evening. But you shall have some help, little monkey, for before you go, I will touch your eyes with the sprig of rue. Then your sight will be sharpened."

Elric and Bridget stared at the glistening spray on the table and asked Wyvern what he meant.

"My children, do you not see? The Book of Brendan is full of power now. All the herbs have magical healing powers. Whatever they would do before, when Father Brendan made medicines from the herbs in the garden, those pictured in the book should do the same as soon as they touch anyone. And if we came out of the book, so can they. Now, this rue is from the picture of Avis, so it must be very special. Rue can be used for healing eyesight as well as for giddiness and pains in the head. I think it will make Babwyn able to see even in darkness."

"Oh, do let's try it now!" said Bridget excitedly.

Wyvern looked at the herb which still lay on the table. Then he lifted it carefully in his claw and handed it to Bridget. "Yes, we will try. Touch Babwyn's eyes."

Solemnly, as Babwyn sat on the table in front

of her, Bridget gently brushed the herb spray over his eyes, one at a time. Then they all looked at him eagerly.

"What is it like?" Elric asked. Babwyn gazed around the cave-like room.

"Everything is very sharp and clear!" He jumped from the table and went to the entrance of the dark passage. "I can see down the passage as though it were lit! I can see every tiny crack between the stones, everything!"

"Let's all try it," Elric said. "I must go with Babwyn as far as the vestment chest to lift the lid and let him out."

"Shall we see if any of the other herbs will come out of the book?" Bridget was about to open it, but Wyvern stopped her.

"No! We must not play with the magic of the book. I am sure if we do, nothing will happen. We must only try to remove a herb if we need it. But you are right, Elric, you will have to go with Babwyn, so Bridget may touch your eyes."

It seemed to Bridget and Elric that the little dragon had taken charge, but they did not mind, for he knew more about magical powers than they did. Wyvern sat looking at her, blinking his bright green eyes. Carefully, she touched each of Elric's eyes with the sprig of rue and waited.

Looking around, Elric was amazed. His eyes felt somehow cool and fresh and he could see every tiny detail of his surroundings. Like Babwyn, he went to look down the passage. He would certainly not need a torch. It was as clear as daylight. He turned back to his friends. "It's wonderful! Let's look outside to see if it is nearly dusk."

He operated the lever slowly, allowing the door to open just enough to peer out. It was obviously evening. They had been talking and planning for a long time. So Babwyn drank some water and ate an apple quickly, for he was impatient to try the rescue.

The two of them went swiftly down the long tunnel until they reached the steps. There they stopped for a moment while Elric remembered to tell Babwyn how to get back to the burial mound and exactly how to open the door from the outside if Father Brendan was not with him. Then, with Babwyn on his shoulder, Elric noiselessly slid open the smooth panel at the top of the stone steps. They both listened but could hear nothing. Pushing the vestments aside, Babwyn climbed into the chest and looked through a crack in the wood to see if there was anyone in the room. He turned to Elric and nodded. Elric's head and shoulders were now inside the chest, but it was an awkward position for lifting the lid. He wriggled carefully inside on his stomach, lying full length. Then, pressing his hands on the base of the chest, he raised the lid with his shoulders, until there was a gap through which Babwyn could squeeze. The baboon disappeared. There was a faint thump as he landed on the stone floor of the room. Elric let the lid down gently, closed the panel and went quickly back to join Wyvern and Bridget, hoping and praying that the brave little monkey would succeed.

Chapter Nine

Babwyn crouched by the side of the huge vestment chest. He was not worried, only excited about his adventure. Dusky twilight filtered into the room from a tiny window. From above him, in the centre of the room, a stout bell rope dangled almost to the floor. Babwyn ran over to the door on the outside wall and tried it. It was locked. That didn't matter, since he wanted to look in the church. He found a narrow door which opened into a well from which three stone steps led up to the space before the High Altar. Babwyn slid out and crouched on the steps, peering over the top one into the abbey church.

All was quiet and the church was empty. The sanctuary lamp still burned with a comforting glow. Babwyn emerged from his hiding place, bowed reverently before the altar, then scampered round the church trying the other two doors. The main door at the end of the church in the right hand wall was locked. So too was the one leading into the passage on the left. He would hear if anyone unlocked them, so he squatted comfortably in a corner of a bench to decide what to do.

"I am safe here for the moment," he thought, "and I can get out through that little window in the room where the chest is, to search for Father

55

Brendan. But I need to distract the enemy, to give me a chance to find him."

Babwyn tapped his forehead with his bony finger, thinking hard. Suddenly he leaped down from the bench and darted back to the vestment room. He had had a brilliant idea.

Inside the room he stood looking up the bell rope. He could see that the small belfry above had openings on four sides and the large bell hung in the space between with a little platform around it. If he managed to ring the bell, the enemy would be alarmed and perhaps frightened. There would be confusion and distraction. He stared at the bell rope, thick and sturdy with a large red tassel on the end of it, and decided to try his plan.

He was about to take hold of the rope when he heard a noise. Someone was opening the outer door of the small room! At once Babwyn disappeared into the narrow space behind the vestment chest. Avaric and Myrddin entered the room. Babwyn listened, trembling in the presence of the magician.

The two men stood facing each other. Avaric was tall and handsome, his reddish beard only sprinkled with grey. Myrddin was taller still, but very thin compared with the sturdy Thegn. His face seemed as grey as his hair, beard and clothes. His expression was cruel and because of his lack of colour, his blue eyes contrasted strangely with his complexion. Avaric was holding a small flaring torch, which made the air smoky. He turned and stepped towards Babwyn's hiding place, to stick the torch into the iron wall bracket above the chest. Babwyn hardly dared to breathe. He looked up fearfully at the Thegn and noticed that his expression was angry. Babwyn froze into absolute stillness and was not discovered.

"I am uneasy Myrddin and so are my men," said Avaric as he moved away. "This abbey is one of the main Christian churches. There could be a great uprising once the tenants know what has happened. The abbot is their Thegn. They will fight to the death for him. It is the custom of my people. I would rather have extended my power in another direction first."

Myrddin fixed his terrible gaze on Avaric, who could not look away. "Fool! These lands are the richest and the most extensive in the kingdom after the king's own lands. You want to rule in Wessex and then in the whole kingdom. To do so you must be guided by me. You cannot gain great prizes without some difficulty. Nothing will go wrong if you obey me, for I, Myrddin, have powers at my command which you have not dreamed of. There will be no uprising. Listen! Tomorrow the monks and the boys will awake, but they will be as those who walk in their sleep. They will obey orders without question. In a short time they will be collected from Woden's Bay in a slave trader's ship and that will be the end of them. It will appear to be no one's fault. The thing will be done and the people here will have to accept you as their ruler."

Avaric was silent for a moment, then asked, "What of the new captive? I have not seen him since you took him in the garden. Why did you destroy the garden? And there is one boy missing, is there not?"

Listening, Babwyn became excited, hoping to hear some answers. Myrddin's voice hissed angrily as he replied. "I will not be questioned like this, Thegn. Do not pry into matters you do not understand. The old man is safely guarded in the infirmary." Behind the chest, Babwyn almost let out a delighted squeak. In his impatience with Avaric, Myrddin had given the information Babwyn needed. Father Brendan was in the small hospital. In the silence which followed, Babwyn risked peering round the corner of the chest. Myrddin was looking in a tall cupboard. The little monkey cowered back as the magician moved to the chest. He lifted the lid, but closed it with a bang when he saw only vestments.

"I had heard that the monks had great treasures, but there is little here at least. Come." The two men left, taking the torch and locking the door behind them.

Babwyn breathed easily again. For a dreadful moment he had thought that Myrddin might find the sliding panel and the tunnel. Now he must put his plan into action at once. Bridget had said that the hospital was near the main gates, so he knew exactly where to go if he got a chance. He leaped to the bell rope and nimbly climbed it. He was light so this movement did not ring the bell properly. It only gave out a few subdued sounds as though swinging in the breeze. Then, holding on with his hands, Babwyn was able to push the bell with his feet to make it ring aloud, sending four loud notes winging away into the night air before he leaped on to the platform to see what would happen.

Babwyn was well-hidden, as still as the stone belfry out of which his little eyes watched. Because Bridget had touched them with the magical rue he could even see the expressions on the faces of Avaric and Myrddin as they looked up from the courtyard. Avaric looked terrified and Myrddin's face was twisted in anger. Other men had run to join them.

"There is someone in there!" snarled Myrddin. "They must not escape!" Avaric raised his voice to rap out an order. "Assemble all the men here! Surround the hall and church!"

Myrddin disappeared into the church as men came running to obey Avaric.

Babwyn grinned to himself as he saw them running around with flaming torches. This was his chance, and a good one. The church was no higher than a house and it was built directly on to the end of the hall. Before the men were organised Babwyn was on the lower roof of the hall. From there he was on the ground in seconds. He had dropped down on the side opposite the courtyard and he could see perfectly. He was so small and quick that he could easily avoid the men. They had been badly frightened by the ghostly ringing of the abbey bell. They all knew that the church had been securely locked and no one was allowed in there. They could see that Avaric was afraid and Myrddin angry, so who had rung the bell? Babwyn knew that they were terrified. His plan had worked. Only one man stood at the door of the infirmary, afraid to move. Torchlight and shadows danced about the courtyard. The little baboon was not afraid. He was enjoying himself.

Flattening himself on the ground, he crawled until he was almost at the man's feet. Then he made a sudden mighty leap into the air in front of the man, spreading out his arms and legs and grinning horribly.

"A devil! A devil!" yelled the warrior. He turned and ran shouting and bumping into the other men. Babwyn, shaking with laughter, slipped into the infirmary.

Old Father Brendan's hands were tied and the rope was securely fastened to one of the wall brackets, long enough for him to lie on the couch nearby. He was sitting there wondering what all the noise was about when Babwyn entered. Babwyn was across the room and untying the rope with his nimble fingers in less than a minute, while Father Brendan stared at him in wonder. Then he said, "It can't be! But, yes. It is my little friend from the cover of my book!"

Still dazed by all that had happened and the loss of his beloved garden, he allowed Babwyn to lead him quickly out of the infirmary and round to the meadow behind the building. They climbed through the hole in the abbey wall and, mounting the wooded slope of the hill, were safely inside the barrow before either of them spoke again.

Chapter Ten

When Myrddin entered the abbey church after hearing the bell ring, Babwyn was already leaving the belfry to climb to the ground. Finding the church empty, Myrddin went to the vestment room where the bell rope hung. He gazed upwards into the tiny belfry and saw at once that there was no one there. It was only a housing for the bell. There was no room for any person to hide in it. If anyone had climbed up there, they would have had to go out on to the roof and would have been seen. He looked thoughtfully at the small window. A man could not get through it, but a boy could. Myrddin was convinced that it must have been the missing boy, Elric, who had rung the bell.

He had found out his name from the list of schoolboys in the book where the abbot carefully recorded the daily life and work of the monastery. He must find the boy quickly. The boy had the book and the book must have some power which could work against his own plans. Myrddin, who did not fear any man, had felt fear in the presence of the invisible bird, when the boy had escaped with the book. He wasted no more time, but hurried out to go and question Father Brendan.

Avaric was outside. Myrddin spoke in his harsh

penetrating voice. "Organise a search, meadows, woodland, village, seashore. The missing boy must be found. He is tall and fair. He wears the black tunic like the other schoolboys." He did not wait for an answer, but strode to the infirmary. He frowned when he saw it unguarded, but went inside quickly, only to discover that his prisoner had gone. Fury seized him. He rushed outside as Avaric came towards the building.

"Fools! Fools!" Myrddin hissed like a snake as the two went back inside. Avaric looked at the scattered ropes lying on the ground. He felt afraid. He hated mysteries. First the bell, now this. Myrddin turned on him. "I am surrounded by fools. Who called off the guard? You did."

"I suppose he ran when the order came to assemble," said Avaric. "They were terrified when the bell rang. I have told you they are uneasy here. They fear the Christian church . . . they fear the black-robed priests."

"Can you not control your own men? What use are they to me if they run around like a pack of hunting dogs, leaving their posts? Is the search in progress? For now we must find the old priest again too!" Avaric nodded sullenly and the magician left him.

Myrddin disappeared behind the hospital. Tossing back his cloak, he took the ends of his black robe as he had done in the garden, but this time he lifted them and swirled them around his head. The robe formed itself into two enormous bat-like wings and he rose from the ground, sailing effortlessly through the night.

He landed on the summit of Holybury Tor. It was bleak and bare there, a stony place, disliked by the local people. It was only called Holybury because of the abbey and was supposed to have been called the Hill of Azab in past ages. The magician strode across the summit. On the opposite side of the Tor from the burial mound, the slope was gradual. Myrddin walked part of the way down it. He examined the ground in several places. With a satisfied nod, he drew a small flask from inside his robe.

Myrddin removed the stopper from the flask. Vapour rose from the neck of the bottle. He began to walk in a curious pattern across the grassy slope, sprinkling liquid from the flask as he went. It hissed as it landed on the ground and smoke rose from the spot where it fell. Myrddin was tracing a shape, or following one already there. At last he stopped, stood perfectly still and began to chant. He chanted in a strange tongue and the sound he made was awful to hear. It mingled with the rising wind, a mournful sinister song, which made all who heard it that night want to stop their ears and run away.

The ground began to glow along the outline of Myrddin's pacing. Soon the shape which he had traced on the hillside could be seen. It was that of a large dog. Brighter and brighter glowed the outline. A fiery red liquid spilled from the lines Myrddin had made until it covered the whole shape. Myrddin's chanting grew more intense and strange. The picture completed itself. Myrddin stopped chanting. He stood with his arms outstretched and, speaking in Anglo-Saxon, cried out, "Arise Azab, ancient Hound of Darkness. Your memory was traced in the chalk of the hill long ages ago by those who believed in you. ARISE!"

Out from the ground sprang a large and terrible hound who immediately went to stand beside Myrddin. It panted and snarled, its whole body glowing fiery red as though it was burning. This glow faded slowly. Only its eyes continued to shine with an eerie red light. In a few moments it had become as sleek and grey as Myrddin himself. He put his hand on its back. It sat down on its haunches, waiting for an order. Myrddin was carrying one of the ropes which had tied Father Brendan. He held it to the dog's nose while it fixed the scent. Then it shambled off, nose to the ground and the grey figure followed.

Chapter Eleven

Inside the barrow they were all happy and excited when Father Brendan arrived safely with Babwyn. Bridget hugged the little baboon, telling him over and over again how clever he was. If he had not been covered with grey-brown fur he would have turned pink all over with pleasure. Then they settled down to hear the story of the rescue and to tell Father Brendan their news. The book still glowed softly, lighting the room, and Father Brendan smiled, showing the wrinkles of his ageing face. He was perfectly at home with Wyvern and Babwyn. He had, after all, drawn them in the first place. Magic did not seem to surprise Father Brendan very much anyway.

He told them about his capture. "When I saw my poor garden, my children, I'm afraid I behaved badly like a very foolish old man. However, we have little time left before we must go to the shore, so I must tell you what happened to me. Myrddin took me to my own dear room. I sat upon my stool not caring what happened to me. I did not want to look upon his evil face so I rested my head on the writing stand.

"He began to talk to me in a very surprising way. He told me that he had no wish to harm

65

me if I would join forces with him. He told me how clever I was and how, gifted with extra powers like himself, I could be his partner. All I had to do was to bring the book to him and the missing boy, you, Elric. He promised that between us we would turn you into a great leader by the time you were a young man. His voice was surprisingly pleasant to listen to. As he talked, I began to feel drowsy and found myself beginning to agree with him.

"Ah! What a clever magician is Myrddin! Just in time I realised that he was weaving his spell of lies around me, flattering and deceiving me." Father Brendan paused and shuddered as he remembered.

Elric spoke. "Of course! He did something like that to Father Abbot and the others."

"Yes, Elric, it must have been so and they were entertaining him as a guest. However, there is no excuse for me. I knew how evil he was. Oh, he is indeed powerful! In the nick of time, I remembered what you had done, Elric. I remembered how you had thought of Avis when Myrddin almost caught you in the same room. I did not have the book, but I fixed my mind on my picture of Avis, at the same time keeping my head down as though I were drowsy. As I pictured the white bird in my head, Myrddin's voice began to fade and nothing he said made any sense. My poor garden floated before my eyes and my anger against him rose once again.

"At last I felt him touch my shoulder. I raised my head and he looked at me suspiciously with those sharp blue eyes. I knew that he was uncertain of the effect he was having. Then someone knocked at the door and Avaric's voice called to him. Because he was still unsure of me I was secured in the hospital. He told me he would come to me later. You know the rest."

Babwyn was about to speak when he and Wyvern suddenly stiffened. The small monkey trembled and the dragon sent out puffs of smoke and sparks. "Myrddin! He is near us," cried Babwyn.

They sat in silence round the table, listening, expecting to hear noises in the passage. Nothing happened. "What if we go out of the door and they are waiting?" whispered Bridget.

"We must leave carefully. It will soon be dawn." Father Brendan pointed to the pile of sheepskins. "There is a satchel among those, Elric. Place the book inside it and put it over your shoulder. I have the sprig of rue."

"Wait," Wyvern said. "Elric and Babwyn can still see in the dark. Let you and Bridget and I touch each other's eyes with it before we go out." They did so and though the light from the book was hidden in the satchel, they could all see every detail in the room.

Father Brendan opened the door slightly. At once they could hear a mournful chanting mixed with the sound of the wind in the treetops, for it was at that moment that Myrddin was raising the Hound of Darkness from the long forgotten outline in the chalky hillside.

Babwyn slipped out first. There was no one outside and the others quickly followed. The chanting was terrible. They wanted to press their hands over their ears and run, but they had to go carefully.

Father Brendan whispered, "See the torches. There is a group searching the woods to our left. There is no one in this belt of trees to our right. We will move through there quickly until we come to the main track near the abbey gates."

He led the way and they reached the track safely, dropping down into the shelter of the bushes near the gates. Just as they did so, the chanting stopped. Looking back towards the hill, Elric could see a glow in the sky as though a fire had been lit. The others followed his gaze. The magic of their keen eyesight would not let them see through obstacles, so they did not know what Myrddin was doing. "He is up to some fearful work," whispered Wyvern. "We must hurry."

They could see that the roadway to the abbey was clear. So too was the wooded slope on the opposite side which rose near the wall of the herb garden. They quickly crossed the roadway into the trees and paused again. Ahead was the slope of coarse grass leading to the top of the cliff path, where Elric and Bridget had met on Friday, almost two days before. They looked at each other, both thinking that it seemed so long ago.

"Stay!" Wyvern said. "I will check the beach." He flew over the sand, his dark shape merging with the clouds. The wind was strong and loud now and the beach was misty, but he could see straight down through the mist. The beach was deserted. He wheeled round and came back to land near the others. "Come quickly down the path."

68

They hurried from their shelter, but their luck did not hold. Something streaked past them, stopping at the top of the cliff path. From behind, Myrddin's voice called, "Stand!"

The terrible hound turned to face them. They could see it as sharply as in daylight. It was a horrible sight. It stood at bay, snarling at them, its eyes glowing red in the darkness. It was huge and grey and its teeth looked frighteningly sharp. They could not turn and run. Elric stepped in front of Bridget. "Get back to the trees," he managed to say before Myrddin appeared.

The magician stood before them, his hood blown back, his robes billowing in the wind. He fixed his eyes on Babwyn and Wyvern. "I see you have friends to help you, Brendan the Healer, but they are not as strong as my hound, Azab. Now give me the wonderful book, whoever holds it, and we shall all return to the abbey."

Behind Myrddin, six of Avaric's men appeared, two carrying flaring torches. Elric could see that they too were amazed and terrified at the sight of the hound. Father Brendan called above the sound of the wind, "You do not need the boy for your wicked schemes. Take me, the book and these creatures and let the boy go free."

He did not mention Bridget, hoping that Myrddin had not seen her, for she was supposedly at home with Ethelburga. Elric knew that as soon as Father Brendan spoke and he had stepped in front of her, she had disappeared back into the trees.

"Silence, old man." Myrddin was speaking to

Father Brendan. "Hand the book to me at once. The boy will come too."

"Give him the book, Elric," Father Brendan said wearily. As Elric began to take off the satchel, a great cloud of gulls descended on the dog, screeching and flapping. The beast was caught off balance. It slithered down the cliff, overwhelmed by the number of birds attacking it. At the same time, a rush of birds knocked Myrddin to the ground and he rolled back towards the trees. Avaric's men did not attempt to help him, but took to their heels, chased by the gulls.

Free again, Father Brendan, Elric, Wyvern and Babwyn ran to the path. They could see Bridget standing on the beach below. The hound was still snarling and howling beneath a huge cluster of gulls. They all ran down to join Bridget and find a hiding place, but they did not need one. As they neared the water's edge a shape appeared.

"It's Sunday!" said Elric joyfully.

Rocking gently on the water was a long curragh, one of the old Celtic boats. On its prow a globe of intense light was gradually becoming more solid. As they stood panting, the small waves lapping their feet, the light formed itself into Avis, the white bird.

"Into the boat at once," he called to them. As the others climbed in, Wyvern rose to settle himself beside Avis.

Bridget leaned over the side and gave a musical whistle. Almost at once a gull appeared out of the mist which still surrounded the boat. Bridget took a small silver bangle from her wrist and as the gull hovered close to her, she placed it in its beak. Then she stroked its feathers and it took off, flying into the lightening sky.

"It is the signal to Mother," she said. "That is one of my special gulls. He will fly home and leave the bracelet on my bed. Mother will know that Father Brendan is rescued and we are safe."

The curragh began to move away from the shore. As it did so, Bridget's gulls rose in a noisy throng from the beach. Warm white mist enveloped the boat, but through it they could see Myrddin. He had reached the bottom of the cliff path and with the departure of the gulls, the hound had risen to stand beside him. The two grey figures watched the departing cloud.

Chapter Twelve

Avis and Wyvern came down into the boat from their perches on the prow. Together they formed a comfortable circle, for there were wooden seats in the boat covered in sheepskins. They were moving swiftly through the water, the brown sail billowing steadily as though there was a good driving wind behind them, but they could not even feel a breeze.

Father Brendan, looking very happy and excited, asked, "Tell me, is this craft a perfect copy of St Brendan's? It is just as I have heard it described in the old tales. That one was made of leather, stretched over a stout wooden frame and greased to make it waterproof. This one is the same."

"This boat is not a copy," Avis told him. "It is the very same boat which St Brendan used on his voyage to the Isles of Truth. After he returned to his native Ireland, leaving his boat by the shore, it disappeared. We, the white birds, took it to our island where it has been preserved in case of a need such as this."

Father Brendan was so delighted, for a little while he could not speak. Then he sighed happily and said, "What an honour this is for me!"

"Also," Avis told them, "although we left the shore at Woden's Bay, the sea beneath is always part of the Sea of Faith. Soon we shall leave your world but you will not feel any discomfort. Then we shall sail to the Paradise of the Birds. From there you must all go on without me to find the help we need to defeat Myrddin. You see, I know all that has happened since I left you. I did not know the extent of Myrddin's power but it is very great. I hoped we could at least protect the garden until your return, but he acted too swiftly for us. Your garden, Father Brendan, is an ancient magic circle of the Druids. Myrddin destroyed its goodness, to use it for some evil of his own. As yet, I do not know how."

Suddenly the speed of the boat increased and the mist changed. Rainbow colours filtered through it, turning it into a beautiful tissue of soft greens, pinks, blues and yellows. Bridget jumped to her feet, plunging her arms into it. "Isn't it beautiful? What's happening?"

"We are out of your world now. In a moment you will see the coast of the Paradise of the Birds."

As Avis spoke, they broke through the mist. There before them stretched the shimmering waters of the Sea of Faith. They all gasped and leaned over the side of the boat, dipping their hands into the warm silky sea. The whole scene was bathed in clear silvery light. Sky and sea seemed to be one at first, but from time to time, the surface of the water gave off sparkling flashes which varied in colour as diamonds do when the light catches them from different angles. In the far distance they could see the faint outlines of two islands and to the right, in the direction in which they were travelling, another island, quite close. Its shore looked rocky and, as they approached, a huge flock of white singing birds rose in the air. It was music of goodness and gladness, which made them realise more than ever that Myrddin's chanting was the music of wickedness and misery.

Without seeming to slacken speed, the boat glided between two large rocks and stopped. Avis and Wyvern spread their wings to fly slowly on to the beach. The others climbed out. The white birds gathered around Avis. They were all golden-crested and very like him but slightly smaller. They gazed at their visitors with intelligent amber eyes. None of them spoke.

"Welcome to the Paradise of the Birds," said Avis solemnly. "Now we must give you some refreshment after your journey." They sat down on the soft silvery sand around a large flat rock. Four of the birds spread a white cloth, carrying it delicately in their beaks. Others brought circular pieces of snow-white bread, which served as plates. On to these were heaped little green shoots. More of the birds brought baskets of fruits, apples, sweet berries and soft golden peaches. Next they were given goblets of crystal water. The meal was so delicious that they were sure they would never taste anything quite so wonderful again.

It was strange and beautiful to sit on the beach sharing a meal with the graceful white birds. They wondered about the food, and it was Bridget that asked, "This food is so lovely, Avis. Where does it come from?"

"Of course you are wondering, little girl. We do

not need food except when we are given the form of birds. So, all we have to do is to place this white cloth in the small cave yonder, where the stream runs out, and the food appears. The good Lord provides us with what we need." Bridget looked along the beach to where the stream ran into the sea. It came from a round opening in the rocky shore. She hoped there would be time to explore the island when they had eaten.

After their meal, Father Brendan placed the book on the cloth so that all the birds could see it. Some hovered in the air above it, as he slowly turned the pages. Then they rose into the air singing joyfully.

"They are glad to see this book," Avis told Father Brendan. "Through it the Magic of Truth made contact with you. They do not speak for it is not necessary that we all chatter. I was chosen to speak to your ancestor, St Brendan, and so I have been chosen to speak with you. Now I must tell you that the magic will never leave the book. All the herbs which you have pictured can be used for good or evil. They will never fade. As they leave the book and are used, more will appear to take their places. It is not the same with the creatures of the book. Babwyn and Wyvern are no longer on the cover, but they will return, as they have told you, when their task is finished. My place will remain empty unless I am needed again and then, my picture will return. After your time, the power to call me will only pass to certain of your descendants. Myrddin could use the book and Babwyn and Wyvern if they allowed him to, but he could never control me."

When Avis stopped speaking, Bridget and Elric felt very serious, though they did not really want to think about the distant future just then. Father Brendan closed the book and said quietly, "What is the next thing that we must do, for you said that we had to find stronger help than yours?"

"You will return to the boat, taking the book. Babwyn and Wyvern will go with you but I shall not. In the Isles of Truth, I may only stay on this island unless I am called to your world. You can see the two islands across the sea. The one on the right is the Isle of St Ailbe. The boat will take you there and you will be told what to do when you arrive. You must leave at once, now you are rested."

"I wish we could see the rest of your island," said Bridget wistfully.

"We must go." Elric sounded impatient. "What about time? What is happening at the abbey while we are away? If we don't bring help as soon as possible, the villagers will probably attack. They could not win. Many people might be killed."

Avis nodded wisely. "Elric is right, I'm afraid. I will answer his question about time. You see, if you were to remain here in the Isles of Truth, you would not grow any older, but in your world, time as you know it continues as normal. We must not give Myrddin too much of it to create more mischief and misery. Never mind, Bridget, you will see the Isle of St Ailbe, and this island is only small. The rocks and sand are the same all around it. The centre is rocky too, with just a few trees. We do not need a large island."

They moved towards the boat, which still rode on the silvery water between the two rocks. They wished Avis were coming with them, as they all climbed into it, but he perched on the prow again to give them some last advice. "Remember to keep your faith and trust in the good Lord and your journey will be a safe one. Lose faith and the boat may drift into the Ocean of Doubt, which surrounds the Sea of Faith. Now go, and God Speed!"

Avis rose into the air followed by the other birds to send them on their way with beautiful singing. The boat swung around and sped across the sea away from the Paradise of the Birds.

Chapter Thirteen

The two islands, one of which was that of St Ailbe, were further away from the Paradise of the Birds than they had seemed. However, the ancient boat moved smoothly through the water and soon they could no longer see the white birds. Bridget was sitting beside Father Brendan and he began to talk to her. Babwyn and Wyvern came closer to listen, but Elric was sitting in the stern looking out across the water.

"I have been thinking about where we are going. Avis called it the Isle of St Ailbe. In his travels St Brendan found Ailbe himself with a group of monks. They held their services in a beautiful chapel where holy fire appeared at evening to light the lamps. I wonder if we shall see that, or if we shall meet anybody. If there are monks there I suppose they will tell us what to do."

Wyvern puffed out small blue flames. "I could make fire to light the chapel lamps."

"Stop that!" cried Babwyn. "You might set fire to the sail."

Bridget smiled at them and turned to Father Brendan, "Did you know about the Ocean of Doubt? Is it in the stories of St Brendan?"

"I have not heard that name before, Bridget,

but not all the monks who travelled with St Brendan kept their faith. Now I remember that there is one part of the story which tells of how they came to a terrifying island. There were creatures there who looked like goblins or devils and they threw hot coals at St Brendan's boat, this very one we are sailing in. Then they saw a high mountain. Smoke and flames poured from its top. The unfaithful monk leaped from the boat and was drawn towards that island. They never saw him again. I think that the monk who did not believe in the Truth caused this boat to be carried into the Ocean of Doubt. Once the unfaithful monk left them, they sailed safely back."

Elric, sitting by himself, had not been listening to Father Brendan. He was thinking of Myrddin and how they could beat him, but he found himself remembering Myrddin's face as he had seen it by the light of the moon in Father Brendan's room.

At that moment, Myrddin was in Father Brendan's room at the abbey. He was seated on the floor in front of a large chafing-dish. The room was full of bitter-smelling yellow smoke. The blackened and bewitched twigs of the elder bush which Myrddin had destroyed in the herb garden were burning in the dish. Many people would not burn the wood of the elder for fear of seeing the shapes of hobgoblins in the smoke. These twigs were filled with the wicked magic of the magician. He sat chanting and muttering, gazing into the smoke until he made out the hazy form of Elric's face. With a triumphant cry he concentrated harder than ever and tossed more twigs into the bowl.

Elric sat staring ahead at the approaching island, but he did not see it. Myrddin's face became clearer and clearer. He could not see Father Brendan, Bridget, Babwyn and Wyvern except, as dim shapes around him. Only Myrddin's face was real. It was surrounded by a yellow cloud. The blue eyes pierced through him.

The boat began to rock. Babwyn fell over in the bottom of the boat. Wyvern perched on the side to see what was happening, but then had to spread his wings to stop himself falling into the sea. Father Brendan and Bridget stood up, but they were suddenly flung backwards as a wave broke against the side, covering them with glistening splashes.

"What is happening?" cried Bridget. The boat veered round, changing course, turning away from the two islands. The silvery light and calm shimmering waters were changed. Elric sat rigid on the seat. Though waves began to toss the boat about, he did not slip or cry out but clung doggedly to the side, staring straight in front of him. The others cowered together in the bottom of the boat. The mist came back, not the rainbow mist, but a cold clinging one which struck through to their bones, making them shiver. It became so thick that they could not see each other, even though they were huddled together.

Elric's voice suddenly rang out. It was harsh and strange, not like his own voice. "We are lost! We should never have left our own world. We have been tricked! We must go back . . . back . . . back!"

His voice trailed away like an echo. The boat began to lurch even more. It gathered speed, plunging forward into a huge wave which practically swamped them. Bridget screamed as she was flung against the seat where Elric sat. Then she heard Wyvern calling fiercely, "Elric! Elric! Think of Avis. Remember to keep faith. You are making this happen!"

Elric felt furiously angry. He felt he was right. He could see Myrddin plainly now, standing in the yellow cloud, beckoning to him, speaking. "Elric, listen to me carefully. Take hold of the book and I will be able to bring you safely back to me. You will become a great leader. But you must hold fast to the book."

"Bridget!" Father Brendan's voice was weak and shaky. "The book! And your golden torc. Try touching them both. Babwyn! Wyvern! Help me! The boat is being attacked."

Bridget reached for her golden necklet with one hand and stretched out her other towards the book which was beside Elric on the seat. She knew where it should be, but the mist was so thick she could not see it at once. As her hand grasped her necklet, however, she dimly saw Myrddin's figure hovering in front of Elric. She could hear his voice clearly. He was repeating, "Take hold of the book. Hold it fast!"

"Elric!" she called. "Don't listen! It is Myrddin!" But Elric was searching for the book on the seat beside him. As he did so the mist cleared slightly. He and Bridget saw it at the same time. They both took hold of it together, pulling in a desperate tug of war. Bridget gasped with the effort of holding on as Elric tried to wrench it out of her hands. Her arms were hurting, but she did not let go. She knew that as long as she hung on the power of her golden torc would help her. The boat seemed to have stopped moving.

Suddenly the mist swirled away, only to reveal another struggle. Clawing and scrambling at the sides of the boat were dull green dragon-like creatures about the same size as Wyvern. Father Brendan, Babwyn and Wyvern were beating them off, pushing them from the edge of the boat into the sea. A dreadful sea! Black and bubbling like a huge pond of tar, it held the leather boat fast.

"This must be the Ocean of Doubt," thought Bridget. "Myrddin has Elric in his power. If I could only touch him with my torc and not lose my hold on it and the book, we might be saved." She gritted her teeth. Elric's face looked different. He was glaring at her as though he hated her. He was much stronger than she was and kept pulling harder and harder.

Bridget snatched the torc from around her neck, but did not let go of it. As the book slipped away from her, she touched Elric's face with the torc, still grasping it herself. He gave a terrible cry, let go of the book and slumped across the seat. Bridget heard a distant roar of rage from Myrddin. Then all was quiet except for the noise of Babwyn sobbing. The boat spun round in a giddy half-circle, then shot forward. Bridget, replacing the torc round her neck, looked up to find that they were once again entering the Sea of Faith. Babwyn was calling to her. "The sea-dragon bit him. He is dying!"

On the bottom of the boat lay Father Brendan. He seemd to be trying to say something. Babwyn and Wyvern were crouched beside him. Bridget stumbled to his side. The old priest had been poisoned by the bite of one of the slimy green dragons which had attacked the boat. Babwyn lifted his sleeve and showed Bridget a large purple bruise and a small gash, where the dragon's tooth had torn his flesh. Father Brendan opened his eyes and murmured, "Green ginger . . . green ginger . . . "

Bridget did not know what he meant. She looked at Babwyn and Wyvern but they shook their heads. She turned to look at Elric, but he was still lying along the seat. He did not move when she shouted to him.

"What shall we do?" she asked Wyvern desperately.

"Green ginger?" the little dragon said, "it must mean something."

Then Elric spoke, shakily, but in his own voice. He had raised his head and was staring down at Father Brendan. "Green ginger, wormwood he means. Give me the book." He struggled to a sitting position as Babwyn passed him the book. "I saw it in here. It's the cure for sea-dragon bites. Here it is, if only I can call it out of the page."

"Quickly!" cried Bridget. "He's getting weaker!" Elric stared and stared at the page, willing the plant to appear. Silently he begged Avis to help Father Brendan. Bright light glowed from the plant. Then it was there on top of its picture, with its nodding yellow flowers and sharp gingery smell. Elric grasped it and passed it to Bridget. She laid it on Father Brendan's wound. The light stayed and the smell of the powerful magical herb grew stronger. Father Brendan began to breathe more easily. His eyes opened. He smiled at Bridget and looked around.

"We are saved, thank God, and I am well again." Sitting up, he removed the herb from his arm. The bruise and the gash had disappeared completely!

The boat was moving swiftly towards a sandy beach, from which sheer cliffs rose high into the air. Tired and bedraggled, but with a triumphant feeling that they had won a battle, the four of them looked at Elric, who sat with his head in his hands. He was ashamed. He knew that he had doubted.

For a short time, he had stopped believing in the Magic of Truth, and Myrddin had been able to contact him. Then he had listened to Myrddin's lies. Now he knew of course that they were lies. Myrddin would not have made him into a leader. They would all have been lost in the Ocean of Doubt, perhaps forever. "Wyvern was right," thought Elric.

"I caused the danger," he said aloud. "Father Brendan nearly died. If it hadn't been for you, Bridget, we'd all have been lost. You were right, you know, I am a coward!"

He sat looking at the bottom of the boat, angry with himself, not knowing how to tell them how sorry he was. Then he coughed. There was a puff of smoke in his face. He lifted his head to see Wyvern's funny scaly face close to his own. Babwyn landed beside him with a tremendous thump and pulled his hair. Father Brendan was laying his hand on his shoulder. Bridget stood in front of him, and said, "It's a good thing you remembered about the green ginger."

Chapter Fourteen

Elric stood up and faced the others as the boat skimmed gracefully into shore. "I want to say how sorry I am that I was so stupid. I know that somehow Myrddin was able to contact me, but I was wrong to stop believing, even for a little while. He nearly defeated us."

They were all silent for a moment, then Father Brendan spoke for everyone. "Thank you, Elric, but now you must not go on blaming yourself. We were in great danger, but we did learn some very important things. We now know that if we only give Myrddin a tiny chance, he can use his power against us even here. We must all be on our guard all the time. We also found the wonderful healing power of the book. It was very quick of you, Elric, to realise what I was trying to tell you. Now, let us go ashore and see what we have to do. First I suppose we must find a way up these enormous cliffs; there must be a path."

On the beach, they all felt very small, for the cliffs were terribly high. The rock was a beautiful reddish-bronze and to their left, two waterfalls cascaded into a river, which flowed into the sea about half a mile from where they now stood. They began to walk towards it to search for a pathway.

Wyvern suddenly said, "I know, if I fly over the cliffs while you try to find a way up, then I can come back and tell you what I have seen." Wyvern rose into the air and flew off.

The air was different. Wyvern found that he could fly higher and faster than when he had flown over the beach at Woden's Bay. He felt wonderfully light. He swooped and turned, making perfect flying manoeuvres. He was enjoying himself so much that he almost forgot what he had set out to do. Swinging round in a beautiful arc, he rose quite gracefully, for a dragon, right above the cliff wall. There he could see that the cliffs encircled a bowl-shaped valley. Its green meadows were sprinkled with flowers. In the centre of the valley stood a hall and a church, surrounded by smaller buildings. He could not imagine what they were built out of, for they glistened and sparkled in the silvery light. Wyvern thought the whole scene looked so peaceful that he wanted to land there at once. He turned to go back to the others. As he flew back over the valley, he saw a procession of white-robed figures moving towards the top of the cliffs. He flew after them, but they disappeared from sight. Quickly, Wyvern sailed down to the beach, making a perfect landing beside Babwyn. They were watching the procession wending its way down a narrow pathway in the towering rocks.

"I hope you enjoyed yourself!" Babwyn said to Wyvern. "You're a nice scout! I should have gone myself. I could have climbed those cliffs twice while you were doing all that fancy flying."

"Ah! Little monkey, since you cannot fly, you do not know how wonderful it was in that upper air."

"Please stop it, you two. Wyvern, tell us what you saw!" Bridget said, laughing at them. "There's some sort of procession coming to meet us."

"There is an abbey, I think, in a lovely green valley. It is built of sparkling stone and the air is so sweet. You have never seen anything like this place in your world."

"Now we shall find out what we must do." Father Brendan pointed at the white-robed monks who were approaching. "These brothers must be descending from the abbey in the green valley."

There were eight men. The leader carried a golden Celtic cross, held high before him. From behind him, a tall old man with white hair stepped forward.

"Welcome, Father Brendan, my children and you good creatures of the book. Your ancestor, St Brendan, came to visit us quite some time ago. Come, follow us to our home, where you must first share our meal."

Bridget whispered to Elric, as they followed behind the procession, "When is St Brendan supposed to have come here?"

"It's over two hundred years ago, I think. Of course! You mean that these are the same monks! Wait a minute. Don't you remember? Avis said that if we were to stay here we shouldn't get any older than we are now."

Although it was a hard climb, they did not feel tired when they reached the top of the cliffs. They were delighted when they saw the green meadows and the shining buildings of the monastery in the distance. The white-haired monk who walked beside Father Brendan turned to them, saying, "We did not build the monastery, but found it ready and waiting for us when we received the call to come here some time before St Brendan's visit. It is built of blocks of crystal. So are the seats and the altar in the church. You will see it when you have eaten."

Before going into the hall, they were taken to a pool beneath some trees. There they washed their faces and hands and bathed their feet. The water was warm and full of bubbles, as the pool was above a spring. Inside the dining hall were long wooden tables and benches. All the monks were assembled for a meal of more of the delicious white bread and green shoots. While they ate, the oldest monk told them that he was Ailbe, abbot of the monastery. All of them kept a rule of silence most of the time, only breaking it for their morning council and to sing in the church and recite the prayers.

"We are very happy to be quiet and go about our work, but this is a very special occasion, so I am going to allow the rule to be broken." He raised his voice. "My brothers, in honour of our guests, you may talk to them and to each other."

The other monks began to talk to Bridget and Elric while Abbot Ailbe was deep in conversation with Father Brendan. However, by the end of the meal, it was Babwyn and Wyvern who were the great favourites. When the food was cleared away, Babwyn hopped on to the table and went along solemnly shaking hands with each monk in turn. He turned somersaults down the whole length of the table. Then he gave a mighty leap and repeated his performance on the other tables. Everyone began to laugh at him, including the abbot. Not to be outdone, Wyvern gave a flying demonstration, zooming around the hall and blowing out smoke and sparks until the room rang with laughter. At last Abbot Ailbe asked for silence.

"Now that you have entertained us so well, I must take you to see the crystal chapel. Before we go I must tell you who is going to help you in your troubles. Listen carefully and do not be afraid. Remember that fear and doubt will cause your strength to weaken. I know that on your way here you entered the Ocean of Doubt and were in great danger. Do not look so sad and ashamed, Elric. Myrddin has great power." He smiled kindly at Elric and continued. "Our very special duty on this island is to be the guardians of the Royal Sleep. In the King's Hall, beyond the crystal chapel, lie King Arthur, Queen Gunamara and the great Merlin. Theirs is a sleep of the highest magic, from which they can only be awakened if the need is great enough and the right people perform the awakening correctly."

Bridget and Elric gazed at him with their eyes opening wider and wider. They could hardly believe their ears. They were going to meet King Arthur and his queen! They were going to meet Merlin, the greatest of all the magicians. Then they were not dead, but lay in the Isles of Truth.

Abbot Ailbe looked straight at both of them.

"You, Elric, and you, Bridget, as members of their two families, must awaken the sleepers. Merlin may be more difficult to awaken than the king and queen. I do not know, but we shall see. Now, are you ready to come with me?"

He stood up and so did the whole company. Bridget and Elric spoke together. "Yes, we are ready."

Chapter Fifteen

The abbot took Bridget, Father Brendan, Elric, Babwyn and Wyvern, out of the hall and across the lawns to the chapel. It was an oddly-shaped church, for it looked as though a smaller chapel had been stuck on to the larger one at one end. They thought that if that were the King's Hall, it wasn't very big.

Inside the crystal chapel, all was quiet and peaceful. As they had been told, the seats were made of crystal and the altar was a solid block, set with precious stones in a beautiful design. Silver lamps hung down from the ceiling and the light was fading.

"Watch and wait," said the abbot. "In a moment the lamps will be lit in a manner you have never seen before."

Almost as he spoke, an arrow with a blue flame at its tip sailed slowly through the open window of the church. The flame was applied to each lamp in turn, then the arrow turned and floated away again out of the window. "We do not question the happenings on this island. We have learned that all is arranged for the best. Now, we must prepare for the awakening. Please lay the book down on the altar, Father Brendan." Father Brendan did so, and they all gathered round. "My friends," said the abbot, "in a few moments we shall go through that door into the King's Hall."

He pointed to a narrow door behind the altar, above which burned one of the lamps. The door was richly decorated, made of silver, and the designs were like those of the borders in the book.

"Now, good Father Brendan, from your book I need euphrasie, or eyebright as you call it. This, together with the sprig of rue which Avis gave you, will awaken the king and queen. I do not yet know if it is powerful enough to waken Merlin."

Father Brendan gave the rue to Abbot Ailbe. Then turning the pages of his book to where the pretty purple and white flowers of eyebright were pictured, for the first time, he himself tested the magic of his book. It was an exciting moment for the good old man. His hand trembled as he gently stroked the picture, fixing his gaze on the flowers, willing them to become as real as they already looked. The soft light, which shone from the book all the time now, grew stronger above the picture. He reached out his hand, as though he were once again in his herb garden picking the plant he needed. As he did so, there, lying on the page, was a posy of the herb. He picked it up and handed it to Ailbe, saying, "A drop of juice must be squeezed on the eyelids."

The abbot bowed graciously and took from his belt a long silver key. He turned and unlocked the narrow door. They all followed him into the King's Hall.

93

*

Beyond the door, they had expected to find a crystal room, similar to, but smaller than, the church they had left. Instead, they found themselves in an enormous hall. The walls were made of the same crystal stone. Father Brendan had been to Rome when he was younger, but had never seen any church like this hall, even there. They stood still in wonder, gazing around them. The pillars which rose to the roof were like fountains of crystal, frozen forever. In the high ceiling, golden decorations made intricate patterns. Elric had always thought that King Ini's hall was splendid but, compared with this, it was plain and small. There were no windows here and the walls were hung with tapestries woven with pictures of the Isles of Truth. The mosaic floor's design contained every shade of blue and purple. Although there were no lamps, the whole hall was filled with the same light which always shone from the book, but this glow was brighter and more golden.

The greatest wonders of all were three couches, two side by side in the centre of the hall and the third positioned across the feet of the other two. Bridget began to feel afraid as she looked at them. She put her hand to the golden torc and kept it there. Elric gazed at the figures on the couches, willing himself not to be afraid. He knew that fear and doubt could cause danger and defeat. After his fears in the boat, he was determined to keep hold of his faith, at least until Myrddin was defeated. They were all glad that Ailbe had told them whom they would find in the hall. Now he spoke to them. "I can see that you children are going to be worthy of the work you have to do."

As they walked to the middle of the hall, Bridget fixed her eyes on the figure of the queen, while Elric looked steadily at Arthur's couch. Father Brendan, Babwyn and Wyvern followed at a little distance. None of them wanted to look at Merlin at first, but the abbot stopped beside his bed. The magician lay on his back, as did the king and queen. He wore his ceremonial white robe, covered with symbols of High Magic in gold and silver. Around the hem was runic writing embroidered in green, entwined with a pattern of oak leaves. He had a noble face with a high forehead, a grey beard and a large, slightly hooked, nose. They were shocked by the resemblance to Myrddin. Bridget trembled, holding her necklet tighter. Merlin slept peacefully, breathing very gently as though he had only just fallen asleep.

Bridget moved to the side of Queen Gunamara. She knew her at once from the dream. How beautiful she was! Her hair was the same red-gold as Bridget's, but gathered into a thick braid which lay over one shoulder. Her robe was green as in the dream. Round her neck was a golden torc, identical to the one Bridget wore.

Elric was beside Arthur, looking at his face. It was calm and handsome in sleep, with wrinkles at the corners of the eyes. His hair was brown and he was clean-shaven, as the Romans had been. He was dressed in a tunic of deep red, over trousers of soft leather. Over all, his mantle was deep purple fastened with a golden dragon-shaped pin. His battle penant, a red dragon on a gold background, was fixed at the head of his couch.

Then Bridget took the flowers which the abbot had handed to her. She selected two from the little posy and leaned over the couch. She wanted so much to wake the queen, wanted to speak to her, as one of her very own family. She squeezed the juice on to Gunamara's eyelids. Then she looked over at Elric, for she needed the rue. It had to be both the abbot had said. Elric was standing transfixed before the king. Now he raised the sprig of rue and brushed Arthur's eyelids with it. He gave it to Bridget, who handed him two more flowers from the posy of eyebright. She touched the queen's eyes and Elric squeezed the dewy drops on to Arthur's lids.

They waited, watching and hoping, but it was Abbot Ailbe who spoke first. "Now the great Merlin. Come."

Abbot Ailbe took the flowers and the sprig of rue from Elric and Bridget. He handed them to Father Brendan, saying, "Father, you must have the honour of trying to wake Merlin. It is you who made the Book of Brendan."

While the others watched, Father Brendan stepped forward. He applied the juice to Merlin's eyes and brushed them with the rue. He had just done so when there was a sigh from Gunamara's couch. Bridget rushed to her side, as the queen moved her head on the silken roll of pillow.

"Your Majesty," whispered Bridget.

"Who wakes me?" she asked. Then she looked

straight at Bridget. "Ah, it is my little Bridget!"

Bridget was too happy to speak. She just smiled and smiled at the queen, as she sat up on her couch.

Almost at the same time, King Arthur awoke. As he sat up, Elric bowed low. The king immediately swung himself off his couch and stood before Elric. Arthur placed his hand on Elric's shoulder. "So you are the son of Imelda who married Eadfrid the Saxon." He turned to greet the queen, taking both her hands and kissing her. The abbot, Father Brendan, Babwyn and Wyvern, all bowed to the king and queen, who both took everyone's hand in turn, even grasping Wyvern's claw. Then all went to stand by Merlin's head. There was no movement. The greatest of the ancient magicians slept on. Something more powerful than the herbs in the book was needed to wake him.

Chapter Sixteen

Two chairs were placed at the end of the hall for the king and queen to greet everyone when they had walked in a solemn little procession from the church. The dining tables were moved aside. Bridget sat on a cushion near the queen and Elric stood beside Arthur's chair. Babwyn stayed at the queen's feet near Bridget. Gunamara stroked his head from time to time and he looked up at her with his odd little face wreathed in smiles. King Arthur had saluted Wyvern as, "My noble and royal dragon", so Wyvern perched on the back of his chair and would not move to any other place. Abbot Ailbe and Father Brendan had seats on either side of the royal couple. The monks sat on the wooden benches, which were arranged in a V-shape, so that all could hear the king speak.

"My Friends, my queen and I have been awakened from our long sleep to help these brave children, this good Father and these two valiant creatures of the wonderful Book of Brendan. We shall remain awake until the evil magician, Myrddin, is defeated and punished. If that task is successful, we shall once again sleep in the King's Hall. I should not say 'if' for together we *must* succeed. In order to do so we need to awaken my great and wise adviser, Merlin.

It is necessary for Queen Gunamara and Bridget to go to the Island of Promise, for the eyebright from the book was not powerful enough to wake Merlin. From the Island of Promise they must bring back a special spray of eyebright, picked by the linnet, the bird which first showed that healing herb to men. They must go at once, for worldy time is passing quickly."

So it was that Bridget and Gunamara were escorted from the monastery. Although it was now the middle of the night on the island and they had not slept since leaving Woden's Bay, none of them were the least bit tired. Nor was it dark, but the silvery light of daytime had dimmed to twilight and the crystal stone of the buildings cast a strong glow across the valley.

They did not go to the beach where the curragh was resting, but followed a much shorter path to the opposite side of the island. There, to Bridget's delight, was a sailing barque, graceful and slim, with red silk sails. The seats were covered with embroidered shawls and cushions. Arthur helped the queen aboard. Following his example, Elric helped Bridget to step into the boat, where she sat facing Gunamara. The whole company stood on the shore to watch them leave. It was all so solemn and beautiful that Bridget did not feel anxious about the journey, especially as she was with the queen.

As they sailed across to the Island of Promise, Gunamara talked to Bridget of many things. She told her about her sister, Mabwen, who had been married to one of the high kings of Ireland and of how she had given the matching golden torc to her on her wedding day. Both the necklets had received their power from Merlin himself. Listening to her, Bridget hardly noticed the journey.

On reaching the island, they sailed straight into the mouth of a river, which the queen explained divided the island in two. Lovely willows and rowan trees dipped their overhanging branches into the water. The air was filled with the song of birds. Meadow flowers grew along the banks. At a point where the river narrowed, the barque stopped. They stepped out on to the grassy bank.

"How shall we find the linnet?" asked Bridget.

"We take this path across the meadow. Soon we shall come to a grove of trees and there, we must call to her."

The meadow on either side of the path was waist-high in silky grass and wild flowers. Many of them, Bridget had never seen. Waves of perfume came from them and she wished she could stay on the island for a long time to explore every corner of it. "Please tell me more about the island," she begged Gunamara.

"You must wait until we have the eyebright, for see, here are the trees. On the journey back I will tell you what I know."

They had arrived at the grove and walked in among the trees. At first, Bridget thought that they were apple trees until she looked more closely. The fruit was bright red and hung in glossy bunches. They reminded Bridget of the grapes which Father Brendan grew, except that these were not purple and were much bigger. The queen plucked two from a bunch, gave one to Bridget and began to eat one herself. They were like grapes, with seeds inside and thin skin, but so juicy and delicious that it was like eating and drinking at the same time. The fruit melted in Bridget's mouth and she was so refreshed that even one was almost too much. Gunamara finished eating. She turned and raised her voice to a lovely singing ringing tone.

> Come brown linnet from your nest,
> To listen to a queen's request.

There was silence for a moment or two, for all the other birdsong around them stopped. Then they heard a single little song. The linnet was answering the queen. From further in the orchard, the small brown bird came flying to them. Gunamara held out her arm and the linnet perched on her wrist, cocking its head and looking at her with its bright beady eyes. Bridget watched fascinated, for she knew that the bird understood the queen as she sang to it.

> Please fetch a spray of sweet eyebright,
> With flowers of purple, edged with white,
> The juice of these on your chick's eye
> Will open it to earth and sky.

The bird gave an answering whistle, spread its wings and flew away. "She will not be long," said the queen. "It was the linnet which first taught men that the juice of these flowers helped to heal sore eyes, for they saw how she cleansed the eyes of her newly-born chicks."

Even as she spoke, the linnet returned, carrying

a small posy in her beak. The queen held out her hands and the bird dropped the flowers. Bridget held out her own hand and was delighted when the linnet perched on it. They gently stroked her as they thanked her. When the bird had flown away into the trees, Gunamara said, "Come, we must return at once to the boat."

As soon as they were sitting in the sailing barque, it turned and began to glide back down the river towards the open sea. Bridget did not want to go, but they had to wake Merlin, so she wondered if the queen would remember her promise. She looked at her, about to ask, but Gunamara spoke.

"I have not forgotten that I said I would tell you what I know of the Isles of Truth. When Arthur was seriously wounded at the Battle of Camlann, he was brought back to Holybury. There was great danger from the Saxons, so the monks hid the king in the little secret cave which looks like a burial mound. Merlin had already gone from us and in those days there was of course no Father Brendan with his book of healing herbs. But as I was caring for Arthur, a wonderful light appeared in the room and a beautiful white bird came out of the light. It was Avis. He told me that we were to be taken to the Island of Promise to live in peace. After a time we should be put into a deep sleep, only to be woken if the land were in great danger. Then Avis touched Arthur's wound with the sprig of holy rue. It was healed at once and he stood up as fresh and strong as when he was young. I too became much younger again.

The bird led us down to Woden's Bay, as you now call it. This sailing boat was riding on the waves.

"We quickly made the journey to the Island of Promise. For us there was then no passage of time as we had known it. We lived in perfect happiness. We needed no house or hall. The same warm golden light was there all the time. That is why I know the birds, the paths and the red fruit groves. The rest of the island on the side of the river where we did not land is, I believe, even more beautiful, but we never saw it. Avis told us that we should go there at the end of time. I do not know how many years of the world's time we lived on the island. Then one day the boat came for us once again. Avis was sitting on the prow. We were brought to St Ailbe, where our couches waited for us in the King's Hall. There we saw Merlin sleeping peacefully. We had thought that he was dead. At once we lay down and fell into the same deep and wonderful sleep, from which you woke us."

Bridget had been listening, spellbound to the queen's story. "So she and Arthur had been in the barrow," thought Bridget, and they had also seen and talked with Avis. "Oh! thank you for telling me, Your Majesty. It's a beautiful story. So you do not know any of the other islands in the Sea of Faith?"

"No, my child, I have not seen any, not even the Paradise of the Birds. I do know that the Isles are called Truth because they are part of Heaven. Certain chosen people live here or are brought here because there are still important things for them to do before time itself ends. The monks on St Ailbe guard our sleep. On the Island of Steadfast Men live many holy hermits who spend their time in prayer. On the Island of Delights there is a banqueting hall, where travellers from earth are allowed to spend some time, as a reward for some special good they have done. They return to earth refreshed to fight against evil. But, look, Bridget, I have talked so much that we are arriving. They are waiting to meet us."

Bridget would have loved to listen to Gunamara for ever, but there was the beach. Only Arthur and Elric were waiting to meet them. When they were out of the boat, King Arthur said, "How alike you are! Bridget could be your small daughter as you stand beside each other."

This made Bridget feel exactly as she supposed a royal princess must feel. She carried her head high as she tripped along behind the king and queen. Elric could not resist teasing her. "Well, Princess Bridget, do you mind if I walk beside you?"

Bridget turned around sharply, a bit cross, but when she saw Elric smiling broadly, she realised that she must have looked funny and they both burst out laughing.

Chapter Seventeen

As Bridget and Elric walked along, she told him about her journey and the story of Arthur and Gunamara hiding in the barrow. Elric said, "Isn't it strange and wonderful, Bridget, that they belong to us? I mean we really are their descendants. We're in the same families from long long ago. We have to be very careful about believing, don't we? I know that now! When we went off course it was because I doubted to begin with." Poor Elric could not stop thinking about the danger he felt he had taken them into.

"But it's strong magic, Elric. You must not go on saying it was your fault. When I touched my torc, in the boat, I *saw* Myrddin! He must have been able to use a spell to *make* you doubt. Isn't Merlin like him, but he has a good face and Myrddin has an evil face? When I saw Merlin on the couch, I had to touch my torc to stop myself being afraid that he might suddenly turn into Myrddin and we would find that we had been cheated. I know that sounds stupid and horrible, but you see what I mean about you in the boat?"

"Yes!" Elric sounded quite excited. "That's it! That's the meaning of the Magic of Truth and the Magic of Lies. You can slip from the Truth into the

Lies if you don't watch yourself. Its awfully hard. It's like looking at things the wrong way up. If you let yourself, you can start to believe that bad people are good and that doing bad things is wonderful. Then you pretend that good people are cheating you." Elric let out a huge sigh and said again, "It's terribly hard to keep it the right way up."

They both felt very serious and walked in silence for a while. Then Bridget asked, "Did the king talk to you while I was away?"

"He talked to me a lot about courage and how it isn't going to be easy to beat Myrddin. I know he was warning me that we are going to meet a lot of trouble when we go back . . . Look! We're going straight to the chapel. There is Abbot Ailbe with Father Brendan and Babwyn and Wyvern."

When they had greeted each other, the whole group went into the chapel. Ailbe at once took out his silver key and opened the door behind the altar. They all followed the king and queen, she carrying the posy of eyebright. Once inside, they grouped themselves around Merlin's couch. King Arthur stood aside graciously and beckoned to Father Brendan. "Come, good Father, together with my queen, you must wake Merlin."

Father Brendan brushed the magician's eyelids with the rue and Gunamara squeezed the juice from the special posy of eyebright plucked by the linnet on the Island of Promise. They all stepped back a little and waited quietly.

At first nothing happened. Merlin still slept and there was total silence in the huge hall. Just as they were beginning to think that even these flowers would not wake him up, a warm breeze stirred in the enclosed hall. It grew stronger, causing the heavy wall hangings to billow slightly. Quickly it became a wind, blowing Bridget's hair across her face. Sharp gusts began to whip around them. They clutched each other and staggered as they were blown off balance by the increasing force. The king held on to Gunamara to stop her falling. Stronger and stronger blew the wind.

"Down, everyone!" commanded the king. They all slipped and slithered on to the blue mosaic floor. Babwyn rolled himself into a ball. Wyvern hid his head under his wings, which was very difficult for a dragon. Huddled together on the floor, they all covered their eyes as a sudden burst of blue flame above Merlin's head lit the whole of the hall. The wind dropped at the same time.

"Who calls Merlin?" asked an echoing voice which rolled its sound around the walls. It was followed by the deep tone of the echo. "WHO . . . CALLS . . . MERLIN . . . MERLIN . . . MERLIN?" Then there was the sound of dancing feet and a chorus of high voices singing, "Merlin, Merlin, Merlin."

The king arose, helping Gunamara to her feet. Slowly the others looked up. Merlin had risen from his couch. Tall and majestic, he stood in the centre of the hall. Around him a whole troupe of figures danced. They were woodland sprites, dressed in tunics made of oak leaves. They carried mistletoe boughs in their hands, waving them as they danced. Faster and faster they twirled until Merlin raised his hand, when they stopped as if frozen into their positions. Merlin strode forward until he reached the king and queen. He knelt before Arthur on one knee, his head bowed. At once all the sprites fell to their knees before the king.

The others felt awe-struck in Merlin's presence. There was something so remote and deeply magical about him. In spite of all that had happened already, they felt that Merlin's magic was on another kind of level.

The king and queen sat on one of the couches and Merlin sat facing them. The sprites gathered around him, some standing, some sitting on the floor. Babwyn stayed close to Bridget. Wyvern, at a signal from the king, perched beside him. Elric and Bridget were also sitting on the floor. Very graciously, Merlin held out his hand to Father Brendan. "Most gifted priest, please do me the honour of sitting beside me." Father Brendan did so, looking very small, but calm and dignified.

The abbot was invited to sit on the other side of Merlin, who spoke to them all in his deep rolling voice.

"Your Majesties and my friends, I know all! I know why I have been awakened. My wicked descendant shall be severely punished when the time comes. I know what Myrddin has done and is doing at this moment. He will not succeed this time, on one condition." He looked directly at Bridget and Elric. "These two children will have to be braver than many grown men. By the laws of High Magic, you, Elric, and you, Bridget, must not lose your faith in the Magic of Truth, no matter how hard it is to keep believing. If you do, the king and myself will not be able to enter the battle at the time appointed and Myrddin will enslave the land for a long time to come. Do you understand this?"

Bridget and Elric thought that they did and answered a solemn "Yes" together.

"Before I give you your instructions, I will tell you about Myrddin, for you should know how very powerful he is. Time, for magicians, is very different from the time of ordinary mortals, so do not be surprised when I tell you that Myrddin was a boy when I was counsellor to King Arthur. He is a member of my family, but from a different branch. We are both descendants of the families of the Gwyddoniaid, the wise men of the ancient Cymry, or Welsh as the Saxons now call them. There were three orders of wise men, the Druids who were priests, the Bards who were poets and musicians and the Ovates who were the men of healing. Many of course practised all these duties, for they all had the gifts. The gifts have been passed down, but some branches of the ancient families have turned to wickedness, using their power for bad ends. Myrddin's family was such a one. As a youth, he loved to make mischief, to cause troubles for others, but then he was only learning his skills. As a boy still, his family took him to the East and I heard no more of him until this time. I believe, I hope, that I am still greater than he, but I do not know what strange powers he has learned in the long years of his travels. I am angry and ashamed that I, Merlin, should have to say that he is a member of my family." Merlin sat still, his face set, his eyes looking beyond them all. As they watched him, Elric thought he would never want Merlin to be angry with him.

"We shall succeed, Merlin, for our friends here are brave." King Arthur spoke with confidence and reached across the space between the couches to grasp Merlin's hand. The magician looked at Bridget and Elric and spoke again.

"That is true, Your Majesty. Also I have talked much and told them little, except to warn them that Myrddin may have much power which he has not used. We have faith and courage and are on the side of Truth. Now, my friends, you must set sail for the Paradise of the Birds. You will not see Avis for it is not possible for the birds to appear always, even on their island. On the shore you will find a basket of food and water left for you. Take it and return at once to Woden's Bay, then the real battle will begin. You will find that you know how to act as each event takes place. We shall be watching over you. When the time is right, you will see us and Avis once again."

He rose, and the rest of them followed.

The whole company on the island took them down the steep cliffs to the shore. Queen Gunamara kissed Bridget and said, "Remember, my child, the torc will protect you. Have courage."

Elric knelt before King Arthur, who handed him the penant which bore the red dragon upon its golden background, saying, "Receive this standard.

Guard it, and you will carry it before me if you do not allow your faith to falter."

It was sad, but exciting, for they were really on their way now to fight against Myrddin, release their friends and win back the abbey.

Father Brendan carried the book and before he stepped into the boat, Merlin took him aside and spoke quietly to him. Abbot Ailbe blessed them and Babwyn and Wyvern insisted on saying good-bye to all the monks separately. As they sailed away, they watched and waved until they could no longer see the shore.

At the Paradise of the Birds, they did not want to land, for it looked so deserted. Wyvern collected the basket, flying with it in his strong claws. They all sat close together, then, as the boat turned away from the island, Babwyn held Bridget's hand. Elric sat clutching Arthur's standard. Father Brendan sat with the book on his knee and Wyvern beside him. The little dragon kept puffing out small clouds of smoke and it made the old priest uncomfortable, but he did not complain.

As the boat began to pick up speed, they suddenly heard singing from the empty trees. Then directly above them, they heard the beating of wings. Though they could not see Avis, they knew he was speeding them on their way. The leather boat of St Brendan shot forward, carrying them back to Woden's Bay and whatever adventures lay waiting for them.

Chapter Eighteen

In this world's time it was almost a month since the friends had escaped from Myrddin and set sail for the Isles of Truth. While they had been away many sad changes had taken place. Myrddin had become the real ruler of the abbey and its people. Inside the abbey walls the monks and the boys went about in silence. They were still under Myrddin's spell and obeyed orders blindly. After working in the garden, fields, or kitchen, all day, they were assembled in the hall. There they would sit for a poor supper. They did not speak to each other or show any interest in where they were or what they did. They ate and drank mechanically, looking like puppets. When they had finished, they sat staring straight ahead until Myrddin came into the hall. As he stood at the end of the room, all heads turned towards him. Dropping his grey hood, he would turn slowly from side to side, letting his gaze pass over them all. Then he would start to chant softly, his voice rising gradually as he increased the power of the spell, to keep them tightly under his control. While he did this, the hound, Azab, was left on guard outside the door. Not even Avaric was allowed to enter.

Avaric himself was becoming more and more uneasy. In the beginning, when Myrddin had lied to him and flattered him, the Thegn had been tempted by the idea of being a great ruler. Now Avaric had begun to hate the scheming, and the magic frightened him. He was also afraid that he did not know how to get out of Myrddin's clutches. When he went home to Wodenswood, his wife, Ethelburga, was silent and sad. He tried to tell her that all would be well. She would listen quietly and say nothing. On his short visits home he did not ask about Bridget. He just supposed she was there somewhere. His own men were terrified of Myrddin and did not dare to disobey the magician's slightest command.

Chad's father, Oswy, had come to the abbey with some of the other men from the village to try once again to find out what was happening. Myrddin had told them to go back to their homes and their work and not to come near the abbey unless they were sent for. That same night, Myrddin had gone out and the next day a mysterious sickness had struck the villagers. No one died, but in every house, the men were sick. They all wished that Father Brendan could be with them. Miserable and unhappy, the women and children did their best. They were very frightened. They dared not step outside their houses for every evening the huge dog would wander around the village. When Avaric asked Myrddin about the sickness, his only reply was to smile cruelly, saying that it would keep the people quiet.

Near the end of the month, in the early evening, a large ship with a colourful sail and many oars slid into Woden's Bay. It was sighted by one of Avaric's men, who ran to the hall to report to him.

"What is it, Wilfrid?"

"My lord, there is a foreign ship in the bay. She looks like a slave-trader to me, for she is the size and kind. She flies a purple flag which I have seen before on such ships."

"Take some men, Wilfrid. If anyone lands, escort them here when they have handed over their weapons. Take no chances. I will go and see Myrddin, then join you at the shore if you have not returned."

Myrddin used Father Brendan's room now for himself. He would never let anyone enter it when he was not there and usually kept the door locked when he was inside. Avaric rapped on the door, calling, "Are you within, Myrddin?" The door was flung open and evil-smelling yellow fumes poured out into the passage, making Avaric cough and sputter. "What foul brew is that?" he roared. Myrddin stepped out, closing the door behind him. "What do you want?" he asked angrily. Avaric faced him.

"What demon's work are you at now, wizard? By Woden, I begin to wish I had not joined forces with you."

Myrddin fixed him with his glittering blue eyes. "And I, Thegn, begin to wish the same. I am tired of your childishness. What is your news?"

Avaric answered him roughly. "The ship is here, but I do not want to carry out the plan to sell the priests and the boys. No good will come of it. Some of these boys are the sons of powerful men. We shall have armies raised against us."

Myrddin answered him coldly. "Listen to me,

Avaric. You are in too deeply now to withdraw. I make the plans and I have the means to carry them out. Take care not to anger me too much. You are stupid, even though you are a brave fighter. There will be no trouble. Slave-traders visit these shores from time to time. It will be a pity that they have raided the abbey. That is the only news which will be found out. Now we will go and meet the captain and I shall drive a good bargain."

They went outside to see if their visitors were arriving. They were met by Wilfrid, running from the gates.

"Well, where are the traders?"

"My Lord, they are gone!"

"Gone!" Myrddin's voice rose. "What do you mean? Speak, man!"

Wilfrid spoke to Avaric. "I took some men, as you ordered. As we reached the top of the cliff path a small boat was making for the beach, from the slave-traders' ship. Suddenly a patch of mist appeared beyond the big ship. It was odd, for the rest of the sea was clear. The cloud was moving towards the ship. The men in the boat stopped rowing to watch it. Then an amazing thing happened. Some sort of bird, or creature, a dark shape, came out of the mist. It landed on the mast of the ship, I think, though I could not see very clearly at that distance. Then, as we watched, the sail of the trading ship caught fire! The men shouted and rowed back to their ship. The sail began to burn fiercely. Men were shouting and one of them climbed the mast. The burning sail was cut loose and fell into the sea.

Then they took to their oars and began to pull away across the bay."

Myrddin said nothing. In a fury he set off for the shore, followed by Avaric. When they reached the cliff path they could see the trading ship as a speck in the distance. Of the cloud of mist there was no sign. Without speaking to Avaric, Myrddin turned and strode back to the abbey. There, he shut himself up in Father Brendan's room. The yellow fumes had gone and he was pleased with the result. In a large bowl, a brilliant liquid cast a green glow around the room. Carefully he poured it into flasks and hid them away.

"So," he thought, "they are back from the Sea of Faith. I almost destroyed them there, but I shall not be defeated by children and an old priest. I shall find them. Once they are in my power and I have the book, their link with the Magic of Truth will be broken. I have this abbey and soon I shall get rid of Avaric. His lands will be mine and I can go to the Court of Wessex and dictate my terms. In a few short weeks this whole kingdom could be mine. The rest will follow."

In his anger, Myrddin had not noticed the gulls gathering high in the sky, when he and Avaric had gone to the beach. Far into the night, the gulls watched and waited. Avaric's men were afraid to go outside, for the birds were everywhere, perching in hundreds on the roofs and circling slowly over the abbey.

Chapter Nineteen

Wyvern was the "dark shape" which had frightened off the slave-traders. The leather boat had arrived in time to see the trading ship standing off, with the small boat pulling away from it. Babwyn had jumped up and down in a terrible state so that Wyvern told him sharply, "Stop that! What's the matter with you, you silly little monkey."

"I remember! I remember! When I was hiding behind the big chest, Myrddin said that they would sell the monks and the boys at the end of the month. That must be the ship come to take them."

"The end of the month!" Elric groaned loudly. "We've been away ages. We should have got back sooner than this!"

Bridget was desperate. "We must do something quickly. Merlin said we would know what to do, but it's all very well for *him*!" She peered through the mist, then turned to Father Brendan. "Please touch our eyes with the magic rue, so that we can all see what's happening clearly."

He did so at once and Bridget pointed, "Look, that little boat is going away from the ship towards the beach. That means they have not taken them on board yet. They're arriving, not leaving."

"Good," said Father Brendan. "There is still

time, but how can we drive away a large ship?"

Wyvern was crouched on the edge of the boat. He said, "They have stopped rowing. A good thing we are hidden by the mist. They are looking at us. I will stop them. I will fly to the top of the mast of the big ship and set the sail on fire."

"I could call up the gulls," Bridget cried.

"Let me first try my fire. If they see a dragon they will be very frightened. Here goes!"

"Take care, Wyvern," Elric called, feeling very anxious about the little dragon. He was, after all, a very small dragon and Elric wondered if they would be all that frightened of him.

Wyvern flew high into the air. Keeping his height, he began to puff and blow very hard so that he would be ready to shoot out flames when he reached the ship. As soon as he felt he could, he dropped at speed and landed on the yard arm. He had to hold on tight with his claws. The brilliantly-coloured green and orange sail hung limp. He wished for a stiff breeze as he shot out short bursts of flame at the canvas. Below him the men were sprawled on the benches asleep, or leaning over the side watching the strange patch of mist which hid the leather boat. The flames caught the canvas, but only smoked a little, flickered and went out.

Desperately, Wyvern blew and panted. With a mighty effort he managed to blow a much bigger burst of flame. As he did so a slight breeze ruffled the sail so that it billowed into the orange fire. It caught! Wyvern kept on feeding the fire with more flames. But he was exhausted now and he had been seen. The men were shouting and two of them began to climb rapidly towards the little dragon.

One of the men reached him and drew his knife, lashing out at Wyvern in terror when he saw his odd shape. The dragon felt a sharp pain in his side, then he plunged down into the cold salty water of Woden's Bay.

Elric saw him fall first and before any of the others did anything, he had leaped over the side of the boat and begun to swim to where Wyvern had fallen in the water. Elric's father had taught him to swim in the river near his home. As he jumped into the sea, he hoped he was not already too late.

"We will lose them both!" Bridget cried. Instinctively, she gripped her torc and asked Gunamara to help her. At once she saw what to do. Grasping King Arthur's penant in her hand, she pointed it towards Elric. The boat swung towards the boy and the dragon, for Elric had seen Wyvern rise to the surface and had gripped his scaly neck, but he felt himself sinking with him as he still tried to swim with one arm. The boat came alongside and, leaning out, Bridget touched Elric with the penant. It stuck to him and he was lifted out of the water, clutching Wyvern, without any effort from Bridget. Elric lay panting on the bottom of the boat and Bridget put her brown woollen cloak around him. Wyvern lay motionless. His mighty effort, the knife wound and the plunge into the cold sea had been too much for him.

Father Brendan bent over him, listening . . . listening . . . Bridget gave Elric some of the crystal

119

water from the flask in the basket and he began to feel better. "Is he dead?" he asked, feeling, in despair, that his rescue had been too late.

Babwyn was kneeling beside Wyvern, moaning gently, stroking his head and dropping tears on to the dragon's snout.

"Quickly . . . the book . . . I think there is life still."

Bridget passed the book to Father Brendan. He opened it at the page where agrimony, the wound herb, was shown with its spikes of bright yellow. On the same page was comfrey with its rough hairy stem and purplish-white blooms. As the light hovered on the page, Father Brendan willed the plants to appear. The light trembled for a second or two. Then he was able to pick up the plants from the page. He placed them both on the wound in Wyvern's side. Then he took the flask of crystal water, lifted the dragon's head and managed to pour a little into his mouth.

Then they watched the brave little dragon. Elric moved into the kneeling circle, still shivering from his cold sea plunge. Bridget was holding her torc with one hand and stroking Wyvern with the other. She noticed the darkness of the dragon's blood. The light over the wound herbs grew brighter and brighter, flared intensely for a few seconds, then began to fade. When Father Brendan removed the herbs, the wound was completely healed. He gave Wyvern some more water. A shiver went through the dragon's body. He moved his head a little and opened his eyes.

Babwyn jumped up and down, then turned a somersault off the side of the boat, landing with a thump beside Wyvern. The others heaved an enormous sigh of relief.

"Babwyn, are you there?" Wyvern's voice was not as strong as usual.

"I'm here, Old Scaly!" Babwyn wrapped his skinny arms around Wyvern's neck and hugged him. Bridget turned to Elric.

"You know, Elric, Arthur's penant is quite magic. It stuck to you and hoisted you out. And Elric, I wish I'd never called you a coward. I'll never, ever do so again."

He answered quickly, "Don't be silly. I'm not really brave. I just jumped in. If I'd thought about it I'd have been too scared."

Father Brendan spoke very seriously. "They are helping us, children, but, as Wyvern and Elric did, we have to make tremendous efforts first, ourselves. Come, let us eat a little, for we are nearing the shore."

He put the herbs into his pocket along with the sprig of rue, for when he looked at the book, fresh pictures of agrimony and comfrey had appeared, just as when he first drew them. They ate some white bread and had a drink as they watched the slave ship being rowed out of the bay. Their own boat swung away and ran ashore a little further down the coast, on a stretch of beach hidden by cliffs, just below the woods. The beach was thick with gulls, as was the sky overhead. It was at that moment that Myrddin and Avaric were at the top of the cliff

121

path, also watching the departure of the slave ship.

The gulls jostled each other to welcome Bridget. They flew, circled and dived around her. She stroked and patted them, making humming noises which they understood.

"Hurry, my child," said Father Brendan. "We must get to the barrow. We shall be safe there as well as being in the centre of things. Here we are exposed to danger."

"What about the boat?" asked Elric, turning round. As he did so, the mist around it thickened, then was shot through with the rainbow colours. They had to watch.

"Listen," Wyvern said. Faintly they could hear the song of the white birds. They were taking the boat back to their island. The singing became fainter, the mist began to dissolve. When it had quite gone, the boat too had disappeared.

They stood together on the shore, feeling lonely. Elric clutched the book more tightly. He was still wearing Bridget's cloak, which looked very funny because it was so short for him. Bridget, in her plain green gown was holding the basket and Babwyn's hand. Father Brendan and Wyvern were worried, so they patted and pulled the others until they turned. Then they all climbed quickly up the low cliffs to the shelter of the woods. As they did so all the gulls rose suddenly and swept in a huge cloud over the headland towards the abbey.

Now that they were back in their own time, Father Brendan, Bridget and Elric felt desperately tired, for in the Isles of Truth they had not slept, but had not needed to. Being magical creatures, Babwyn and Wyvern did not feel tired. Even so, no one dared to stop until they had made their way to the boulder door at the foot of Holybury Tor. There, Father Brendan pushed the gargoyle's head and one by one, they slipped inside. By that time, the humans were too tired to speak. Sinking down on the warm sheepskins, they fell fast asleep.

Chapter Twenty

The dragon and the baboon sat beside each other talking quietly.

"I need no sleep, little monkey. What about you?"

"I am not tired either, Wyvern. It is because we are creatures of the book. I like to sleep sometimes, but I don't need to do it every night like the humans. I wanted to ask you something, Wyvern."

"What is that?"

"If you had not been healed by the wound herbs and had died, what do you think would have happened to you?"

"I believe I should have simply gone back to the book as a picture on the cover, but I should never have been able to come alive again."

Babwyn thought about that for a moment. "Yes, I think you are right. If we can come through this adventure, even if we are sealed back in the book for ages, we shall be able to be called upon again for help if we are needed, by the right people."

"Yes, I believe that to be so. Now, Babwyn, we must decide what to do. You and I must find out the position of the enemy. We do not know what has happened while we have been away. It is night-time here and it seems that we have been gone for three weeks of human time. We know that we have foiled

Myrddin's plan for selling our friends in the abbey as slaves. We know that he has a great and dreadful dog to help him. We know he destroyed the garden because it is a magic circle, but we do not know how he will use it. We do not know how things are at the abbey."

Babwyn nodded his funny little head. "You are right, Wyvern. We must try to find out as much as we can tonight. I can move secretly and you can fly. We can be back by the time our friends wake up, for they are very tired. Shall we go together or separately?"

"It will be best if we separate, Babwyn. You go into the woods and talk to the creatures there to find out any news from the village. I shall go to the abbey. I can consult the gulls. The magic of the rue will last until daylight. We must be back by early light."

Without disturbing their friends, they opened the door, slipped outside, closed it carefully and parted silently.

Babwyn crossed the grassy slope of the Tor, keeping low. He moved swiftly in the direction of Wodenswood, which gave its name to Avaric's estates. It stretched to the right, down to the shore and to the left, extended for about a mile. Through the centre of the wood ran a broad stream which marked the boundary between the abbey lands and those of Avaric.

As soon as Babwyn entered the woods and paused, he knew that everything was wrong somehow. Although it was still summer, there were no night noises, no rustlings, no movement of any of the night folk. He could not see any birds roosting, though he sprang up into the trees and moved through the branches, leaping and swinging. Muttering to himself in dismay, he searched everywhere, but he seemed to be alone in the woods. Quickly he went to the stream, thinking that perhaps he might find a vole or a water rat, a frog or a toad.

Crouching on the bank, at first he could only see the fishes gliding silently or lying beside stones on the bed of the stream. Then he caught a suggestion of movement on a large flat stone just below the bank. He peered down, then called softly, "All's well, Toad. I am a friend, but I find the woods empty. Where are all the night folk?"

There was silence for a moment, then a hoarse croaking voice answered, "I have never seen your like before, stranger. What are you?"

"I am Babwyn, a monkey. You do not know my kind, Toad, but I am no ordinary animal. I have been released from the Book of Brendan, the good priest. Are you alone here with the fishes?"

The toad made some more noises to himself, then startled Babwyn by suddenly leaping on to the bank beside him. He could see then that the toad was large and very old. Its skin was coarse and wrinkled, and the leap seemed to have exhausted it, for it did not reply for a long time.

Babwyn wondered if it were dying and tried again. "Where are the woodland creatures? I know that the wizard has taken over the abbey and imprisoned the good monks."

At last the toad replied. "It is good to sit beside you, Nunkey. I can sense the good magic, though I must say I've never heard of nunkeys before. Still, if that's what you are, I suppose it's all right. I am lonely now. You can feel the bad magic, can't you? This wood is no longer fit for any living thing. The great hound of Myrddin stalks here. It has been through tonight. But I am very old. I could not go with them when they all left. We toads have come back to this stream and the pool in the village every spring from the overwintering land on the heath since before my time and my father's and grandfather's before me. This is my home and I shall die here this summer."

Babwyn asked, "Tell me, Toad, what of the people in the village?"

"Sick, Nunkey, all sick."

"Is there a plague in the village, Toad?"

"It is the wizard's doing, Nunkey. The men are all sick and the women and children little better, for they must do all the work and look after the men. None of them get better. I am careful and clever in my way, for I have crept into the houses and seen what a sad state the people are in. But I feel that tonight is different. First I heard the gulls, many of them, for they darkened the sky. Now you have come. You bring good magic. Tell me, Nunkey, can you drive away the wizard and his great dog?"

"Not by myself, Toad, but I have friends with me and we will do our best. Do not talk of dying, Toad. Have courage and stay clear of the hound. I must go now, but I shall be back to tell you what is happening and perhaps to ask for your help."

"Come back soon, Nunkey." And Toad jumped back off the bank on to the flat rock at the edge of the stream. Babwyn made his way to the village to see for himself.

Almost as soon as he parted from Babwyn, Wyvern rose in the air to fly over the abbey. He could see nothing. All was shuttered and silent. He had thought there might be guards posted, but there was no one in sight in the courtyards between the buildings. He landed carefully on the roof of the church, near the belfry.

Close by, there was a gull perching. Wyvern spoke softly to the bird. "Do not fear me, gull, though I look so odd. I am a friend of little Bridget. She is safely hidden from Myrddin."

The gull turned to face the dragon. As it did so, the moon shone from behind the clouds, outlining their two black shapes on the church roof. "I know you, for you were in the boat with Bridget. I keep watch in case she needs us quickly."

"Tell me, gull, are there many men at the abbey?"

"Listen, Dragon Bird, for we, the gulls, have waited and watched. After your boat returned, Myrddin and Avaric saw the slave ship leaving, but they did not see the cloud of mist which hid your boat. We saw them return to the abbey. We saw you land safely and disappear into the woods. Myrddin has not appeared since, but a large company of Avaric's men left and rode away towards Wodenswood. They have not returned and soon it

128

will be dawn. These are bad times. The monks and the boys walk around like dreamers and the hound stalks the countryside. The people are afraid. They do not come near the abbey."

"But the Thegn himself, is he still here?"

"He has not left . . . Wait! Listen!" The gull and the dragon, close together in the shelter of the belfry, listened and watched in the moonlight. Wyvern could still see perfectly because of the lasting effect of the magical rue. From the track leading to the abbey gates came the sound of horses. The figure of Myrddin appeared from the hall. He opened the gates himself and stood waiting to receive the horsemen. The riders entered and dismounted. Wyvern was shocked to see that one of them was a lady. She was helped from her horse by one of the men. Myrddin spoke to her and she hurriedly followed him inside. Myrddin came out again and stood speaking to the men for a moment. They re-mounted, rode away and, closing the gates after them, Myrddin disappeared again into the hall.

The gull spoke to Wyvern. "That lady is Ethelburga, the Thegn's lady and Bridget's second mother. She has come at this hour because the Thegn is sick."

"How do you know?"

"I saw him. I was perched in the rafters of the hall when he came in from the beach. He looked angry. He sat down and called for something to drink. It was brought to him, but almost as soon as he had drunk, he slumped in his chair as though he were dead. He was carried out by some of his men before they all left."

"Ah!" said Wyvern. "Myrddin must have planned that and made sure that he was given something in his drink to make him ill . . . Look! Here comes Myrddin again. He is going towards the herb garden. Come, Gull, we must follow."

Myrddin walked swiftly to Father Brendan's deserted and dreadful garden which had once been so beautiful. It was the still dark hour before dawn. He carried with him the two flasks of luminous green liquid which he had prepared so carefully and kept safely locked away. As he entered the garden he did not know that Wyvern and the gull were already watching from Father Brendan's little hut. Myrddin threw aside his grey cloak and hood and, standing once again in his ceremonial black robe with its gold and silver symbols, he could be seen clearly by Wyvern.

The dragon had never seen him like that and shuddered in the darkness of the hut. Myrddin's face was triumphant and excited. His glittering blue eyes made twin points of cold light. He raised his arms, holding up the flasks, one in each hand. They sent out such blinding flashes of green that Wyvern could not look at them directly. Myrddin began his chanting. It was the same strange language and the same awful sound that they had heard from the hillside on the night they were escaping to the boat. The gull trembled next to Wyvern and hid its head under its wing, trying to blot out the sound, but Wyvern was determined to see everything.

As he chanted, Myrddin now began to walk around the garden. He stopped beside what had been the first bed, uncorked one of the flasks and sprinkled drops on the garden. As he did so his chanting grew louder and harder to bear. Passing along the narrow paths, he walked and scattered drops of the fluid over all the plots. When one flask was empty, he opened the other and continued until that too was gone.

When he came near the doorway of the hut, Wyvern and the gull retreated further into the darkness. When Myrddin moved on, they crept back to the doorway to watch. What they saw terrified them, for the wizard was again standing in the entrance to the garden, his arms outstretched, singing his dismal sinister spell. The whole of the herb garden had begun to glow brightly as though the ground were on fire. They dared not go out and could not take to the air from inside the hut. Fearfully they waited.

The glow from the ground became more intense. Then fiery liquid, like molten metal, began to bubble all over the ground. The earth trembled and shuddered. The sight was so terrible that Wyvern wanted to run away and hide. The gull crept underneath the dragon, shivering with fear, but Wyvern was grimly determined to know what Myrddin was doing. He needed to know so that he could best help his friends. To give himself courage, he thought of them and of Avis. Then he fixed his thoughts upon the great Merlin. He felt steadier and more able to bear the sight of what happened next. The chanting stopped suddenly. Then from all over the garden, columns of fire rose into the air, each one as tall as a man. They stayed still in the places where they rose. The fire began to fade and as it did so, the columns became solid. They were men! Fighting men, dressed like Avaric's warriors and armed with swords and shields!

There were about thirty of them and they formed themselves into rows, their heads all turned towards Myrddin. Wyvern could not see their faces. If he had, he would have seen that they had blank expressions, except that their eyes glowed with reddish gleams. Myrddin gazed at them, delighted with his success.

Raising his voice, he cried out in Anglo-Saxon. "My fine warriors of the underworld, no one shall defeat you. I know now that I can raise a whole army if I need it. This ground is the ancient magic circle of the Druids. No wonder the priest's plants thrived! But once I had destroyed its goodness, I knew I could use it for my own ends."

He was silent. Then rasping out an incomprehensible command to the dreadful company, Myrddin turned and left the garden, followed by his marching warriors.

Chapter Twenty-One

Babwyn and Wyvern, as they had planned, were back in the barrow by first light. Father Brendan was sitting quietly at the table, studying his book, while Elric and Bridget still slept. Once inside the cave, Wyvern's strength left him for a while after all he had seen. He crouched on the table near Father Brendan. His wings drooped. No puffs of smoke came from his nostrils and from time to time he shook so much that his claws rattled on the table. Father Brendan did not know what was the matter with him. He woke Elric and Bridget. The friends gathered round Wyvern stroking and patting him. Bridget gave him some crystal water and he began to feel better. Father Brendan said that Babwyn had better tell his news first to give Wyvern more time to recover. They shared the remains of the bread and fruit they had brought from the Paradise of the Birds while Babwyn told them about Toad.

He then went on to tell them that he had been to the village after leaving Toad. There he had slipped, unseen, in and out of the houses. In every house the men lay without even lifting their heads. The women and children looked worn out and dreary. A horrible smell rose from the pond, for Azab had breathed his foul breath into it. Most of the animals had strayed to find fresh water and stayed away because of the dog.

Although this was bad news, when Wyvern told his tale of the raising of the warriors from the ground, Father Brendan, Bridget and Elric were so sad and angry that they sat in silence, not knowing what to say or think. Babwyn jumped about restlessly, muttering to himself. At last Father Brendan spoke.

"My children, for you are my children too, Wyvern and Babwyn, I know you understand how sad and angry I am that my lovely garden should be used for such wickedness, but," he straightened his thin shoulders, "I will cleanse and purify the ground and grow my herbs again, God willing." Father Brendan looked at the four sad faces around him and he suddenly felt cross with himself. He said briskly, "I am a selfish old man to think only of my garden, when the villagers are sick, our friends are captives and now it looks as though Avaric and Elthelburga are prisoners too. We must decide how to act. Come, Elric, what do you suggest?"

Elric had been thinking that he must devise some action or he might slip into the same hopelessness that he had felt on the journey to the Isle of Ailbe. He took a deep breath and put forward a plan.

"If you all agree, I think we shall have to separate like Babwyn and Wyvern did last night. If you, Father, and Bridget and Babwyn could take the book and go to make the men better in the village, Wyvern and I could make our way to Wodenswood. I know that seems to be part of the enemy camp, but

I don't really think that it is any more. I think Avaric has turned against Myrddin, Bridget, and that we can rally his men to our side."

Excitedly, Bridget broke in. "Oh! I'm sure he has, Elric. He is not wicked. I'm sure that Myrddin deceived him. When you get to Wodenswood, find Wilfrid, for he is Father's best man and has served him for years. He hated what was happening and would do anything to get rid of Myrddin. Mother told me that he only stayed because he is loyal. He could collect men from the other villages too. We might have a good force, Elric."

Wyvern, who could not help thinking of the terrible warriors he had seen rise from the ground, asked solemnly, "But even if we do raise a force, how can ordinary men fight against those soldiers of Myrddin?"

Babwyn leaped on and off the table, then back on to it. He flung his long skinny arms wide and said, "We must not be hopeless, Wyvern! We do not know when Arthur and Merlin will come to help us, do we? We've got to try to do something. Look how you got rid of the slavers' ship. Look how Elric rescued you. We've got the book and Bridget can always call up her gulls!"

"You're right, little monkey," Wyvern began to puff out his smoke. "I must not lose hope and start to doubt. Elric's plan is a good one. Let's do it."

Carefully Father Brendan wrapped the book inside an animal-skin bag and slung it over his shoulder. "We must be very careful now that it is daylight. It will take you some time to walk to Wodenswood,

Elric. Take care, my boy, for there is great danger all around us."

"There is more danger for you, Father, for we are going away from the abbey. I hope Myrddin is too busy to appear in the village this morning and that hound too."

Once outside the barrow in the early morning light they all wished that somehow they could be invisible, for they could feel the heavy atmosphere of evil magic hanging over the whole countryside. They parted, arranging that whoever returned first would wait in the barrow until the others came back. Bridget gave Elric a gold bangle which Wilfrid would recognise as coming from her. Elric had cut a hole in one of the sheepskin rugs. He pulled it over his head so that his black school tunic was hidden. He carried Arthur's penant. He and Wyvern went swiftly into the shelter of the wood. Wyvern flew low, skimming over the ground, for walking was not an easy way for him to travel.

Inside the woods they stopped to decide their quickest and safest route. "I wish I had my horse, Thunder," Elric said. "We should soon be there with him to carry us. I wonder what has happened to him? He was grazing in the meadow as usual the day Myrddin came. I suppose he's wandered away. I brought him from home when I came to school here."

"He'll come back, Elric, when things are put right again. Now, you know the country. Which way?"

"We must stay in the trees as much as possible

until we are well away from the abbey. We'll follow the stream up to the heath and then strike out across open country to Wodenswood. It's a very large village, with a fine hall and not far from the end of the woods there."

They went quickly through the woods noticing the awful silence, as Babwyn had done. They soon reached the stream and began to follow the bank. Suddenly from Elric's feet, a hoarse voice croaked, "More strangers! I know that's a boy, but what's that thing?"

Elric and Wyvern stopped dead at the sound. Then they remembered. Toad, of course, Babwyn's friend from last night. "I'm not a thing, Toad, I'm a dragon, friend to the monkey you talked with last night."

"Ah! Nunkey, with the furry face and long arms. Well, my friends, boy and dragon, you had better hide for a time, for each morning early, the hound comes through the wood. Be advised by Toad. Follow me."

Elric and Wyvern wanted to hurry on, but felt that they should accept the toad's advice for a short time, as he was so certain that the hound would be coming. So they followed him along the stream to a place where, over the years, the earth below the bank had been washed away. There, a rowan tree hung down almost touching the water, its roots still holding the upper part of the bank together. Behind the branches was a large cavity and into this Toad led them. Except when the stream was swollen in the winter, there was only a trickle of water there. It was a perfect hiding place.

No sooner had they hidden themselves than there was an outburst of noise downstream. Mixed with the thudding of hooves and the whinnying of a horse was the terrible snarling of a dog. Elric and Wyvern peered through the branches. Then Elric froze. Slithering and galloping towards them upstream came a chestnut horse, *his* horse! Thunder! Bounding after it was the hound Azab. As the horse drew level, with a mighty leap the dog landed on its back. Through the branches Elric saw his horse stumble to its knees in the stream, the open mouth of the vicious dog about to sink its teeth into the chestnut's neck. With a cry of "Thunder", he rushed from his hiding place to try to save his horse. His sudden appearance distracted the dog for a few seconds. Thunder scrambled up in panic and reared, throwing the dog sideways. Water splashed over Elric and Wyvern, who had followed him. Azab turned on the boy with a ferocious snarl. Wyvern flew at the dog clumsily and at the same time Thunder recognised Elric. Turning, the horse reared and plunged at the dog. Horse, dog, dragon, and boy seemed to tumble together for a brief moment as water and small stones flew everywhere. The poor old toad hopped up and down croaking helplessly.

Elric staggered back against the branches of the rowan tree as the hound turned on him. He flung out his arm to save himself, without even realising that he still held Arthur's penant in his hand. As he did so, the penant touched the dog. Its growl was cut

138

short. It fell heavily and lay still, half in and half out of the water. All at once there was quiet, apart from the panting of the horse.

While Elric stroked Thunder and examined his back where Azab's feet had landed, Wyvern and Toad peered at the dog. "It still lives, Elric," Wyvern said. "Ought we to kill it?"

Elric had ripped a piece of his tunic and was bathing Thunder's back with water from the stream. The horse was calmer now, so Elric looked at the dog. It was an ugly sight. Its grey coat was slimy, nothing like the fur of an ordinary dog. Its mouth was slightly open and Elric shivered as he thought of those fangs killing Thunder. He stood thinking for a moment, then answered Wyvern's question.

"No, we must not kill it. If it were meant to die now, I think the penant would have killed it. But I think it may stay as it is for a while. Let's cover it with branches, then Toad won't have to look at it. I'll push its bottom half on to the bank."

They found fallen branches and covered the dog. Then they thanked Toad and continued on their way. Elric did not ride Thunder as the horse's back was sore, but the two were happy to be together again. When they reached the limit of the wood they could see the clustered buildings of Wodenswood in the distance across the heath. Wyvern flew above Thunder's head as the boy and the horse walked wearily to the village.

Elric had no trouble in finding Wilfrid. The sight of Wyvern made several of the men run to bring him out of the hall, for, in Avaric's absence, he was next

139

in authority. As soon as he saw Bridget's bangle, he ordered that Thunder be fed and watered and took Elric and Wyvern into the hall. Wilfrid was pleased to meet Wyvern and laughed heartily when he realised that it was the little dragon who had set fire to the sail on the slave-traders' ship. Then Elric told him that he had come for help.

Wilfrid was older than Avaric, with steady grey eyes and a curling grey beard. He was still straight and tall and could handle a sword better than many younger men in the Thegn's service. He now spoke quickly and seriously.

"You are a brave lad, Elric. I am thankful that you were able to stay free along with Father Brendan on that dreadful night. I am right glad that little Bridget is with you, for, yes, her parents are prisoners now. Avaric has realised at last that to join with Myrddin is to become steeped in wickedness and dishonour. I have many times thought of leaving, but stayed for Lady Ethelburga's sake. It would be dishonourable for me to leave my service. So I have kept quiet and obeyed orders." He laughed. "Ay, and often changed them, so that our people who were supposed to have gone as slaves are safely hidden, in the hope of better times. Well, you know the state of things at the abbey and in the village. We must act quickly. Avaric is supposed to be sick, but I believe that Myrddin has poisoned him. When the news reached Lady Ethelburga, she insisted that I take her to him at once."

"I saw that from the roof of the church," said Wyvern.

140

Wilfrid could not help smiling. "We shall win with you on our side, little dragon."

Wilfrid paced up and down suddenly as though he were angry. Then he turned and sat down again before continuing. "If only I had been at the abbey when he collapsed! I should have slung him over my horse and brought him home. But I was here. Some of the other men obeyed Myrddin of course and laid him in a room at the abbey. They were all sent away then. You saw what happened, Wyvern. I took a few men to escort my lady, but Myrddin did not even let us into the hall. Anyway, enough talk for now. You must go back to Father Brendan. If he has cured the men at Holybury, that is well. Today is Saturday. I shall gather as many men as I can and meet you with your force on the heath at dawn tomorrow. Then we shall march on the abbey and take what comes. We dare not leave it longer, even though Myrddin has got magical forces. I know that you can produce strange helpers too. I saw the gulls attack Myrddin and the dog."

Elric was excited and happy that this strong man was joining with them. He began to tell Wilfrid about Avis, wanting to tell him all about Arthur and Merlin, but Wilfrid stopped him. "I shall learn all in good time, Elric. There is too much to be done and already I have taken up too much of your time. Go now, and go carefully."

Elric was able to ride Thunder back. They were given a large satchel of food and some rousing cheers, as they left Wodenswood.

Chapter Twenty-Two

Father Brendan, Bridget and Babwyn made their way carefully along the side of the track leading to the village of Holybury. In normal times the men would have been out in the fields. The women would have been working and talking while the children ran in and out of the houses. But this morning the village was silent.

The little group stopped at the edge of the trees to stare at the deserted village. The smaller wooden houses were grouped around a larger one. This belonged to Oswy, Chad's father, who farmed more land and owned more animals than the other villagers. Father Brendan decided that it was best to visit this house first, for Bridget and Ethelburga had told Chad's parents something of the happenings at the abbey on the day after Myrddin first took over. Having caused the sickness, Myrddin had then left the villagers alone. As he had said to Avaric, the sickness would keep them quiet.

"Come," said Father Brendan. "They know me well, so we can go straight into the house." Inside, Oswy's house was like a miniature hall, built to the same design as the great halls. Although the weather was warm, a low fire burned on the central stone hearth, making the room slightly smoky. Near the fire was a bed, on which a man was lying quite still, with a lady sitting beside him on a wooden stool. It was Chad's mother, Winfred. As they entered, she turned, gave a little cry and jumped to her feet.

Recognising Father Brendan, she ran to him, holding out her hands. "You have come back. You have come to help us. I knew you would. I knew you would not desert us." Then she began to cry.

Father Brendan patted her shoulder gently. "Of course, Winfred. I came as soon as I could. Now sit down and recover yourself and I will attend to Oswy. See, here is little Bridget and my funny friend, Babwyn. Do not be afraid of him when he speaks, for he is not an ordinary animal."

Winfred looked at Babwyn, who put out his hand and took hers, shaking it solemnly. For the first time in three weeks, she gave a little smile.

That morning was the happiest time in the village since Myrddin had arrived. The magic of the book's herbs was marvellous. Father Brendan gathered angelica from its pages, the Root of the Holy Spirit, to cleanse the men of the poisonous sickness. On Winfred's fire, he brewed medicine for them to drink. Winfred and Bridget went around the houses giving some to the other men. Oswy, to Winfred's delight, was fit and well again so soon that before they had finished, he was helping them. Babwyn took a bunch of penny royal to scatter on the pond. This purified the water from the evil breath of Azab. Then he hung a sprig in the rafters of each house to drive away the bad smells of the sickness. The medicine worked wonders and by mid-day all the men were well again.

Everything was done stealthily in case Myrddin should appear. When Babwyn had done his job, he kept watch at the edge of the village until everyone had crowded into Oswy's house. Then Babwyn joined them to listen to Oswy. They were all packed very tightly into his little hall and, though they were delighted that all the men were better, everyone spoke in whispers for they knew that they were still in great danger. Oswy only raised his voice slightly to speak to them all.

"Friends, thanks to our good Father Brendan and his wonderful herbs we are cured of the terrible sickness which was caused by the evil Myrddin. Father Brendan has told me that a force is being raised at last to turn Myrddin out of the abbey. Now it is best for us all to remain quiet for the rest of today, just as though nothing had happened. If we stay in our homes, even if Myrddin comes to the village, I do not think he will suspect anything. It is more likely that he will not come, for since we have been sick he has left us alone, except for sending his hound to frighten us. It is strange that the beast did not come this morning, but it usually stalks here at sunset too. Go carefully back to your own houses now, but have any weapons you can at the ready and we will join the force as soon as the word is given. We can fight bravely even though we are farmers."

It was arranged that as soon as Father Brendan knew Elric's news, Babwyn would bring a message to Oswy. The villagers accepted the talking monkey as their friend and the children loved him. Winfred walked as far as the track with them. She gave them some food and a jar of fruit cordial and watched them safely cross the roadway into the trees on the opposite side, before she returned to the village.

Elric and Wyvern were waiting for them in the barrow and since Elric had been given food as well they had quite a feast. Both their missions had been successful and when they had listened to Elric's story of Thunder and the hound Bridget asked, "Where is Thunder now?"

Elric laughed. "I wish you could have seen them. I rode him back as far as the stream, but I couldn't bring him here. The hound had gone, but Toad was there and told me that the great dog had awakened after some time, scrabbled its way from under the branches and slunk away. Toad is funny! All the excitement seems to have given him new life. I'm sure he won't die this summer now. He insisted that he would take Thunder somewhere safe. He hopped on to my hand and I put him on Thunder's neck. He talked into Thunder's ear, then off they went together after Toad had said that they would meet us at the stream at dawn on Sunday."

Father Brendan spoke seriously. "Everything seems to be ready for what we hope will be the defeat of Myrddin. Wilfrid is mustering what forces he can. The villagers are well and, if you, brave Babwyn, will slip to the village as soon as it is dark tonight, you can tell Oswy to meet us on the heath tomorrow. Everything depends on Myrddin

145

not making any move until then. I do not think he will. I hope I am right."

Elric agreed. "No, why should he? He has the abbey. His prisoners are quiet. He can raise more men from the magical ground of your garden, Father. That is probably what he will do. With forces like that he can take over all of the seven kingdoms, or he thinks he can."

Bridget was looking very anxious. "Wyvern saw them and said that ordinary mortals could not fight against them, didn't you Wyvern?"

Wyvern did not answer her at first, then suddenly his green eyes glowed and he said, "That is so, Bridget, but we are not ordinary, are we? Babwyn and I are from the book. Father Brendan, Elric, and you, are not ordinary mortals. If only we do not give in, we shall have Avis, Merlin and the king and queen to help us."

Father Brendan was watching Bridget with his kind old eyes. He said, "You are very worried about your parents, Bridget, and you have been full of courage from the beginning. Do not begin to lose hope now, my child. At midnight it is possible that Avis will appear, so now that we have eaten it is best for us all to rest before the battle tomorrow."

"We do not need to sleep," said Babwyn. "Wyvern and I will keep watch. It will soon be dark and I will take the message to Oswy."

The three humans lay down for what they hoped would be the last time in the burial mound. Babwyn did not disturb them when he scampered off on his errand to the village.

146

The three sleepers were given pleasant dreams. Father Brendan dreamed that he was once more in his garden, which was blooming more beautifully than it had ever done before. Elric dreamed that the battle was won and he was riding through the gates of the abbey on Thunder, with King Arthur riding beside him. Bridget's dream was that her second mother and father were free and happy again and that she was sitting with them and Queen Gunamara in the hall at the abbey.

The brightness of the light in the barrow woke them. There on the table beside the book was Avis, their lovely white bird. It was after midnight, and the day of the battle. They greeted Avis with delight and were going to tell the bird all that had happened, but he already knew.

"You have all done well and tried so hard, but there is still great danger to be faced today. Everything depends upon your keeping your faith and courage high. Listen carefully. Elric, you must lead the forces beside Wilfrid, carrying Arthur's penant. Wyvern and Babwyn, watch for the hound, for you, Wyvern, can attack from the air, and you, Babwyn, are small and quick. You can distract it and escape yourself. Father Brendan and Bridget, stay with the book at the side of the heath, at first. You may need to tend the wounded quickly. You will know when and how to join the battle. You all look puzzled, for you thought that you were going to storm the abbey. But the battle will be fought on the heath beyond the woodland. The time has come and the place is chosen. I go now to challenge Myrddin. While he is engaged in battle I shall have much to do at the abbey. Soon it will be time for you to go. Have courage and believe that you will win, no matter how hopeless it may seem."

"Will Arthur come?" asked Elric.

"It is hard for you, I know, but you must not ask any questions. I shall take this sprig of rue with me, which I held in my beak in the picture." Avis finished speaking and the light dimmed quickly as he disappeared, leaving them sitting silent and serious.

Chapter Twenty-Three

The abbey church now looked completely different. The lamp no longer burned on the altar. All the hangings had been taken down and were piled in a corner. The seats had been moved to the side so that there was a large empty space. There, standing to attention, were Myrddin's warriors. The magician had not been sure of success when he first went to the herb garden to raise them from the ground. Since that first triumph, he had found that the ground was prepared. He had returned to the garden again and again during Saturday and had found that the special chant he had used only needed to be repeated to raise more troops from the ground. The whole church was filled with them. They stood perfectly still awaiting his slightest command.

At first glance they looked like ordinary warriors dressed for battle, with helmets, leather tunics and leggings, their black cloaks slung round their shoulders. But on their black shields was the figure of a leaping hound and one look at their faces was enough to terrify anyone. From either side of their nose shields their eyes glowed with a red fire in the dimness of the church, like those of Azab. They made no sound and each stood in exactly the same position, one hand holding the shield, the other at the ready on the sword hilt.

Myrddin himself sat in Father Brendan's room. It was past midnight and the sun would soon be rising. Myrddin was pleased with himself. He had glanced into the room next door a few moments before and smiled cruelly at the sight of Avaric lying still and sick. Ethelburga sat beside her husband watching for any sign of recognition. In the dormitory building the monks and the schoolboys, still in their trance-like state, lay sleeping until given the order to rise. In the church his troops stood at the ready. He flung back his grey hood and gazed straight ahead as though looking into the future. Full of pride, he saw himself ruling the whole of Britain, bringing to their knees before him the kings and the proud Thegns. But for Myrddin this was only the beginning. Greater dreams were yet to come.

"All is well for me. This abbey will serve as my headquarters for here I have the sacred ground of the Druids. Now I must have the book, the old priest and the children. I know that the girl is with them, for when I sent for the mother, the child should also have been brought to me. Those stupid men said that she was not at Wodenswood and her mother will only say that she is with friends. She foiled me when I almost upset them in the Ocean of Doubt. She has power too, and although they have returned she is not at home, so she must be with the old priest. They returned in time to drive away the slave ship. No matter, now that I have my warriors, I am sure that by tomorrow night I shall have them in my power . . . "

Suddenly there was a fluttering sound in the quiet room, the same sound as on the night Myrddin had tried to catch Elric. Startled and angry, he turned his head from side to side. Then immediately in front of him he saw an intense patch of white light. Fascinated, Myrddin waited, his cold eyes riveted on the centre of the light, for he could not withdraw them. The light caused him pain, yet he could not close his eyes. As the light slowly faded, Avis appeared. He landed on the window ledge, his pale golden eyes fixed on Myrddin's face. He bent his head, laid the sprig of rue down beside him and spoke to the magician. "The time has come, wizard and is not of your choosing. As soon as dawn breaks, you must go to the heath beyond Wodenswood. There you will meet your fate. A battle awaits you."

As Avis spoke, Myrddin, angry and proud, recovered himself and replied, "A battle! I can win any battle. My troops are unbeatable. And whom do they fight? An old man, two children and you and your creatures of the book. Your power is limited, angel-bird. You cannot join in the battle. You could help them escape, yes, and take them to the Isles of Truth, but you are not allowed to fight in this battle. Who else dares to challenge Myrddin?" He laughed. "Willingly I shall come, bird. It will suit me well. Now I need not trouble to find them. By tonight I shall have them and the book. You know, though they do not, that to rule in this island is only the

151

beginning for me. Before long I shall control the Isles of Truth. The Ocean of Doubt shall surge around their shores. The Magic of Lies will be all powerful! The book has opened the door for me to enter the Kingdom of Truth!"

Myrddin was becoming more and more excited as he spoke. Avis waited for him to pause. When he did, the bird said simply, "We shall see, Myrddin. For the present, only obey the call to battle." Then, taking up the rue once more in his beak, Avis melted away and the grey light of dawn began to creep slowly into the room.

Still excited, Myrddin strode out of the room. He did not doubt that victory would be his. He knew the legends of the resting place of the king and queen and Merlin, but had always dismissed them as the foolish stories of the people. With Azab at his heels, he went to the church to feast his eyes on his troops, before ordering them to the heath.

Chapter Twenty-Four

As dawn broke over the heathland, the forces of Truth looked brave but few. It was a fine summer morning and all were in their places. On the edge of the woodland, Bridget and Father Brendan had made a small tent with branches and the animal skins from the barrow. Toad sat with them. In neat formation Wilfrid had arranged his fighting men behind himself and Elric. There were about sixty men, half of them on horseback. Behind these were another fifty men from the village. Some had swords but most had only wooden staves and clubs. Elric rode Thunder. He carried the penant and Wilfrid had provided him with a short sword. Wyvern perched behind him, ready to take off and attack the great dog as soon as it appeared. Babwyn sat on Oswy's shoulder, but kept jumping down and darting among the men from the village, calling, "Keep your lines straight! Weapons at the ready!", which was his idea of rallying the villagers.

As the morning light increased, they began to feel uneasy, for they could not hear the sound of anyone approaching from the abbey road. Bridget, standing anxiously beside Father Brendan said, "I shall call the gulls to help us, for I know that they are standing by." She began to sing, softly at first, then she raised her voice so that her song rang out over the heath and woodland. The sea gulls answered her call at once. Groups of birds began to appear in the sky high above. More and more joined them until there were hundreds of gulls. Then to her dismay, Bridget saw Myrddin. She stopped singing abruptly. "Oh no! Look Father, look!"

Myrddin, his black robe swirling about him, was among the gulls, flying like some terrible bird of prey. Billows of dense black fog started to pour from the robe. They watched helplessly as the gulls scattered, shrieking and wheeling. Many dived clumsily to escape. Some fell to the ground, while others swooped low over the heath and away. The cloud of blackness was descending, casting a dreadful shadow so that it seemed as though twilight had fallen on the battlefield. It stopped suddenly, hanging in mid-air. Myrddin landed and stood in front of Elric and Wilfrid. His harsh voice resounded over the field.

"Your defeat is certain. You have seen only a small example of my powers. Surrender now or you must face my army, which will destroy you. I cannot lose. You can see that it is useless for the girl to call up the gulls. The cloud above you will also descend at my bidding. Then in the darkness, my warriors will swarm over you."

Elric looked at Wilfrid, who placed his hand on his sword hilt as a sign. Though he was afraid, Elric spoke to Myrddin for the very first time. "We shall not surrender to you. We must fight to free our friends and keep our freedom."

The magician looked straight into Elric's eyes.

"You are brave, boy, but your courage is foolishness. You, the little girl and the priest will be my honoured assistants if you give up this fight now. Then these men can return to their homes."

This time his voice was calm and soothing and Elric could not take his eyes off Myrddin's face. He felt his fierce determination slipping. Wilfrid removed his hand from his sword and wearily rubbed his eyes. Then a voice called, "Elric! Elric! Do not listen to him!" It was Bridget calling. Elric turned his head and she ran forward, carrying one of the fallen gulls.

As Elric looked at her, away from Myrddin, his courage began to return. He raised Arthur's penant and cried, "He lies. Do not listen to the wizard. It is better to fight!"

Myrddin turned his back on them and, raising his arms, began to chant. His warriors appeared from the abbey road, marching up the slight slope of the heath in perfect formation. In front of them stalked Azab. The magician called them to a halt only yards away from Elric and Wilfrid, who held their ground, though their horses were trembling and Wyvern sat frozen with fear. The sight of the warriors was so frightening that the other men could not move or they would have turned and run for their lives.

At that moment, as Bridget and Father Brendan watched, all seemed to be lost before any fight had begun. The forces of evil waited ready to pounce. Overhead hung the black cloud. The gulls, ever faithful, kept trying to return, but could not. Many of the poor birds had fallen and Bridget had run about collecting them into the little tent, so that they could be healed with angelica from the book. Now Myrddin, his robe glittering in the dim dreary light, began to laugh, hollow sinister laughter, as he enjoyed the spectacle, before deciding to wave his troops forward to finish the battle with one swift blow.

Bridget stood helpless next to Father Brendan. Toad was croaking dismally. The men suddenly began to call out in terror. "We shall have to surrender!" cried Oswy.

"Let us go home!" chorused the rest. Elric sat rigid on Thunder's back. The warriors were more terrible than anything he had expected. They were silent. Their eyes glowed in the dimness. Desperately he tried to think, but the whole atmosphere was polluted with evil magic. Where was Avis? Where was the help they had been promised? The horses began to whinny with fear. Myrddin, delighted, raised his arms and began muttering to himself. A few streamers of the awful cloud floated down like long black ribbons among the horsemen behind Elric and Wilfrid. They wound themselves around those they touched causing the men to cough and choke, their horses to snort and stagger blindly from the field. There, the animals tossed their riders to the ground and bolted into the woods. Myrddin watched, smiling cruelly, feeling sure now of an easy surrender as he looked at Elric.

Leaving the book in the tent and carrying a bunch of angelica, Father Brendan ran to the first of the half-dozen men who had fallen. He called out to Bridget, "Bring more angelica from the book. It is strong against witchcraft."

As Elric heard Father Brendan mention the book he wrenched his mind free from the evil magic of lies which surrounded him. Merlin's voice came back to him, " . . . you, Elric, and you, Bridget, must not lose faith in the Magic of Truth no matter how bad things seem to be."

"Seem!" Elric thought. "I must remember that Myrddin can spin a web of lies! The book is filled with the Magic of Truth!" In a flash, as he saw Myrddin wave his troops to advance, he shouted to Bridget, "Bring the book, Bridget . . . on to the field. Your torc will protect you!" Then, gripping the penant tightly, he held it high, calling as loudly as he could, "Forward, in the name of King Arthur!"

Bridget was in the tent with the book open at the page where angelica was pictured, but Toad heard Elric's call and hopped inside to fetch her. At the same moment, Azab sprang forward leading the warriors. Elric charged at the front line, holding the penant like a javelin. Wyvern flew at the hound and Babwyn darted across its path. It turned aside to strike at the monkey with the little dragon puffing flames and smoke at its back. Wilfrid and a few of his horsemen joined Elric, but the others hung back. Elric urged poor Thunder straight at the phantom troops, saying to himself, "Lies! lies! They are all lies!"

Myrddin, with a howl of rage, stretched his arms to the black cloud, commanding it to descend.

Elric flailed about him with the penant, while Wilfrid cut to right and left with his sword. They were surrounded by glowing eyes and shields on which the figures of the dog glinted. The blackness was just above their heads, when it suddenly stopped and rays of soft light filtered through the whole gloomy scene.

Bridget was walking into the battle, holding the Book of Brendan in front of her. Her fear had left her and, gripping the book tightly, she marched steadily right through Myrddin's troops. If the light from the book struck any of them, they fell to the ground, disappearing in a hiss of molten fire.

Seconds before, Elric and Wilfrid had seemed to be fighting real soldiers, but now the penant and their swords slashed empty air and on the field around their horses the red fire bubbled and went out. Elric gave a shout of triumph and raised Arthur's standard high. Seeing it and seeing that their leaders had not fallen, Wilfrid's men rallied and rode forward, followed by the foot soldiers and the villagers.

Myrddin saw that the battle was turning against him. He began his weird singing and more of the phantom figures came from the abbey road to replace the ones which had disappeared. But all the men were fighting now and as long as Bridget steadfastly held the book, the troops fell before her. The men who had first been stricken by the deadly vapour were recovering and Father Brendan now joined Bridget. Between them they held the book high. Wyvern and Babwyn were keeping the hound

Azab on the edge of the heath, harassing and chasing it.

In his rage, Myrddin strode into the battle. He reached Elric first and grasped Thunder's mane. The horse reared and Elric fell from his back. The penant flew from his hand and Myrddin seized it.

As the magician grasped the penant, there was a blinding flash of white light which pierced the black cloud above them, dissolving it in seconds. There, in the midst of the battle, on a mighty white horse, rode King Arthur! He drew his sword, but made no stroke. As he held it over the heads of Myrddin's troops, they melted away as the cloud had done. Myrddin dropped the red penant with its golden dragon and cowered on the ground. The battle was over.

Elric had staggered to his feet. Weary but triumphant, he leaned against Thunder's quivering flank, stroking his valiant horse gently. Sunlight burst over the heath as King Arthur sat resplendent on his charger and a mighty cheer rose from the forces of Truth, ringing out across the heath and woodland. It was answered by the abbey bell pealing out across the countryside. Hearing it, the women and children came from the village shouting and laughing.

When they arrived, King Arthur raised his hand for silence. "Clear a space around our prisoners."

They all obeyed, making a huge semi-circle around Myrddin and Azab. The gulls had returned, clustering in the surrounding trees. Father Brendan sat on a low rock with the book on his knees. Bridget and

Elric sank to the ground beside him with Wyvern, Babwyn and Toad. Thunder and the other horses rested and grazed on the edge of the crowd. Then Arthur spoke to the silent, angry Myrddin.

"Evil Myrddin, I do not intend to try to destroy you. Your punishment is to be decided by another, whose power is much greater than mine or yours." Arthur pointed down the heath. There, a procession was approaching. Avis flew steadily above the figure of Merlin, tall and imposing as he strode beside another white horse, on which rode Queen Gunamara. Following them walked Abbot Benedict with Avaric and Ethelburga and behind them the monks and schoolboys of Holybury Abbey. The abbot lead a hymn of thanksgiving and everyone joined in the singing.

Chapter Twenty-Five

Myrddin stood transfixed at the sight of his great ancestor. The hound lay down whimpering at its master's feet.

When the hymn ended, Merlin stood with King Arthur and his queen and waited until the prisoners, all free and happy now, had been welcomed. Bridget ran to hug Ethelburga and Avaric. She was overjoyed to find Avaric was just as he used to be, cheerful and smiling, swinging her off her feet and calling her "My little Bridget" once again. Elric and Chad shook hands very hard and both started talking at once. Father Brendan was greeted as a hero by his abbot and brother monks. Then Merlin called for silence once again.

"Your Majesties, good people. The time has come for me to speak to my wicked and unfaithful descendant, Myrddin. The faith and courage of Bridget and Elric, of our dear Father Brendan, and of Wyvern, Babwyn, and all of you, has delivered you from the Magic of Lies. Today is a great victory for Truth." Then Merlin looked straight at Myrddin. "You, Myrddin, whose name is so like my own, have disgraced your ancestors and abused your power. Have you anything to say?"

All the time Myrddin had been standing in the

centre space, seething with rage over his defeat. His face was terrible to see. With a mighty effort he seemed to overcome his fear of Merlin. Defiantly he lifted a clenched fist and shook it at the great magician.

"Do your worst! I planned a great scheme, O Merlin. I have not been beaten by an old man and by children. You and all the magic of the Isles of Truth were needed to overcome me. Had I succeeded I should have taken over those islands and enslaved you and your king and queen."

"Silence!" commanded Merlin. "As always you speak lies. You have been defeated by the forces of Truth working together. Now, since you are not sorry for your wickedness, justice shall be done." He turned to Father Brendan. "Good Father, be kind enough to bring me the book."

Father Brendan came forward carrying his precious book and handed it to Merlin, who opened it at the page where ivy leaves bordered the writing. Everyone watched as he passed his hand over the page. The open book glowed more brightly. Then, as though it were growing very fast, long streamers of fresh ivy sprouted from the open page and trailed to the ground. There was the sound of sweet singing in the air and the dancing sprites appeared as they had done in the King's Hall. Four of them took the strands of glossy green and, still dancing with the others, began solemnly to wind them around Myrddin, pinning his arms to his sides. Then one placed a collar around Azab's neck and stood holding the hound on an ivy lead. Myrddin was powerless to stop them. He stood as though turned to stone.

The ivy was sufficient. Merlin closed the book and handed it back to Father Brendan. Then he strode down the heath, calling, "Bring the prisoners and everyone follow."

A long and stately procession made its way to the road leading to the abbey. When Merlin came to the gap in the trees and the grassy slope leading to Holybury Tor, he turned to the right and led them all to the far side of the Tor, to the spot where Myrddin had raised Azab from the hillside. On that slope he stopped and addressed Myrddin.

"This is your punishment. You shall be imprisoned in this hillside next to the hound for a thousand years. At the end of that time, if you are found to be sorry for your evil ways, you will be taken to the Isles of Truth to be cleansed of your wickedness. The dog shall never rise again."

The sprites, at a sign from Merlin, led Myrddin and Azab up the slope near the summit. They placed them side by side, still secured with the streamers of ivy. Then they stood back to watch with everyone else. Myrddin suddenly cried out in a terrible voice, "I shall never repent! I shall never repent!" over and over again.

Merlin faced him and beckoned to Avis. The white bird rose in the air and flew to the prisoners. It remained hovering straight above them. Then, with his arms raised, Merlin began to cast his spell in the ancient language of the Druids. As he did so, white light from Avis' wings poured down on the prisoners. The hound gave one long howl and was gone. Myrddin disappeared from among the green ivy, but the echo of his voice was heard for a moment.

"I shall never repent . . . never repent!"

All stood silent and afraid too, for there was strong magic in the air. But it was not like the fear they had felt on the battlefield.

Merlin waved everyone forward after Arthur and Gunamara. The crowd moved up to file slowly past the figures of Myrddin and Azab, pictures in chalk, with the wind blowing the strands of ivy across them.

When all had passed the sight, Merlin passed his hand over the ivy which lay on the chalk figures. As he did so it began to grow, covering them in a dense mass of tangled green.

Chapter Twenty-Six

The crowd stood staring at the overgrown patch near the summit of Holybury Tor. Elric and Bridget had stood together with Babwyn and Wyvern as the imprisonment was carried out. "A thousand years!" whispered Bridget.

"I wonder if he will be sorry," murmured Elric. "Somehow, I don't think he will be and in a thousand years Merlin will have to destroy him."

They were both feeling rather sad. Although there had been great danger, they almost wished that it was not over. It meant saying goodbye to Avis, to the king and queen, and to Merlin. They didn't mind that too much, but they hated the idea of losing Babwyn and Wyvern. Bridget suddenly took hold of Babwyn's hand and he knew what she was thinking. Elric looked down at Wyvern, who opened his bright green eyes wide and puffed out quite a lot of smoke. He was thinking that he must soon be sent back to be a picture on the cover of the Book of Brendan and he loved being alive. Bridget gave a very big sigh and Elric, knowing why, said, "Let's stop thinking about the book cover, at least for a little while."

Toad hopped in front of them. "Listen," he croaked, "the woodland animals are coming back."

He was right. Behind them in Wodenswood there was a sudden chorus of birdsong. Then a murmur ran through the crowd and everyone started talking. The atmosphere had changed. The shadows of Myrddin's magic were swept away. The people smiled, straightened their shoulders and took deep breaths.

Merlin faced them. His voice rang out across the hillside. "Come! Let us all go to the abbey."

This time the procession was not solemn and stately. Laughing and talking, the crowd surged back to the road and then into the open abbey gates.

During the battle, when Avis and Merlin were in the abbey, they had awakened the schoolboys and the monks from their long trance. It had taken the holy rue and Merlin's power to break the spell. Then they had all set to work to put the church in order again.

There was hardly room for everyone to fit in for Thanksgiving. It was the strangest and most beautiful service ever held there, for the ordinary mortals were beside their magical visitors from the distant past. Even Abbot Ailbe and his monks were there. In the rafters the gulls mingled with the golden-crested birds from the Paradise of the Birds and no such singing was ever heard again in Holybury Abbey.

Afterwards there was to be a great feast in the hall, followed in two days time by another at Wodenswood, to which all were invited by Avaric and Ethelburga. But before they left the church, Merlin spoke. "My friends, you must all go and enjoy your feasting without us. We must bid you 'Good-bye', and this is the best moment to do so. Peace and happiness to you all for many years to come."

Father Brendan, Elric and Bridget, Wyvern and Babwyn, did not go straight to the feast. They went first to the herb garden with the whole company from the Isles of Truth. They all waited at the gate while Merlin and Avis took Father Brendan into his garden. Great was his cry of joy when he saw it, no longer blackened and destroyed. Merlin had renewed its beauty and all the herbs were blooming even more brightly than before. Father Brendan stood in the middle, thanking Merlin over and over again. Then he walked about touching his plants gently. It was so good to see him that no one wanted to leave.

In the middle of this happiness, Elric and Bridget realised that the moment had come, for Merlin was holding the book and beckoning to Wyvern and Babwyn. They came forward at once.

"This book," he said, "written with such care by Father Brendan, is to be placed in the secret barrow where you hid so safely. Father Brendan agrees that this should be so. The penant of Arthur will be placed there with it. They will always keep their magic, but their power must only be used if the people are ever threatened again by the Magic of Lies and wickedness. As you know, the picture of Avis will remain empty, only to return if Avis is needed again. These two brave creatures know that they should return to the cover of the book." He paused. Father Brendan smiled as Merlin continued,

"But because of their great courage, they are to be allowed to remain alive during the lifetimes of Bridget and Elric. Only after that will they return to the picture."

Wyvern and Babwyn solemnly thanked Merlin. Then they rushed back to their friends, hardly able to believe the wonderful reward they had been given. All the way to the barrow, Babwyn and Bridget skipped along together and Wyvern kept soaring into the air and shooting out flames. Elric carried the penant and when Father Brendan had operated the lever with the gargoyle's head, King Arthur received the penant from him.

He told Elric, "You carried this with the greatest honour and I am proud that I gave it into your keeping." The king went into the barrow with Queen Gunamara to look once again at the place where they had hidden, from where Avis had taken them to the Isles of Truth. Father Brendan entered to place the book on the table beside the penant. When they came out, Bridget and Elric went in to look at their hiding place again, but it was not to be sealed, for it was a good place for Wyvern and Babwyn to live. They would be the guardians of the book and the penant, living between the abbey and Wodenswood.

Their work finished, the boulder door was closed and the group walked down to the shore.

Moored at the water's edge was the leather boat of St Brendan and the sailing barque with the red sails. Swirls of rainbow mist played around the boats. Abbot Ailbe and his monks stepped into the leather boat.

Avis told his friends, "Remember that I shall be watching over you. Elric, if I am needed you will find me again in the picture as you did that day in Father Brendan's room. My sprig of rue is in Father Brendan's keeping. Plant it in the garden, good Father, and it will then be protected for always."

Avis rose into the sky with the other white birds and they hovered singing above the boats. Gunamara kissed Bridget. "Treasure the golden torc," she said, "and do not be sad, for one day you will meet me again."

Before the queen, King Arthur, and Merlin stepped into the royal barque, Merlin went to the white horses which had been led down to the beach. He touched their heads and pointed to the sea. They pawed the beach for a moment, tossing their silky manes. Then they took off at a wonderful gallop right into the white breakers of Woden's Bay. One moment they could be seen, still like horses, then, though Bridget and Elric strained their eyes, they could see nothing but the white horses of the foam.

It was over. The singing of the Paradise birds became fainter. The rainbow mist cleared for a moment as everyone waved farewell. Then the two boats slid gently away to become two patches of mist on the surface of the sea, which dissolved as they watched.

The gulls came, as they had done on the morning when Elric had first seen Bridget singing to them. They clustered around her again and sat on Elric's shoulders too, this time. Babwyn and Wyvern were happy to be alive. Father Brendan looked at the boy and girl, the baboon, the dragon and the gulls and said, "Come, all my children of Truth, let us go to the feast!"

N O R T H   T O W N

Lorenz Graham

NORTH TOWN

Thomas Y. Crowell Company

New York

By the Author

South Town

North Town

Whose Town?

Tales of Momolu

I, Momolu

David He No Fear

Every Man Heart Lay Down

God Wash the World and Start Again

A Road Down in the Sea

Copyright © 1965 by Lorenz Graham

All rights reserved. No part of this book may

be reproduced in any form, except by a reviewer,

without permission of the publisher. Published in Canada

by Fitzhenry & Whiteside Limited, Toronto.

Designed by Albert Burkhardt

Manufactured in the United States of America

by Vail-Ballou Press, Inc., Binghamton, N. Y.

Published in Canada by Fitzhenry & Whiteside

Limited, Toronto

Library of Congress Catalog Card No. 65-12503

ISBN 0-690-58750-3

6 7 8 9 10

To my daughter, Jean Graham Jones,
and to her daughter, Stephanie

NORTH TOWN

O N E

David Williams was going to school in North Town for the first time. He was alone and he was colored, a newcomer from the South. Sixteen years old and reaching for six feet, he was neatly dressed, his dark brown skin washed clean and his crinkly hair pressed down as tight as he could get it. He thought that people would know he was new and be watching him. He was not sure what he was supposed to do, for he had never gone to a school with white students. He had never ridden on a bus where colored passengers were not separated from white. That was why he was walking this morning.

Groups of boys and girls were walking in the same direction, and he looked at them curiously. He was also watching to see how they looked at him. He wished he'd see a colored fellow he could join. The white boys did not seem unfriendly. No one laughed at him or made unkind remarks; they seemed not to notice him at all.

He had walked all the way from the Williams family's new home on East Sixth Street. He was wearing his good wool suit, and he felt uncomfortably warm, even though it was the first day of October. Last evening his father had shown him where to get the bus and where to get off it a block from the North Town Central High School, but David had chosen to start early and to walk.

As he came in sight of the school, he suddenly realized that it would be the largest building he had ever entered. Probably all the people of his hometown would fit into it at one time, he thought. Built of handsome light-colored brick and stone with a central tower, it reminded him of a great church or castle. Students were moving toward its doors from all directions. Greetings were exchanged, and David caught scraps of conversation. Some students hurried, but many lingered as though unwilling to give up their freedom.

Nearby in front of a candy store a crowd of boys, some of them smoking, filled the sidewalk. Clowning, they jostled two girls, forcing them to step off the curb into the street. As David approached, trying not to look as though he expected trouble, he heard a loud outburst of laughter. He did not slow down but went on, his eyes straight ahead, though he was afraid someone might strike him from behind. There was a quick scuffle on his right. Two or three bodies smashed hard against him, spinning him across the walk and into a metal newspaper rack.

"Look out!" someone shouted.

David caught his balance just short of the curb. He straightened up and looked around angrily. He could not fight the whole crowd, but he was ready and willing to take them on one by one. But the boys who had shoved him were already running toward the school. The other students laughed as they watched a stout man in a white apron come out of the store to collect the newspapers that lay in disorder on the sidewalk.

"Juvenile delinquents, Daddy!" one of the boys taunted.

David did not join in the laughter. He was not amused and he wanted to avoid trouble. He had expected some of the white boys to be mean, and he determined grimly he would be watching for them and ready to fight any time he had to.

He walked on, but now the school seemed less beautiful. It looked more like a fort than a church.

A bell was ringing as he started up the wide steps. It was not late, but he started running, taking the steps two at a time. He slowed as he neared the door. Some other colored students were going in, but they did not notice him, and inside the building everyone seemed to be in a hurry. Not wanting to draw attention to himself, David tried to act as though he knew where to go and what to do. He turned to the right and walked down the hall.

There, along the wall, was a large glass case filled with athletic trophies—silver cups, bronze plaques, and statuettes of runners and players. He stopped and studied the inscriptions. North Town Central High seemed to hold championships in nearly every sport. There were photographs of the winning teams, too. Studying the picture of a baseball team, he thought he saw some colored boys, though caps partly covered their faces and he could not be sure. But in the first row of a football photo there was definitely one dark fellow, his jersey pulled tight over shoulder guards, a football in his hands. He read the list of names; fourth from the left was Sam Lockhart, the varsity's co-captain.

He had heard of Sam Lockhart. He had read about him in *Ebony.* Lockhart was now playing football at Michigan, and they said he would be All-American. So this was Lockhart's high school.

David pulled himself a little straighter. He would like it here, and perhaps he, too, would play football.

He moved on down the hall until he saw a door with a brass plate marked Office and joined a line of students waiting there. School had started three weeks ago in North Town, and David gathered from the conversations going on around him that most of those waiting wanted to make changes in their programs. He hoped he was not in the wrong line, but he asked no questions.

"I got old Peterson again for English," the boy ahead of him was saying to a girl whose curly blonde ponytail was tied with a bright red ribbon.

"I had her last year," the girl exclaimed, "and was she ever a tight marker! All she cares about is description and she loves to give 50's. She won't ever give anybody over 89—says the kids don't do half enough in her course."

David thought that they sounded just like the

boys and girls he had gone to school with in South Town. Only it was funny the way they pronounced their words, especially those with *r* sounds—*year* and *her* and *course.* He pursed his lips to imitate the sound, but when he silently repeated the words, they were not the same.

"Course," he said again, aloud, but he knew that his *r* was muted.

The boy ahead turned. "Did you get Peterson?" he asked.

David was embarrassed. "No, I don't know," he tried to explain. "I didn't get anybody yet."

"You must be new. Are you a freshie?"

"Yes— Well, not exactly. I'm new here, but I've already been to high school."

"Where you from? Detroit?"

"No. I went to Pocohantas County Training School. I just— My folks just came to North Town."

"Never heard of Pocohantas County. Whereabouts is that?"

"It's down South."

"Oh, say! Were you on television in those sit-in strikes? I saw a lot of those pictures."

The line moved forward before David could reply. Perhaps it was just as well, he thought.

"You play football?" the boy continued. David nodded. "We had a colored fellow here last year as halfback, made all-state. He graduated. Now we got Buck Taylor. Do you know him?"

David shook his head. No, he had not heard of him.

"What kind of team did they have at your school?" the girl asked with interest.

"We didn't play football so much at home," David answered. He wished now that they had. "We played baseball and basketball mostly."

"Well, say, you ought to go out for football anyway," the boy suggested. "You got size now, and you ought to be fast." He went on to describe the past successes of Central High's football team.

David found himself surprised at how easy it was to talk to him.

"What year are you?" asked the girl.

"I'm supposed to be a senior."

"Yeah, but they put you back when you transfer," she announced. "They always do that. Like no other school could be as good as ours."

David took a deep breath and looked around. Inside he felt funny. He was entering a high school in the North, and while it was not a "colored" school, it was not a "white" school either. Here he was, talking with white people who did not treat him as inferior or as anything special. He had never before talked with anyone white this way—just as students together, friendly and equal. But, he told himself, this boy and this girl were probably unusual. He must not be foolish. There were those who had nearly knocked him down a little while ago.

The line moved forward again, and the girl passed through the door. David could see people inside the office checking records, looking up information in file cabinets, and marking the students' course cards.

When it was his turn, a girl who looked like a student glanced at his report card from Pocohantas County Training School and, after a few questions, sent him with another card to a counselor in an inner office.

Until now, David had not realized how many courses a school in the North offered and what a wide range of choices students had. At his school in the South, everyone in the same class had to take the same subjects, and almost all of them were taught by the same teacher. His principal had prepared a typed statement describing his work and the studies at the Training School. The counselor now studied it carefully, and although David told him he hoped to go to college after high school, the counselor enrolled him in the vocational course, rather than the college preparatory. Later, he said, David might make a change. He classified him as a sophomore.

His first day so many things were new that at times David was confused, but he still hesitated to ask questions. He wanted to talk with some of the colored boys he saw, but each one seemed busy with his own affairs. With the white students he was even more uncertain. Fearing he might be rebuffed or considered forward, he was very unsure of his place.

At lunchtime he lingered outside the door of the school cafeteria until he saw another colored student approaching. The boy was almost as tall as David but heavier, wider in the shoulders, and he was lighter in color. He and the redheaded fellow with him wore white pullovers with red C's on them.

David followed them into the cafeteria and, watching carefully, did just what the colored fellow did, even to selecting the same food for his lunch. After paying the cashier, he sat down at the same table with his guide, who looked at him for the first time. His look did not make David feel welcome, and he did not respond when David said, "Hi!"

The redhead, on the other hand, seemed less annoyed than startled. "Are you a freshie?" he asked.

"Well, I'm new," David answered. "I transferred."

"So you didn't know, huh! Didn't anybody tell you that freshies and new men don't eat in here?"

David looked at the colored student, who made no response. "No," he said, "nobody told me."

"Well, that's the way it is, but since you have your tray, you can take it with you. You'll have to go to the fire basement. You go out that door and go down the hall. Halfway there's a red button marked *Fire,* and you push that, and when the elevator comes, you go down to the fire basement with the other new boys and freshmen."

So there was a special place for new people, David realized. It was with the freshmen in the basement, probably next to the boiler room. They were not sending him away because he was colored. He smiled to show that he was not angry. As he walked toward the door, he noticed two tables full of colored students and wished he had seen them before.

Halfway down the hall, just as he had been told, he saw the button. Balancing his tray in his left hand, he pushed.

Instantly it seemed that all the fire sirens in the world had gone off.

Doors flew open, but in no door was there anything like an elevator. Within seconds, the hall had filled with people. It was a fire drill.

The two sweater wearers were suddenly on each side of David; the white boy took his tray from him and laid it on a radiator. Laughing, they each took him by an arm and hurried him down the stairway and out to the street. They had thought he would know better and they were sorry, they said; but they still laughed.

For the rest of the day David was less interested in what he was doing than in what might result from his awful blunder.

When he got home that afternoon his mother and his sister, Betty Jane, were anxious to hear about his first day at the new school. He poured himself a glass of milk, took a handful of cookies from the cooky jar, and sat down at the kitchen table opposite them. After talking some about his classes, he tried to describe the huge gymnasium, the well-equipped shops, and the science room with its gleaming modern laboratory. When his mother asked him about the other colored students, he told her that he had spoken to one, but he did not say that his greeting had not been returned.

It had been Betty Jane's first day at school, too, and she was full of enthusiasm.

"I don't mind getting put back," she said. "I'm still no older than most of the kids in fifth grade. Besides if I was in sixth grade, I might have had one of the meanest teachers in the whole school. As it is, I got one of the best."

David was tall and dark like his father, but Betty Jane was like her mother. She was lighter than David, and her hair was sleek and glossy like an Indian's. Mrs. Williams was just medium height, and Betty Jane was still small for her ten years.

Before she married, Mrs. Williams had taught in a two-room school. She had had more formal education than her husband, but he knew more about city life for he had worked on factory jobs in Southern cities before coming North.

"My school has a gym, too," Betty Jane hurried on. "And a cooking room for the girls. And guess what? A library with just hundreds and thousands of books. And I can bring them home and don't have to pay. Nobody at home in South Town could ever imagine such a school," she concluded in a burst of enthusiasm.

Mrs. Williams laughed and kissed her.

"How did you get along with the others?" she asked. "You know, the white children?"

"Oh, they were all right," Betty Jane replied quickly. "Tenth Street School is mostly colored. We have some colored teachers, too, but they're just like the others and nobody pays any mind. That is—" Betty Jane paused. "That is mostly nobody pays any mind, but it looks like going to school and coming home the colored kids all walk together and the white kids walk together."

The Williamses were living temporarily in a four-room flat in a dingy two-story building. It was the last in a row of identical frame houses, all of which badly needed a coat of paint. Farther out on Sixth Street, on the east side of North Town, colored people owned comfortable one- and two-family houses, and Mr. Williams hoped some day to be able to buy one for his family. They had lived in their own house on their own land down South, and apartment-living seemed crowded. However, the flat had been freshly painted, and, after their furniture was installed, they found the place livable.

They had never had a bathroom before, and Mrs. Williams particularly enjoyed the kitchen with its running water and white enameled sink. David was glad he didn't have to carry water from a pump in the backyard, as he had at home. However, he no longer had a room of his own. His room in South Town had been small, but it had been his own. Here he had to sleep on a couch in the living room and to double up with Betty Jane on the closet for his clothes.

The Williamses were on the first floor; another family lived across the hall, and two more on the second floor. The Williamses thought it might be nice to have neighbors so close, but they missed not having a porch and a yard.

David also missed feeding the hens, the pigs, and the cow and gathering the eggs and doing the milking and the other country chores he'd done down South. He missed them, but he was glad to be free. City life, up North, looked good.

When his father came home from work and the family was eating dinner, David jokingly told about his misadventure with the fire alarm. He laughed, but his father did not think it was funny at all.

"Didn't anybody ask who rang the bell?" he asked. "Didn't your principal say anything?"

"No, sir," David said. "After it was over, the fellows said they thought I would know better. They were all right, I guess. I found out afterwards the colored fellow's name is Bruce Taylor, but they call him Buck. He's a senior, and he plays football. The white boy is Mike O'Connor, and he's the captain of the football team."

"I do hope, David," Mrs. Williams cautioned, "that you won't be getting into any trouble. As a new student you've got to be extra careful. Try to get started right."

"Yes, and being colored, too," his father added. "They'll be watching you extra hard, colored and a newcomer from the South."

David reminded himself silently that he would be watching, too. He had said nothing about having been pushed that morning, but he had not forgotten. He would be watching, and if they came at him again, he would be ready.

T W O

*T*he next morning on David's way to school, two colored boys left the group of friends they were walking with and crossed the street to greet him. Jimmy Hines and Alonzo Wells were their names. It was an act of friendship that David welcomed. They asked David where he was from and how he was classified. Later, in front of the school, Alonzo introduced him to the other members of the group.

"We saw you in the lunchroom yesterday," one of the boys said. "Figured maybe you was a friend of that Buck Taylor."

David said he hadn't known Buck before.

"Buck thinks he's so big," the boy continued.

"Our crowd don't run after the white kids," Jimmy Hines explained. "We know we're just as good as they are—better than lots of them—because they're treacherous—smile in your face and laugh at you behind your back. We figure to leave them alone, man."

"Oh, Jimmy," one of the girls protested, "you're always talking down the white kids!"

"I'm just trying to let our new friend know what the score is," Jimmy defended himself. "He's just come from down South, probably thinks up North we got the race problem solved— Well, I want him to know what's coming. These paddies going to be down on you, man. You got to watch it!"

Some of the students left, but four or five others chimed in, agreeing with Jimmy. The white people, practically all of them, teachers as well as students, they insisted to David, would try to make life hard for him. He would be given lower grades and fewer chances. They would try to make him look inferior. He wouldn't have a fair chance to make a team, and if he was so good that he had to be put on one, they would still try to make him look bad. The only thing for him to do was to stick with "our crowd."

"They don't bother none of us," one of the boys told him. "They know we're ready, and we don't take no stuff."

David had little time to think about what he had

been told. He had to hurry to reach his homeroom before the final bell rang, and then everyone left immediately for an all-school assembly. It was very much like other assemblies he had seen. David was seated at the back of the auditorium, and they all rose to sing "The Star Spangled Banner" and salute the flag. Then they were seated, and Mr. Hart, the principal, spoke, his words coming out loud and clear over the amplifiers in the big room. He made a few announcements, and there was general laughter when he said that he hoped everybody was now fully recovered from the effects of vacation.

"Yesterday," Mr. Hart began, "yesterday during the lunch period someone set off the fire alarm. We are happy that our building is fireproof, and we are proud of the discipline and good order shown by the faculty and student body in promptly emptying the building, but we cannot allow such potentially dangerous jokes."

He went on to describe the possibility of accidents, the inevitable disruption of programs, and the evils of undisciplined action.

"I want the student, whoever he or she is," he concluded relentlessly, "to stand now so that all of us here can know where the responsibility lies."

Heads turned, and there were murmurs of curiosity, but no one stood.

David was positive that others knew of his guilt. Mike O'Connor and Buck Taylor, the two responsible for his action, would certainly not have kept the story to themselves. To stand up before the whole school seemed impossible. Now they would stare. Afterward they would point him out. They would identify him as the bad colored boy, a newcomer from down South, ignorant and stupid. A lump rose in his throat. He would be expelled. His mother would be ashamed of him. His father would be disappointed and angry. But they already knew, and it was too late now.

He pushed himself to his feet. "I did it, sir," he said in a voice so low and husky that only those close by heard him.

Around him, a sea of white faces turned to look. David's eyes were blurred, but he knew they were staring at him. He heard a buzz of talk and the sound of laughter. Then he heard the principal's voice over the public-address system saying that he should report to the office after assembly. He sank into his seat utterly miserable. At last the assembly was dismissed, and he was free to leave the auditorium.

David waited in the principal's outer office. His dejection was so deep that he didn't look up until someone stood right in front of him.

"Hey, fellow," Mike O'Connor greeted him with a big smile. "It took guts to stand up and take it like that, but you didn't have to do it. I was going to tell old Hart myself—later—not naming any names."

David did not answer. "But I'll tell him now," Mike volunteered. "He'll understand. Everything'll be all right."

After Mr. Hart had led both boys into his private office, Mike told him the whole story, taking all the blame. He talked as though he knew no one would be punished. He said it was just a joke that had gone too far.

But Mr. Hart did not smile. Finally he dismissed Mike, telling him he would send for him again.

The principal seated himself behind his desk and told David to take a chair. He wanted to know David's name and then asked about his earlier schooling. David tried to answer all the questions.

"We had all the grades," he said, "from first grade on up through high school. They had other elementary schools in the county, but ours was the only high school—I mean, for colored."

Mr. Hart seemed pleased when he learned that David hoped to go through college and medical school and become a doctor.

"That was one reason," David explained, "that my folks wanted to come North, so I could get better schooling."

There were more questions about his family. David was polite, but he made his answers short and was careful about what he said. He might have said that his family had been caught in the storm of hate and violence that was sweeping over his native state, that in his own hometown, just a few weeks ago a white friend of theirs had been killed by a sudden volley of gunfire from night-riding men. He might have told him that as a result they had been jailed, all of them, even his little sister, and that his father had been so badly beaten in jail that he still was not completely well. However, although these things were very much in David's mind, he said nothing about them.

"Why did your father decide to live in North Town?" Mr. Hart asked.

"Well, I guess he didn't decide that at first," David answered. "We were supposed to drive to Detroit, but we stopped here overnight with some friends who used to live near us at home, and they said this was a better place to live than any of the big cities, better for work and better for schooling. And this friend, Mr. Crutchfield, said he could help my father get a job where he worked. My father had his trade, and the next day he got hired right away at the Foundation Iron and Machine Works."

A bell was ringing. The principal stood, ending the conference.

"David," he said with kindness, "you might have trouble getting adjusted. Let me know if I can help. I don't mean for every little thing—somebody might call you a dirty name, and you may think you're getting pushed around some—but if there is anything important, just walk in the door and tell them out front you have an appointment with me. I'll see you."

Even the principal seemed to feel there would be trouble.

THREE

*D*avid did not tell his parents what Jimmy Hines had said about the unfair treatment at Central. First of all, he didn't believe all of it, and anyway, he decided, it was up to him to keep his eyes open and make up his own mind.

The next day in the general science lab, one of the colored boys he had met asked him a question about an experiment they were doing.

"I don't think I've got it figured out," David replied. "I missed the first month, and I've got to do a lot of extra work to catch up."

"Aw, there's nothing to this," the boy bragged. "I had all this stuff before in grade school. I even flunked it last year 'cause I never turned in no notebook."

"But I never had science before," David ex-

plained, "not like this anyway, not in a real laboratory. I'll have to study."

"It don't mean nothing to me, man. Besides, I'm
going in the Air Force next year. I'll get my science
there."

The two got acquainted, and the boy invited David to join his friends at noon for lunch. They
turned out to be the same group of colored students
David had noticed on his first day in the cafeteria,
and they were friends of Jimmy's and Alonzo's. No
one had told them to eat in one place, and they knew
they were not being segregated. It was rather that
they chose to keep together. They seemed to be more
comfortable that way. David found himself enjoying
their company for they made him welcome. They
laughed a great deal. They laughed loud, and they
talked loud. They seemed to be trying to show they
were not afraid.

The conversation turned to football, and David
couldn't help asking Jimmy Hines, who had joined
the group, how Sam Lockhart got to be co-captain of
the team. "He was colored," David said.

"Yeah, old Sam made it," Jimmy admitted, "but
you don't know how it is. It's one of two things: You
got to be twice as good, or else you got to play Uncle

Tom. Now you take our boy, Lonzo Wells. He's good, better than that Buck Taylor, but Lonzo don't take nothing off of nobody."

An argument developed about Alonzo, and whether or not he was always looking for trouble. David said nothing, but he decided in his own mind that he was going to succeed at Central. Others had done it, and he believed that he could, too.

For physical education in the gymnasium that afternoon, David took off his leather-heeled shoes and stripped to the waist. He had no gym shoes or gym uniform yet. With the other boys he performed some calisthenics, and then he was made part of a squad with a student leader. He was awkward and self-conscious on the parallel bars and rings because he had never used them before. Some of the fellows laughed at him. He laughed, too, to cover his embarrassment.

After class was dismissed, the instructor beckoned him into the office that opened directly off the gym floor.

"Ever do any apparatus work before?" the instructor asked, and when David was slow to answer, he added, "Do you know the shoulder roll or the flying Dutchman?"

"No, sir, I've never heard of anything like that," David said.

"You new here? Where did you go to school before?"

David told him it was in the South—in the country, really—and they did not have a gym there.

"Have you played any football?" the instructor asked.

"Well, sir, I played. But our school was small, and we didn't have a real good team like you all."

The instructor encouraged David to try for the squad; and as a result, a few days later, David reported to the team locker room and was issued football equipment.

However, the only gear that was left so late in the season was in poor shape, held together with extra cords and lacings. When Alonzo Wells saw David struggling with it, he crossed the room to offer him a hand.

"They shouldn't give you this crap," he complained. "Hey, manager!" he shouted. "You got two left shoulder guards here, and both of them busted. What you expect this new man to do?"

"Tell him to keep driving to the left, Alonzo," someone joked.

Mike O'Connor looked up from the bench, where he was putting on his shoes. "Hi there, Fire Chief," he said, smiling. "Get your signals straight out there!"

The freckle-faced team manager tried unsuccessfully to lace the two left shoulder guards together, and then agreed that David would have to get along without them.

David's helmet fitted badly and the front was broken, but just the same he felt pretty good as he ran out to the field with enough other fellows in uniform to make four or five teams. He jogged around the cinder track with Alonzo, trying to look like one of the regulars and wondering how they ran so well with all their gear and with heavy cleats weighing down their feet. Buck Taylor loped easily past them, but he did not turn his head.

"You tired?" Alonzo asked, puffing, as they neared the end of the second lap.

"Not much," David said shortly, though he really was.

"Supposed to make this five times around."

Five times! David knew he could never do it.

He ran on, not talking, trying to save his wind. Alonzo pulled ahead. Halfway round again, David's heart was pounding hard. He slowed still more, wanting at least to get back to the starting point, but before he could finish the third lap, he gave out and dropped panting on the turf. He lay on his back, his eyes closed, his wind coming in hard gasps.

"Can't you make it?" Alonzo asked a little while later. "The man don't want you to rest too long. He'll tell you to keep going. Course, I know how it is, first time out. Still it's better to keep going."

David pushed himself to his feet; he had his wind back. Some of the others, having already completed their laps, were walking in tight circles or jogging in place. Across the field, under the direction of a coach, players were tackling a dummy suspended on a line. Others, each carrying a football, were diving and rolling. No one was scrimmaging. It all looked like work, hard, steady, driving work, David decided.

Alonzo took his place at the foot of a line practicing passing and receiving, and David fell in opposite him. The ball zigzagged down the line as far as the fellow on David's right. Instead of passing it to Alonzo, who would have thrown it across to David, he quickly shot the ball back up to the top of the line again. Once more the ball worked its way down.

"Kirinski, here!" Alonzo called out.

But again Kirinski fired the ball to the other end. Then he turned with a look of mock surprise on his face. "You call me, Lonzo? What you want?"

"I don't want no mess. That's what I don't want."

"Man, neither do I," Kirinski said. "I sure don't want no mess."

Somebody up the line cautioned, "Watch it, Kirinski!"

The ball came down the line. At the very instant that it started toward Kirinski, Alonzo leaped forward. He and Kirinski collided, and they both went down.

"Bastard," Alonzo shouted. "Stinking Polack bastard!"

A whistle blew. Some of the boys helped Kirinski to his feet.

"You didn't have to do that," one of them said angrily to Alonzo.

"Just who do you think you are?" another demanded.

David stood rooted in place, wondering what he should do.

"I told you no tackling," said the coach, pushing his way through the crowd. "You there!" He

pointed at Alonzo. "Get off the field! You might as
well turn in your uniform. We can't use people like
you at Central."

"I only showed him," Alonzo argued, defiant.
"He was playing tricks, and I showed him."

"I'm the coach here. I'll do the showing and I
know all the tricks. You get off the field!" He
watched suspiciously as Alonzo turned and started
away. "And if anybody don't like it," he added,
looking directly at David, "he can go along with
you."

David wanted very much to go, to leave with his
friend, but he also wanted very much to stay.

Kirinski was saying that he was O.K., that he
didn't know why the crazy joker had jumped him
like that.

The coach was still looking at David. "All right!"
he said. "I guess you want to go along with your
buddy. So get going, huh!"

Yes, he certainly would go along with his buddy.
David turned; walking with what dignity he could
command, he left the field. He was angry. He was
angry with the whole crowd; he was angry with the
coach who had asked no questions but just assumed
that the colored player was the one at fault; and he

was angry with the other players who had failed to defend Alonzo. He was angry, too, at himself because he had not left the field before the coach drove him away.

"Wait, Lonzo," he called and broke into a run. "I'm coming."

F O U R

*I*n the locker room after practice was over, the coach called the whole squad together.

"All of you know how I feel," he announced. "I don't care what color a man is if he can play football and be a part of a team. If green men from Mars show up and they can make the team, I'll play them. But a team can't hold hotheads who want to show how bad they can be. We threw one man out today. Then his buddy chose to go with him. Well, that's all right with me. Maybe it saves trouble up ahead."

Buck Taylor, who was listening carefully from the back of the locker room, believed that what the coach said was true. He felt that he had always been treated fairly. He knew that he wasn't as good as some of the other players. He was fast—that was his one great talent—but sometimes he fumbled, and often he drew penalties for the team.

The coach had always been fair to him, Buck felt, and Mike O'Connor, the present captain, was one of the finest fellows he had ever known. The rest of the guys—most of them, anyway—had always been O.K. A few had ignored him, and some maybe had tried to be mean, but he had always been able to get along without fighting. He had learned how to do this from his father.

"White people will respect you if you respect yourself," Mr. Taylor said. "Trouble with the colored man is he often wants more that he has earned or more than he deserves. He expects somebody to hand him something. I don't want anybody to hand me anything. I'll go after what I want, and I'll get what's mine."

Buck admired his father's forcefulness, but he was somewhat awed by his father's brains and the stories he told of his early struggles. Born on a farm in Georgia, Mr. Taylor had worked his way through trade school in the South, then married and supported his family as a carpenter. Later, after moving to North Town, he had developed a real-estate business and studied law, finally passing the bar examination.

Buck believed that other colored men could have

done what his father had done if they had only tried, but he also believed that he was quite different from other colored boys of his age. Being a football player helped to support his feeling of superiority. He knew that most of the other colored students didn't like him, but he didn't care. He had a small group of close friends. Jeanette Lenoir, whose family was from New Orleans, was one of them. Jeanette's father, a postal clerk, had been transferred North two years ago. Through Mr. Taylor's real-estate office, he had bought a comfortable house on the west side, two blocks from Buck's home.

"Paid spot cash for it, too," Mr. Taylor often said when he pointed out the Lenoir home to his prospects.

During football season, Buck kept training rules—in the house by nine every night and in bed by ten. However, he didn't always go right to sleep, and that night he felt like telling Jeanette what had happened that afternoon on the football field. He brought the phone into his room, and shut the door on the long cord. Sitting cross-legged on his bed, his bare chest showing dark against his blue pajama jacket, he dialed her number.

After listening to the story, Jeanette wanted to

know more about the background of David Williams.

Buck was sure that he had David all figured out, and he told her so. "The first day I saw him I said to myself, Another one of them scared spooks from down behind the sun, ignorant and dumb."

He listened, frowning, then he went on.

"I've told you before, even if you and your folks did come from the South—well, mine did, too, as far as that's concerned—that these down South farm people are really trouble. First, they're so scared they can't do anything for themselves. Then they think they know so much nobody can do anything with them."

Buck swung his feet over the edge of the bed and stood up.

"You take what happened today," he argued. "This guy Wells jumps bad, and he deserved what he got. He asked for it. Probably this new boy put him up to it— Yes, they were working together— and Kirinski is a good guy, you know. He's all right —Hunh?— No. What is there to say?— No I don't mean to ask Wells or this guy Williams anything. I don't have anything to say to them— Because they don't have anything to say to me— They'll be griping. White folks don't give you a chance, white folks

down on us poor colored folks— Yeah— Well now
you know as well as I do . . ."

He was silent for a while.

"Look, Jeanette, now look," he said, interrupting
her. "You know I'm as sorry as anybody for those
people over in the flats, but my dad's got plenty of
houses that they can buy if they really want to get
out of the slums. They like it, I tell you. My dad says
the same thing, and if they move out into a nice
neighborhood, they bring the rest of the lot right
along with them— Well, I know, but you're the ex-
ception."

He scowled.

"No!" He was short with her. "No, I'm not going to ask David Williams anything— Well, I hope
you won't— First thing you know he'll be wanting
to date you— No, you wouldn't— No, you wouldn't,
for one thing your old man wouldn't let you— Listen, Jeanette, if you do ask him, if you carry it that
far, you know what'll happen to you with all the
bunch of decent guys? They'll drop you like a hot
potato. Yes— and maybe I do mean that— What?
—Jeanette? Jeanette?"

He took the receiver from his ear and looked at
it with a frown. It only buzzed.

The next morning, after he reached school, Buck waited for Jeanette at her locker. Some of his friends, who knew that he liked her, saw him standing there and smiled. They thought that Buck and Jeanette made an attractive pair. He watched as she hurried up the hall in a bright yellow rain cape and hood, her steps firm and quick. Her smile was warm and friendly as though she had not hung up on their conversation. As she shrugged out of her wraps and dug into the locker for a book, she spoke of her need to hurry.

"I'll see you later." he said abruptly. Without waiting for a reply, he turned and walked away.

Jeanette, with an armload of books, made her way to science class. She saw David going in the door ahead of her, as she stopped to greet her friend Maybelle Reed. Of the two, Maybelle was the one everyone noticed first. She was very pretty with light brown skin, naturally straight hair, and a pleasant, easy smile.

Jeanette was tall for a girl, and slim. In color she was as dark as David. She had large eyes and highly arched eyebrows, which gave to her face a questioning look. She smiled often, but she seemed also to be thoughtful and serious, and she walked as though she knew where she was going and what she would do when she arrived.

This morning at the end of the class period she waved at David to indicate that she wanted him to wait for her. She left Maybelle and walked across the room, meeting him as they both neared toward the door.

"You seem to like this study about plants and pollination," she said.

"Well, it's kind of interesting, I guess." He tried to seem casual. "I've seen it working before, but I never did know what was going on, not really."

"Your father wasn't a farmer, was he?"

"Well, he wasn't much of a farmer, and while we didn't do any cross-pollination, they had it on the big farms, and I always wondered about it. Seems funny," he went on, "to be studying about growing things and fertilizing and pollinizing up here in a big city high school."

"Yes," Jeanette agreed, "lots of things seem funny. We've only been here for about two years. I know what you mean."

They moved down the hall, not saying much. At the end of the hall, she turned toward the stairs.

"I have first lunch period," he said hastily.

"So do I," Jeanette answered.

"How about—" He stopped. "How about meeting you—"

"Yes, I'd love to." Jeanette was smiling. "We could meet right here and maybe go over to the Nut House. I like hamburgers."

Later, while they ate in the crowded confusion of the lunchroom across the street, David found himself telling Jeanette all about Alonzo and the football coach.

"I know how white folks are," he concluded. "I learned about them down South, but I'm going to get my schooling just the same. Only I'd like to get the chance to try like anybody else. I don't want any special favors. I just don't want white people holding me back all my life."

He wondered afterward if Jeanette agreed with him. She did not say.

In the locker room that afternoon as the players were dressing for football practice, Mike O'Connor said to Buck, "You know I've been thinking about that guy Williams. Thought I'd try to talk to him, but he wasn't in the cafeteria today."

"I don't know what there is to talk about," Buck said, not trying to hide his annoyance. "He had his chance just like anybody else. Nobody did anything to him."

"I know. Just the same maybe he thinks somebody did. He's from the country, you know."

"Lots of guys are from the country."

"Why don't you try to talk to him, Buck? Maybe you could help him."

"Who, me?" Buck was really angry now. "Why should I? He's not my baby. He's nothing to me, less than nothing."

"O.K., O.K." Mike watched while Buck stamped into a shoe and bent to lace it with swift hard motions. "You don't have to bust a gut about it."

FIVE

Getting up Sunday mornings without having a regular round of duties was another thing that made David realize that his new life was very different from his old. He had grown up knowing that regardless of the day or the weather, good times or bad, sickness or even death, the livestock had to be fed and the cow milked. He had been taught the Ten Commandments, and he could recite the one about the Sabbath by heart: "In it thou shalt not do any work, thou, nor thy son, nor thy daughter, thy manservant, nor thy maidservant, nor thy cattle, nor thy stranger that is within thy gates." But down South he had never heard anyone preach against doing the necessary farm chores.

"Seems funny not to have to worry about feeding and milking and cutting firewood and all that," David said at the breakfast table on Sunday morning.

"It's all just what you get used to," his father replied. "I guess we couldn't go back to wood stoves if we wanted to. Right, Dave? And where would we find the wood?"

"One thing," Mrs. Williams said, a wistful look coming over her face, "we didn't have to pay for fuel, and we always had eggs and most of the time vegetables out of the garden."

"I guess you do miss the things around home," Mr. Williams admitted.

"It's more the people," Mrs. Williams tried to explain. "It looks like we don't have friends here. We don't know people. We don't really even know the people who share this house with us. Yes, I miss my friends."

"How about the Crutchfields?" David reminded his mother. "They're real friends now, and after they take us to church today, you'll be making a lot more new friends."

"They'll be wanting you to teach Sunday school as soon as they get to know you." Betty Jane remembered with pride how the students and older people, too, had admired her mother's teaching. "You must have been a good teacher, Ma. I wish I could have been in your school."

"You're right, Betty Jane." Mr. Williams leaned back in his chair, smiling. "Your mother was one of the best, and she could still do it."

"Your father's a little biased in my favor." Mrs. Williams was laughing, but David could see she was pleased, as she got up and started clearing the table. "We've got to get a move on. The Crutchfields will be here soon to pick us up, and we don't want to keep them waiting. Ed, you'll go with us, won't you?"

Mr. Williams shook his head slowly. "Honey, you and the children go along. Maybe I'll get a sermon on TV," he said.

"Is your head hurting?" David asked.

"Not just now. It's not bad, but when I sit still, like in church, then it gets worse."

"Ed, I want you to see a doctor." David had often heard his mother say the same thing before, but today she sounded particularly anxious.

"Nothing for a doctor to do." Mr. Williams shrugged and spread his hands wide on the table. "He'd give me some aspirin or something, or he'd tell me I need a rest. Might tell me to get a change of climate, go South, take a trip to Florida. Yeah!" he elaborated as he saw the smiles around him.

"That's just about all I need, a nice trip South."

All of them tried to laugh, but David could see in his father's eyes the look of deep pain mixed with anger and bitterness. David knew that he was remembering the horror of those days before they had moved when, because he had defied a white man, he had been jailed and beaten and his family had been terrorized by a mob. Now they tried not to think about what had happened, but they could not forget it. The subject was never openly discussed, and they did not talk about how they felt. When anyone mentioned the matter at all, it was referred to as "the trouble," and everyone knew what was meant. They spoke of events "before the trouble" or "after the trouble."

As the family started to dress in their Sunday clothes, Mr. Williams caught some of their enthusiasm, in spite of his headache, and decided he would come with them after all.

"Can't have my family going out to meet the public like they didn't have a daddy in the house," he said.

Betty Jane was watching at the front window when the Crutchfields drove up. She waved and ran to the door. Everyone was ready to leave except David who complained that he was always the last one to get into the bathroom.

Mr. Crutchfield was standing beside his car when the Williams family reached the sidewalk. He held the door open for them like a servant proud of his employers.

"My, my!" He bowed and smiled broadly. "Don't you all ladies look fine this morning! Don't know when my old hack has hauled such beautiful ladies and such well-set-up gentlemen."

They exchanged pleasantries, and the Williamses piled into the back seat.

"Don't mind Andy," Mrs. Crutchfield said. "He goes on like that all the time."

"Course," Andy Crutchfield retorted, as he settled his large body behind the wheel, "you all know that this fine lady sitting up here beside me is my real boss. Like the man said, I the one drive the car but she the one drive me."

Andy Crutchfield had left South Town many years ago, and was now firmly established in North Town. Without skills or special training, he had found work at the Foundation Iron and Machine Works as a janitor. For seventeen years, he had survived layoffs and cutbacks, boasting that he never

missed a day except at vacation time, which was always spent among his old friends in the South. Like
the Williamses, many families making their way
northward had stopped overnight at the Crutchfield
home.

As they entered the church, people in the vesti-
bule greeted the Crutchfields as friends. An usher,
wearing white gloves, led them down the center
aisle to a pew near the front. The service of wor-
ship had not yet started. David sat very straight and
tried to look as though he had been there before.
Betty Jane, openly curious, turned and twisted in
her seat. She peered at the painted angels and cher-
ubs on the ceiling and studied the leaded patterns
of the stained-glass windows.

The organist played a few bars softly and then
started a hymn. The voices of the choir members
sounded melodiously from the back of the church.
From the pew behind them, someone passed an
open hymnbook to Mrs. Williams. David reached
for a book in the rack and found his place.

It was a song that David had liked to sing at
home. Now it seemed quite grand with the pipe or-
gan and a large choir of good voices.

"Holy, Holy, Holy!" they sang, *"Lord God al-*

mighty! Early in the morning our song shall rise to Thee." At the start of the second verse everyone stood up and the choir began to file, two by two, down the center aisle. *"Holy, Holy, Holy! All the saints adore Thee."* The singers, like the organist, were robed in dark red. As they passed, David clearly heard the sopranos, *"Cherubim and seraphim, falling down before Thee"*; the altos, *"Who wert and art, and evermore shall be"*; the tenors, *"All Thy works shall praise Thy name in earth and sky and sea"*; and the basses whose voices seemed to rumble and growl, *"Holy, Holy, Holy, Merciful and Mighty."*

At the front of the sanctuary the procession divided with practiced smoothness, one line going to the right and the other to the left to take their places in the choir sections. When the last verse came to an end, the minister walked to the pulpit. He quoted one passage of Scripture, and the congregation responded with another.

"The Lord is in His Holy temple: let all the earth keep silence before Him."

The minister bowed his head and quietly said a short prayer. It was as though he knew that God was there and it was not necessary to shout to get His attention. As he concluded the prayer, many joined in saying, "Amen."

David knew that some of the worshipers, perhaps most of them, had once lived in the South. They were Negroes who had decided that "going North" would mean better opportunities to earn a living and to educate their children. Some, like the Crutch- fields, had come North many years ago. Others, Da- vid guessed, were probably newcomers like himself. He imagined that most of them had more education than the people left in South Town, more money too. They earned more and they lived better.

The sermon was also different—there was much more about citizenship and voting than in the ser- mons David was used to. The Reverend Mr. Hayes, who was over six feet tall and very thin, had bushy white hair which stood out from his head. At first, he preached about Moses and the children of Israel. David knew the story well, but this time the minister had taken his text from a less familiar part. It told how the people complained after Moses had led them out of the land of Egypt. Once he freed them of their bondage to Pharaoh, they blamed everything that went wrong on Moses.

Probably no one in the church was old enough to

have been a slave, but they had all heard stories of that time. They often sang songs that came down from slave days and heard preachers compare the Bible stories of slavery in Egypt with the history of slavery in America.

The Reverend Mr. Hayes was saying that the lesson to be learned from the Bible story did not apply only to the physical slavery of the past. It applied as well to people here and now. He talked about the slavery of poverty and unemployment and contrasted it to industrial prosperity. Then he compared the slavery of ignorance with the liberty of knowledge and understanding. There were many, he said, who complained when they achieved freedom and opportunity because they then had to meet greater responsibilities.

Among the responsibilities all must meet, he claimed, was that of citizenship. An election was pending, and campaign speeches were blaring forth from radio and television sets. The Reverend Mr. Hayes told the congregation that voting was more than a right and a privilege. It was a duty, and every citizen had a responsibility to consider the candidates and to examine the issues and then to vote for good government.

"Our prophets," he said, "Frederick Douglass, Booker T. Washington, and W. E. B. DuBois cried out, 'Let my people go!' We have come out of the land of bondage. We are called to new tasks and new responsibilities, in conduct and industry, in thrift and education, in citizenship and brotherhood. Many of us in North Town today are complaining like those lost children in the wilderness, complaining and refusing to use what we have to make life better, complaining about what our leaders do not give us, what our politicians will not do for us, never thinking how much we can and should do for ourselves."

After church the Crutchfields joined the Williams family for dinner. They talked enthusiastically about the sermon and the church program. Andy Crutchfield was loud in praise of his pastor, and Mrs. Crutchfield applauded the missionary society's work, caring for the needy at home and raising money for churches in Africa.

"How long does a man have to be in North Town before he can vote?" Mr. Williams asked.

"I don't know," Andy Crutchfield said. "I don't mess with politics. Never voted yet, and don't aim to. That's one thing I don't go along with Reverend

Hayes on. Voting! Only place I vote is in church meeting. I vote there, and I know what I'm voting on."

"Down South, they didn't let us vote," Mr. Williams said. "I always figured that if they ever would allow it in my county I'd want to be among the first to walk in there and express myself."

"What difference you suppose your one little vote is going to make?"

"Might not make much difference to anybody else, but voting in a public election, whenever I get the chance, is sure going to make a big difference to me." Mr. Williams pushed his chair back from the table and stood up. "I'm going to say: Here I come, me, Edward Mansfield Williams! I'm voting as a free-born citizen. It won't be anything more than others are doing, but it will be the first time for me, and when I vote, then I'll know I've got some real equality, 'cause my one vote will weigh as much as any other man's, be he high as a Georgia pine or white as new cotton."

SIX

*I*n November, at the end of the first marking period, David was again called to the principal's office. This time Mr. Hart was smiling as he greeted him. He glanced at a paper on his desk and remarked that David had made some good grades.

"At our last meeting you told me something about your parents, David," he said. "How are they getting along? Are they settled yet?"

"Not really," David replied. "They're still looking for a better place to live," he explained. "We'd like to buy a house."

"Is your father still working at the Foundation plant?"

"Yes," David said, adding that they had joined the First Baptist Church and made some friends there.

"How do you like Central?" Mr. Hart was persistent.

David hesitated. "I like it very well, sir," he said after a moment's thought.

"I know it still seems new," Mr. Hart said. "And I don't pretend to know how you feel about us," he continued, "but I'm sure there've been problems in getting adjusted. Do you think you've adjusted to us? To the school in general?"

"I guess so." David was noncommittal.

"Have you made many friends? Close friends, I mean?"

"No," David answered, "not really. Not like I used to have."

"Have you been out for any sports? You look like good football material."

For a minute David wanted to tell Mr Hart what had happened that day on the football field.

"Yes, sir. I went out one day," he said slowly. "I guess I didn't do much."

"Well, the basketball season is coming up. Maybe you'll want to try for that team."

David did not look at the principal. "I don't think I will," he murmured.

After he had gone to bed that night, David thought of some of the things he should have said in answer to Mr. Hart's questions.

Problems in getting adjusted? Yes! Why couldn't he, David Andrew Williams, age sixteen, be recognized as a student who was a human being, just like any other at North Central?

In his classes he was proving that he could do the work. In geometry he did better than most of the white students. In science and in English, he kept up easily. He had been behind in mechanical drawing because he had never before used drafting instruments, but in the machine shop he had caught on fast, and evenings at home he discussed the work with his father who gave him pointers.

One thing about the school, he could not understand. In class, when he recited, he was listened to with interest. In the classrooms and shops the white boys and the girls, too, talked readily with him. They seemed to respect his opinion in discussions. However, in the halls or outside the building everything was different. White boys seldom spoke to him, and they never walked with him or stopped to talk. The white girls were even more distant. When he met one he knew from a class, she often seemed not to recognize him. Sometimes they deliberately looked away, or even worse, they acted as though he were not really there.

He told himself that he did not mind. He knew that there was a book written by a Negro about Negroes called *Invisible Man.* He knew something about how the invisible man must have felt.

He told himself that he did not mind. But deep inside of him, he did mind. He minded very much. He minded, and he was hurt.

Any friends? The people he knew best at North Central were not his friends. He knew without being told that Alonzo and Jimmy and their crowd were not going anywhere in life. They were not interested in an education. They had no real goals. He did not belong with that unhappy group, although they had befriended him and he spent much of his free time with them.

Jeanette had seemed friendly, but he had not really talked with her since that day they had had lunch together. She seemed to be always busy with her own affairs and with her own friends like Maybelle Reed and Buck Taylor.

David wished that he could talk to Buck Taylor. Buck excelled as an athlete and as a student, but Buck, like the white students, showed no interest in David.

There were other colored boys who, apparently

easygoing and relaxed like Buck, were active in school affairs; but they, too, appeared indifferent to David. Certainly he did not want to be friendly with white people—he did not trust them—but he did not want to be totally ignored by them, either.

If only he could do something important in the school, David thought, then they would know that he was there. If only he had made the football team, or could play the trumpet, or maybe the drums in the band, if only he could do something to make them recognize that he belonged, that he was a person who had something to share. He was looking forward with the best of them to getting an education, and he knew he was capable of doing it.

He should have said all this to the principal, and now he was angry at himself because he had not been able to speak out.

One morning after science class, Jeanette surprised him with an invitation.

"I'd like you to come to Guild meeting at church next Sunday," she told him. "The son of our rector will be the speaker. They say he's very smart. He teaches in one of the church schools in the South."

"I guess I know what he'll be saying," David an-

swered. "I don't have to hear it from anybody else.
I could tell them what happened with my family."

"Yes, guess you could." Jeanette was serious.
"Most of the people here think that Abraham Hamilton is crazy to be teaching in the South when he
could be teaching here."

"I don't. Somebody's got to do it. I figure to go
back, after I get my education," David announced
firmly.

"That's what I mean. He might need somebody
from the South to help him get his point over."

David arrived at St. Cyprian's parish house after
the meeting had started and took a seat at the back.
Jeanette saw him come in, and she smiled her welcome. He noticed Buck Taylor sitting next to Maybelle Reed, who, with one or two others David knew,
turned and nodded in greeting. In the front seats
with the older people was the rector, Father Hamilton, in his white clerical collar and black suit.

Mr. Hamilton, the speaker, was describing the
poverty and the ignorance in the section of the
South where he was principal of a mission
school. It seemed there was no public high school
for colored children in the county, and very few of

the people sent their children to the church school.

"As I stand here speaking to you about our people, I know that it is difficult, if not impossible, for you to realize the conditions there. But I can say that when I stand before an audience there and describe the schools you have and the homes you live in, they do not understand. They cannot believe me. Sometimes they say that not in heaven itself will white children and colored children attend the same schools, study the same books, and work together on the same problems."

He closed with an appeal to young Negroes to prepare themselves to go into the South to teach, or at the very least, to try to understand the problems. With understanding they would find ways of helping. They could share their benefits through the church mission programs and welfare activities. Through political activity, they could bring about legislation for better public education.

There was only light applause as he took his seat. The young woman in charge of the meeting expressed her thanks to the speaker and called for questions. There were none, and the meeting was adjourned.

After the meeting, hot chocolate was served.

Jeanette brought a cup to David, and then they both went forward to join the group around Mr Hamilton.

"I'm from the South myself," a man was saying to the speaker. "When I was a boy things were pretty bad in some places, although they weren't so bad for my parents. They weren't sharecroppers. They were landowners, and my father sent every one of his children off to school. From what you say, they haven't made much progress in your section. What about integration? Aren't the school authorities working on that?

"Where I am," Hamilton replied, "most of the people have never heard the word, and the authorities have never done anything about it. In the cities, yes, they have done something." He smiled grimly. "In the state capital they have passed new laws, all designed to prevent any action in support of the Supreme Court's decision of 1954."

"Well," Buck Taylor interjected, "it looks like the Southern Negroes really don't want to help themselves. You say yourself that the parents won't send their children to your school. It looks like they don't care."

"Yes, I know what you mean. It does look like

the people don't care." The others looked surprised that the speaker had agreed with Buck. "This
is what I mean by understanding. Can you understand that in their ignorance, in their poverty, in
their lack of vision, these people are without hope?
They aren't happy, but they don't know how to improve their conditions. It's hard, often impossible,
for them to realize that education might open the
way to a better living. In most families, the work of
the children in the fields is necessary for survival.
If you ride through the country, you'll see that not
only men are working in the fields, planting, culti-
vating, harvesting, and picking cotton, or whatever
it might be, but women, too, and children, children
six, seven, and eight years old."

"Oh, I can understand that," Buck said easily,
"but what I can't understand is why when those people come North they want to go on living like they did
down South. They want to live in the slums. They
crowd together in places like East Sixth Street.
When they go to our schools, they try to make trouble. It looks like even here they don't try to improve
themselves."

David was jolted, and found himself disliking
Buck Taylor. He could understand very well what

Mr. Hamilton was saying. Although his own parents had been landowners, most of his friends' parents had been sharecroppers. He knew how pupils stayed out of school at planting time and at crop time, and how they dropped out for good as soon as they had learned to read and write.

Yes, he knew just what Mr. Hamilton meant and felt that it was brave of him to spend his life working in the South. This was what he himself had always dreamed of doing. After finishing high school, he would go to the state university and then to medical school. Once he became a doctor, he would go back to the South. He would be interested not only in people's physical health but also in what they thought and felt. He would try to help them to understand themselves and to see the possibilities in their lives, to work and sacrifice to get an education and make a better living in the future.

Mr. Hamilton was saying some of the very things that David himself would have said.

"I'm from the South," Jeanette said, plunging into the discussion. "My family moved here from New Orleans, where conditions were not too bad. We had good homes and good schools. There are three colleges for Negroes right in the city."

"Yes." Mr. Hamilton was quick to agree. "You are quite right. Perhaps I did not make myself clear. I was not speaking of all the South. What has happened in New Orleans, in Atlanta and Nashville and Richmond and many other Southern cities shows what can happen. People are making progress in understanding, and now oppression is diminishing. There is growing appreciation for human rights. There is more recognition of worth. It is for this we strive. It is for more light in the dark places that we pray."

"Then I guess," Buck spoke again, "you don't recommend that all those ignorant Southern people come up North and make it harder for us who don't have any problems."

David saw a look of deep sadness come over Mr. Hamilton's sensitive face.

"There is something you will have to learn," he said earnestly, "something you will learn sooner or later. The problems of those who come here, whether they are from the South or from across the seas, their problems are ours. They are more than the problems of race. They are the problems of all mankind.

"Some of us live in fine houses," he went on.

"We drive beautiful cars. We go to school, and we think we learn. We think we have no problems. We delude ourselves when we say their plight is not ours. Their mistakes, their ill health, their ignorance—yes, even their violence and their crimes— are problems for all of us. We cannot, we must not think that the problems are theirs alone."

As David walked home, and for a long time afterward, he thought about all that he had heard.

For the first time he realized that where he lived was considered a slum area and that people like Buck looked down on him. He knew that someday his family would move to a better neighborhood, but he hoped he would not forget that others would be left behind. It would be like moving out of the South. He did not want to forget the people there, either. Someday he would return to help them.

SEVEN

David began to spend more and more of his free time at the Carver Community Center. He had gone there first with some boys from his block on a Friday evening for the Teen-Time Club.

When they arrived, a record would be put on and a few couples would be dancing. Most of the time, though, the boys just stood around and talked about sports or jazz or the girls across the room.

Some evenings there was basketball practice, and David worked hard to make the Carver team. He wasn't used to playing indoors on a hardwood floor. Still, he had speed, and by Christmas he was playing on the team as a forward with Head. Head, whose real name was John Henry Healey, was six feet two, well coordinated, and fast on his feet.

Nearly everyone who came to the Center was colored, though this was not because white people were barred. Occasionally during the afternoons, white kids who lived in the neighborhood stopped in to play Ping-Pong or work in the shop. Visiting basketball teams with all white players brought their own rooters, some of them girls. If there was a social hour after the game, they would share refreshments and listen to music, but no one would dance.

After practice one cold Monday night in January, David dressed quickly. He was hoping for a ride home with one of the other players, Billy Atkinson, who lived near him. There was no hot water in the showers, and he was eager to get home to a warm bath.

"I'll see you, fellows," Billy called over his shoulder as he headed for the door.

"Which way do you go?" David asked pointedly.

"I'm not going home direct," Billy replied, and David knew he had been rebuffed. He was sorry he had asked.

Head was tying his shoes.

"Some people I know!" he exclaimed. "Probably wheeling over to the west side. He's crazy about that girl Maybelle Reed where they had the New Year's Eve party. You know her?"

David said he did.

"Did you go to her party?" Head asked.

David shook his head. He had spent New Year's Eve at the Crutchfields with his family.

"They got a nice basement," Head went on. "She's got plenty records. Only nobody likes her much."

"Why not?" David asked, surprised.

"Her old man's a cop. When she pitches a party, he invites all his friends." Head pulled a red sweater over his head. "Millie Robinson was there," he went on, "and her old man was supposed to pick her up about one o'clock. They say when he came up and saw the squad cars he thought the house was being raided. He rushed in there, shouting. He was going to save his daughter."

David laughed with Head at the picture.

The lights were dim as David and Head left the dressing room and skirted down the side of the gym to save the varnished floor from their metal-tipped shoes.

David liked Head. He seemed like a fairly intelligent guy who desperately needed a break. Head had left school a couple of years before, and was out of a job most of the time. Once David had suggested night school to him.

"Yeah, I'm going to take that up," Head had replied, "just as soon as I get something steady to carry me along. See, if I get a job working at night, I'd have to drop out."

Sometimes, Head said, he was able to get work cooking at one of the downtown hotels. David guessed that what Head actually did was wash dishes, but he did not say so. Head always managed somehow to have enough cigarettes and spending money. The younger boys at the Center admired him for his skill as a basketball player, and he sang in a quartet which he had organized. He was a natural leader, and had friends among the older fellows outside the Center, too.

When they walked down the steps of the building that evening and Head suggested, "Come on down the street," David willingly followed him.

"It sure is cold," he said, and pulled his scarf closer around his neck.

Under a swinging sign labeled Café, Head stopped. He pushed open the door and went in, David right behind him. In the dim light David saw two men at a marble-topped table, their empty plates before them. A fat man with his hat on the back of his head was talking loudly to the aproned proprietor behind the counter. Then he noticed a fellow, perhaps a little older than Head, sitting by himself with a cup of coffee.

"You know Hap, don't you?" Head asked.

David had never seen Hap before, but he had heard about him. He knew that Hap had been "away" and that at one time he had been the leader of a gang. A fuzzy white sports cap was pulled low over Hap's face, and he wore dark glasses. David could not see his eyes, but he could feel them looking him over.

"What you say!" Hap greeted them. "Want anything to eat?" When Head hesitated, he added, "I'm straight, man."

Head ordered a hamburger and a Coke. David did, too, but resolved to pay for his own. While they ate, Head and his friend spoke in brief exchanges which did not include David.

After they left the café, Hap led them around the corner to a car, and jumped into the driver's seat. Head opened the right-hand door and motioned for David to take the place in the middle. Hap bent and reached under the dash before he pushed the starter button and the motor pulsed into action. He backed the car away from the curb and then turned left, away from the business district.

Flipping on the radio, Head found a station with some good modern jazz. He snapped his fingers and moved his head to the steady beat. No one spoke for a while. Then Head got out his cigarettes and offered the pack to Hap and David. Hap reached toward the dashboard and, after tugging at two knobs, located the cigarette lighter which he pushed in. Suddenly David knew he was riding in a stolen car.

The three of them smoked in silence. Head was moving his hands with the rhythm of the music.

"Lots of power," he said, inhaling deeply.

"You ought to feel it," Hap replied. By now they were in the suburbs. He let the car slow until the speedometer read twenty-five. Then he pushed his foot down hard on the gas pedal, and the big machine leaped forward. It seemed to David that pressure was coming through the back of the seat. The dial registered forty—and then fifty, sixty, sixty-five. The indicator crept up to seventy, where it held steady.

Head's body stiffened. He leaned far back, his eyes closed in ecstasy. "Drive me 'til I sweat!" he cried.

David sat tense and fearful, his eyes on the road.

He had to admit that Hap was a good driver. The car stayed on the right; the lights were dimmed for oncoming cars; they easily overtook and passed a truck.

Bright lights ahead illumined a highway intersection with a cluster of service stations, a diner, and a few houses. A traffic light controlled the intersection, and Hap slowed for it. The light turned from green to orange and then to red. The car braked to a stop. The music from the radio was loud.

In the instant before the light again turned green, a siren sounded close behind them. The glow of a blinking red light was reflected in the windshield. Hap drove slowly across the intersection and pulled off on the right of the pavement.

For a short space of time, David was able to tell himself that everything was all right. It really was Hap's own car, or maybe one of his friend's. It was going to be all right. Hap wasn't even trying to get away.

"Speeding!" he said, "they got us for speeding. We were going too fast."

"Shut up!" Head spoke harshly. "You don't know nothing. You don't say nothing. Not nothing."

It wasn't exciting. It wasn't even a chase. It was

just bad. It was the worst thing that had ever happened to David. The police officers in the car asked only a few questions. Hap did most of the talking. A friend had loaned him the car. He didn't know the name of the friend or his address or anything like that.

Then Hap and Head and David were all three handcuffed. Hap's hands were handcuffed behind his back; David's right wrist was linked to Head's left. They were put in the patrol car, and with a short salute of the siren, the car made a U-turn through the intersection and moved swiftly back toward the city.

EIGHT

At police headquarters, it was soon determined that David Andrew Williams and John Henry Healey were under eighteen and that Hap, whose real name was Percy Johnson, was twenty-one. A different procedure was required for booking minors, so the handcuffs were taken off Head and David and they were led upstairs to another office. There juvenile officers questioned them.

They sat side by side on a hard bench without a back. A round-faced sergeant with light hair asked the questions while a younger man, who was swarthy and lean, wrote down the answers.

David could hardly speak. He had to struggle for every answer, even those of the simplest sort.

"Have you ever been arrested before?" the sergeant asked brusquely.

David hesitated.

"You might as well tell us," the sergeant said. "We'll find out anyway."

"Not really, sir." David could hardly hear his own voice.

"What do you mean 'not really'? Were you or weren't you?" the sergeant pressed him. "Were you ever picked up on anything? Were you ever booked? You don't have to have been convicted."

David did not answer. Engulfed by shame and despair, he dropped his head in his hands and closed his eyes. The officers seemed far away. Their voices seemed unreal. He was not sure what their words meant. When they asked him where he got in the car and how long he had been with Hap, he did not answer, and when they pressed him, he could only shake his head slowly and mutter, "I don't know."

With Head, it was different. The officers knew Head. They addressed him by his nickname, almost as though he were a friend. David was glad when they left him and turned their attention to Head.

Finally, the officers moved away to a counter on the opposite side of the room. David was still slumped against the wall, his eyes closed, Head close beside him, when he felt Head's elbow nudging him.

"You did good, man," Head said, congratulating him in an undertone. "They'll charge us with grand theft auto, all three of us, but we can beat it."

Grand theft auto! Beat it! We can beat it! The words filled David with terror.

Head poked him again. "You going to stick by Hap, ain't you? You ain't going chicken out?" he asked.

David did not answer.

"You been busted before?"

"Busted," David knew, meant arrested. Why did they keep asking him that? Would they call what had happened to him and his family busted? Anyway, that was down South. It shouldn't have happened. It didn't count.

"Well, have you?" Head asked again.

David shook his head.

"So they can't do nothing to you. They can't do nothing. This is the first time, and you're a juvenile. They can't do nothing more than put you on probation. That's the law in this state."

David felt some slight relief. He hoped it was true.

"Hap's got a prior. Course you probably knew

that, and I'm glad you ain't going chicken out on
Hap, 'cause they'd just love to put him away for a
long time. And they will, too, if we don't stick together."

Head put his hand on David's shoulder. "All you
got to do," he advised, "is keep on playing dumb.
They can't use what you don't say against you. Besides, like I said, they can't do nothing to you. That's
the law."

Head spoke rapidly in a low voice. He seemed to
know all about the laws for juvenile offenders, and
he was very sure of himself, referring to names of
friends and cases he had heard about. He talked
about judges and probation officers, and he gave de-
tailed instructions about what to say and what not
to say to inquiring "juvies," as he called the special
officers on the youth detail.

"It'll be like this," he explained. "The juvies
will make a case and write up a petition. Then
they'll take you to court, and the judge will ask you
if it's true what they say in the petition. Best thing
you can do is just what you done here—play dumb.
'Cause even if you say you not guilty, they say you
is. So play real dumb and say you don't know nothing, you don't remember, or something like that.

Then there's the probation officer. Some of them cats try to be real cute—make you think they're on your side and they want to help you and all that jive." He took out a cigarette and matches as he talked.

"Don't let them snow you, man. They're just educated cops. They don't mean you no good unless you want to play it their way." He paused and struck a match.

"No smoking here!" the sergeant called out.

Head continued to light the cigarette as though he had not heard. He took a deep drag. Then he pushed the cigarette into David's hand.

"What you say, sir?" he asked innocently as he looked up.

The sergeant moved quickly from behind the counter, and David cringed, expecting a blow. Frightened, he dropped the cigarette on the floor and covered his face with his hands.

But no blow came.

"Pick it up!" the officer ordered. As David bent over, he heard, "Not you! I mean Head!"

"I don't put nothing on the floor, Sarge," Head said calmly, his arms folded. "I don't pick nothing up."

"I did it," David said hurriedly. "I didn't mean to. I'll get it."

"No!" The officer's leg blocked David, and his hand grabbed the back of Head's neck. The muscles of Head's face tightened with pain as his body was forced slowly forward. David watched the officer's white fingers pressing hard against Head's dark skin. He drew away, hating the cop. He hated the other cop who was standing there watching, waiting for Head to move. He hated them all. White folks!

"Pick it up!" The sergeant's words came through clenched teeth. David was glad when Head's right hand reached out and retrieved the still-smoking cigarette butt.

"On your feet now," the sergeant commanded. Head was half turned, half pushed toward the hall. The second officer flicked a switch on the intercom and reported, "One coming in for lockup."

David was sure that now Head would be beaten. He had never witnessed such defiance of law. He had never before seen a Negro refuse to carry out a white man's order. He listened fearfully, expecting to hear blows and cries of pain. It wasn't worth it, he decided. Head shouldn't have asked for it like that. This was one of the times when Head should have done what he was told, knowing what a white man would do when he had the chance.

The sergeant came back, half-smiling. "He can smoke back there," he said to David.

At that moment there was the sound of more footsteps in the passage. David turned to see his father coming through the door with a policeman in blue overcoat and cap.

David saw in his father's face an anguish that had nothing to do with physical pain or beating or threat of death.

"Son!" Mr. Williams exclaimed.

"They'll tell you about it," the policeman said. Taking Mr. Williams by the arm, he turned him toward the counter.

"Yes sir," the swarthy officer said, rising to his feet. "Are you this boy's father?"

David heard the questions the officers asked his father, and he heard the answers his father gave, and then he heard his father's questions and the officers' account of the arrest, the fact that the car was stolen, and their very low opinion of both of David's companions.

"If your boy's the kind of kid you say he is," the sergeant said, "if he's a decent kid, then he sure is running with the wrong kind. Sometimes they do, you know. It wouldn't be so bad if the good guys didn't try to act like the bad guys. You know what I mean?"

"You know, Mr. Williams," the other officer said, "this boy of yours hasn't been very cooperative. Not at first, anyway. He clammed up. Looked like he was trying to cover up for his pals. He should know what these hoodlums are like, both of them."

"You mean he wouldn't talk?" Mr. Williams asked in disbelief. "He wouldn't answer questions?" He turned to look at his son, but David did not return his gaze.

"Aw, it doesn't matter," the sergeant shrugged. "But under 'attitude,' we're going to have to spell it out—'sullen, withheld information, uncooperative.' Know what I mean?"

"I guess I do, but I'm surprised." Mr. Williams shook his head. "I just don't understand it. I can't understand it."

"You and the other fathers!" The sergeant laughed. "Nobody understands nowadays what makes juvenile delinquents, but I bet your father did—and I bet he knew how to handle his son, too."

Mr. Williams did not join in the laughter. "May I talk to my boy?" he asked.

"Sure, all you want," the sergeant replied. "You can take him home with you. Only have him in court, let's see"—he checked a calendar. "Probably the eighteenth. Have him in juvenile court when they call for him. That's the second floor of the county building. You'll get a notice."

Mr. Williams gave his solemn assurance that he would be there with David. He was then told to sign the "Promise to Appear" form, and he reached eagerly for the pen, but his hand shook so that he was ashamed of his poor writing. They would think he was an illiterate, he thought.

He crossed the room to David and stood before him; David did not look up. Mr. Williams laid his hand on his son's shoulder. "We're going home, son," he said.

David half raised his face. His father spoke again, "We'll talk about it later. They say we can go now."

David motioned with his head toward the hall. "They're doing something bad to my friend," he said.

Mr. Williams quickly sat down on the bench beside him. "What? What are you saying?"

"They took Head, John Henry. They beat him

up. They'll try to kill him. You got to do something, Pa. You know what they do."

Mr. Williams rose. His voice was hard as he spoke to the sergeant, "What about the others?"

"Oh, we had to put that Healey boy in the back." The sergeant was casual about it; too casual, it seemed. "His folks won't be coming down for him. There's only his mother, and she can't do anything with him."

"They hurt him," David blurted out.

"Well, we had to use a little restraint. He broke bad." The sergeant got to his feet. "Want to speak to him? Come on, both of you."

David and his father followed the officer out the door and down the hall. They turned right into another corridor and finally stopped before a gate of heavy steel bars. Here the officer summoned a guard. "They want to see Healey," he explained.

David figured it was a trick, and he wanted to turn back. Maybe they would all be held, he thought wildly. The guard slid a thick metal key into the lock and then swung the gate open. David and his father walked through, and the bars clanged behind them. Now David could see dimly lighted barred sections, stretching on both sides of the corridor.

The bunks in most of them were unoccupied, though some held blanketed forms of men who might have been asleep.

Before the last section on the left, the guard called, "Healey, on your feet!"

David saw that, inside, only one bunk was occupied. On it a figure stirred, and Head turned his face toward his friend. He swung his bare feet to the floor, stretched, and walked forward, smiling.

"What you say, man? This your daddy? You going home?" Head asked.

This time it was surprise that kept David from speaking. He could only nod.

"Don't forget what I told you. You know." Head looked at Mr. Williams and back to David. "You doing all right, man. Say, you got any smokes? Let me hold them. You can get plenty more."

As Head reached out his hand, David removed a pack of cigarettes from his pocket. The guard nodded and took the pack from David, then passed it to his prisoner.

David did not look at his father as he turned and walked away.

David Williams had never lied to his father. He would have admitted that when he was a little kid

he had sometimes twisted answers and evaded questions, not telling all the truth about just where he
had been or some such, but he had never really lied.
He might not have been able to explain the reasons
for this. The main reason was that it had not been
necessary. His father was not what you would call a
hard man, unlike the fathers of some of David's
friends. He was intuitive and understanding, and he
seemed always, or almost always, very reasonable.
Perhaps the time would come when David would deliberately tell his father a lie. Perhaps this might
be the time.

On the way home that night, riding in the faithful old family Chevrolet, David explained what had
happened; then he answered, as well as he could,
his father's questions.

Yes, he had known Head for a while, and he had
thought he was all right; that is, he had never
heard anything bad about him. Yes, he knew that
you couldn't always tell who might be a juvenile delinquent or even a criminal. No, he just hadn't
known Hap well enough to know he didn't have a
car. Even some of the boys still going to school had
their own cars—ones they had bought themselves
or old cars of their parents. Yes, of course, if he had
known the car was stolen, he would never have gone

in it with the others. All of this, which was true, he told his father. He did not tell him that he had seen Hap reach under the dash before he pushed the starter button, nor did he speak of Hap's difficulty in locating the cigarette lighter. In fact, David said nothing to indicate that he was anything but a completely innocent bystander. He knew he was not telling the whole truth.

As they stopped for the last traffic light before reaching home, Mr. Williams said, "Your mother is going to be very upset."

"Couldn't we not tell her?" David asked. "Or maybe not tell her everything?"

"Not hardly." The light turned green, and the car rolled forward. "Not hardly. The policemen came to the house and she heard it from them. I don't see how we could keep anything from her," he concluded with sorrow. He put on the brake and drew up to the curb in front of the house. "It will hurt her, but one good thing, it won't be like you were really guilty. She'll understand that."

"Pa, let's go on. Don't stop. I'd like to talk."

"We can talk in the house."

"No, I'd rather talk to you first. Can't we just drive a little?"

Mr. Williams looked questioningly at David, then started the motor. He could see that his son was miserably unhappy, and he sensed that there was more to tell. They rode several blocks in silence.

Finally he spoke. "What is it, son? Why don't you tell me?"

"It's no use," David muttered. "I might as well admit it. They're going to say I'm guilty anyway."

Mr. Williams pulled up so abruptly by the side of the road that the tires squealed.

"What did you say?"

"I don't mean I'm guilty, but I can't prove I'm not," David said.

"You can prove you never stole anything before, and this fellow that stole the car has a record. Besides, you were at the game tonight until almost the time the three of you were picked up. You sure don't have to admit to something you didn't do."

"It's no use, Pa. John Henry was telling me. They'll charge all three of us anyway, and we might as well admit it and get it over with. They'll put me on probation, that's all."

"So that's what your friend told you," Mr. Williams said. "That you'd all three go down together? These toughs! These hoodlums! I guess they'd like to have you tied up with them. Don't do it, son! Don't do it!"

In his desperation Mr. Williams held tightly to David's arm, trying to arouse him into a realization of what a plea of guilty implied. David did not argue, but he did not agree with his father. He felt defeated and hopeless.

Mr. Williams, his voice taut, spoke of the necessity for David to tell the truth, of the evils of having a record as a thief. He forced David to recognize that Head's plan was for the sake of Hap who might otherwise be sent to prison. David knew that his father was right. It would be bad to have a record. He listened to all that his father said, glad that he was not scolding, only advising and urging, though he was clearly trying to get David to do what Head would call "finking out."

"I'll get a lawyer," Mr. Williams said. "He'll fight for you. He'll probably want to get your case tried separately. He'll speak for you. He'll show the judge that you're not a juvenile delinquent. He'll prove it. Everybody will know that you don't have anything in common with the others."

Out of his bitterness, David spoke. "Pa, that's what we'd like to think," he said. "Maybe you don't know, but I'm learning. It's just the same, Pa. It's just the same as down South. I've got plenty in common with those others. We're all colored together, and the whites will prove we're guilty together."

"Don't say that!" The back of Mr. Williams' hand smashed across David's mouth. "Shut up, I won't hear it! Don't tell me that what we went through in South Town has got to happen all over again. It ain't so. There's law here. I got a decent job. You're going to a decent school. You've got a chance to be somebody here. To live decent. Don't tell me it's just the same!"

The blow hurt. David's lip was cut, but the hurt was more than just that. David had not been hit by his father since he was a young boy, and never before had his father struck him with such anger.

But David was sure of his point. His father was blind, just dumb fool blind. He would prove it.

"Pa, listen to me! Will you listen? Look at where we're living. Can you get a decent apartment anywhere in North Town? They got lots of places advertised, but not for us. Even to buy. Can you buy any but the old rundown houses, or pay double if you get something halfway decent? You know you've been saying that yourself."

"But we're still better off. And we will get **some-thing**," Mr. Williams insisted.

"But you don't know how it is— How they act like they're your friend, and then as soon as they get the chance they're ready to give you a dirty deal. I've seen it at school, on the football field, and every place, and I know that judge'll just take one look and say, 'These guys are guilty.' It's no use, I tell you." David was almost crying. But his father was determined to change his son's thinking.

"Boy," he said, "if I thought you were right, I'd pack up and go to the farthest county in Mississippi, and I'd hire out as a field hand for the rest of my life. It ain't so, I tell you. And you got to learn better. I'll prove it. You'll see I'm right. Tomorrow morning, first thing, I'm going to call a lawyer. That real-estate man, Mr. Taylor, is a lawyer and a good one, they say. I'll phone him from the job. We're going to fight this thing!"

He reached over and started the car. A few moments later he pulled up at the curb in front of the drab two-story house in which they lived. After turning off the ignition, he sat gazing straight ahead with both hands on the wheel.

"Dave," he said, "I'm sorry I hit you. I truly am.

I never meant to strike a child of mine in anger, and you're not even a child. You're most a man now. You got a right to your opinion, I guess, but if I thought you were right I'd be the most disappointed black man that ever lived."

As they walked up the steps, Mr. Williams held his son's arm. They opened the door to the dimly lit hall, and from the apartment above came the wail of a blues song.

Before Mr. Williams put the key in his own lock, he turned again to David.

"You don't have to tell your ma what I done— in the car. Maybe later, sometime, I'll tell her."

"Don't tell her, Pa," David begged. "I hope you don't ever tell her."

NINE

Buck Taylor first heard about David's arrest the following evening at the dinner table. Although Mr. Taylor was an ethical lawyer and never discussed the confidential business of his clients even with his wife, the affair of the Williams boy was now public knowledge.

Mr. Taylor's law practice was not large since his real-estate business gave him ample income, and demanded most of his time. However, he took pride in his knowledge of the law and in his personal contacts with North Town judges and politicians. He sometimes felt that his son did not show him proper respect, that in his own house he was a prophet without honor. So, when he talked at home about a case, he consciously tried to emphasize the fact that in the halls of justice he was a man of status and that white people, as well as colored, looked upon him with respect.

"The police picked up three fellows in a stolen car last night," he volunteered at an appropriate break in the conversation. "One was an old customer and two were juveniles. The father of one of the boys has asked me to represent him."

He put salt and pepper on his meat. "The boy came to see me this afternoon. Bruce, maybe you know him." Mr. Taylor wanted to learn what kind of reputation David had at school, so he added, "Says he goes to Central. Name is Williams, David Williams."

"Yes," Buck acknowledged, "I know him. He's new—from the South."

"I have to go to juvenile court with him on Thursday. What's he like? Get into any trouble in school?"

Buck told what he knew, believing his report to be completely honest. He mentioned the trouble on the football field, adding that David ran around with fellows from the east side. He was kind of dumb, he said, and real Southern.

"But they say," he added, "he gets pretty good grades. Of course, he doesn't go out for athletics and student activities."

"Usually I don't like these juvenile cases," Mr.

Taylor said. "They have special laws of procedure. The judge runs his court informally and doesn't follow the rules of evidence."

Mr. Taylor related some of his experiences in juvenile court; then he went back to David. "Now the way this boy talks! It's as though he were afraid of something," he said.

"Maybe he belongs to a gang," Buck guessed. "Those gangs are pretty tight."

"I asked about that." His father shook his head. "He says he doesn't, and yet he keeps avoiding the issues. Says he doesn't remember. I think he's trying to protect the others."

"Who are the others? Maybe I know them."

"There's a John Henry Healy and a Percy Johnson."

Buck smiled at the names. "Yes," he said, "I know Head—that's what they call Healey. And everybody knows Percy Johnson, but they call him Hap. Anybody might get hurt calling him Percy. He hates it. Lots of the boys are afraid of him. With Hap in it, I can see what Williams might be afraid of. Maybe he's got good reason."

"What are his people like? The new boy's, I mean," asked Mrs. Taylor, who was serving dessert.

"Do you know anything at all about his family?"

"Oh, they're just some more common Southern people, I guess, living over on the east side like the rest of them," Buck answered.

"Bruce, I don't know what you mean by that." Mr. Taylor was annoyed. "Maybe you think 'some more common Southern people' are not worth bothering with. When I was your age, I lived in the South—yes, and on a Georgia farm."

"But, Daddy, you say yourself that these newcomers are ignorant and don't know how to live. You're always having to help them. Getting them out of jail, like now, and finding them homes they can buy and arranging their mortgages."

"But that's my work," Mr. Taylor said. "And I get paid for getting them out of jail, and I make a commission every time I sell a house or place a mortgage."

"I bet they thought they were coming to the Promised Land when they left down there," Buck said, laughing.

"I don't understand you, Bruce." Mr. Taylor looked at his son with surprise. "Maybe you're too integrated already. You know, the Jews have an expression, some of them, that is. They say of another

Jew who has succeeded and who now looks with scorn on the struggling poorer Jews, 'He forgets the ghetto.' I'm afraid many of us with some success and some schooling 'forget the ghetto.'"

Buck did not want to be offensive, but his father had always invited discussion, and now when Buck could not agree he felt he should say so.

"I, for one, would be very happy to forget the the ghetto, and the old tales of slavery days and the South and Jim Crow and discrimination. I'm doing all right. At school everybody treats me O.K. I'd just as soon forget that I'm a Negro."

"Oh, Bruce!" Mrs. Taylor's hand went to her throat. "How can you talk like that?"

Mr. Taylor laid down his fork, marshaling his arguments. Buck turned to his mother. It was easier to talk to her than to his father.

"I mean it," he stated vehemently. "Around here we're always talking about race and Negroes, race pride and Negro history. So what? Why can't we just be Americans? This is a democracy. I'm a senior at Central High School. My father's a lawyer. I'm just like hundreds of others at school. I don't see why I should make something different out of myself."

Mr. Taylor shook his head sadly. "Bruce, if I've led you to believe that by going to Central you can overcome bigotry and race prejudice, then I'm sorry. And if you believe your daddy is the big business man and the eminent lawyer that means success in American life, then, boy, you're so wrong. Your daddy is a very little fellow who scarcely makes enough to live decently and to plan for the future of his family. And let's face it." Mr. Taylor raised his hand in protest as Bruce tried to interrupt. "I make my living off the people you would like to forget. The parents of your white friends at Central don't come to me for help. They aren't even aware of me. And you're going to find out that white people won't let you forget your color, no matter how much you want to. And you'll have no ghetto to remember. Some people get lost like that."

The conversation was interrupted by a telephone call for Mr. Taylor, and Buck took the opportunity to excuse himself. He wanted to see Jeanette and be the first to tell her the news about David. He bounded upstairs and slipped into his new award sweater with the scarlet C and two scarlet stripes on the left sleeve. He knew it looked well on him.

"Don't forget your coat," his mother called. "It's

cold out tonight." But Buck insisted he'd be warm enough in his sweater. He ran all the way to Jeanette's house.

Mr. Lenoir opened the door at his ring, and led the way back to the dining room where the family was finishing dinner.

"Hello, Buck," Mrs. Lenoir said smiling. "Pull up a chair and have some dessert with us."

Mrs. Lenoir was very dark in color. She had strong, sharp features that softened when she smiled. Her hair was pulled back from her face and fastened neatly in a French twist. Jeanette looked very much like her.

Mr. Lenoir, who sat at the head of the table, was much lighter than his wife. He might have been a Creole. Jeanette's older sister was light, too, and could easily have passed as white.

The Lenoirs liked Buck. Mr. Lenoir admired Buck's father and gave him generous praise. All of them thought it was wonderful that Buck did so well at school. Both Mr. and Mrs. Lenoir welcomed him to their home and considered him good company for their younger daughter.

Although Buck announced that he had just finished dinner at his house, Mrs. Lenoir went to the kitchen and returned with a dish of peach cobbler topped with ice cream. He accepted with only a minimum of protest.

In reply to their questions Buck answered that his family was well, that school was all right, and that he was not going out for basketball.

"I got behind during the football season," he explained. "Can't afford to have any low grades this year."

"Have you decided about going into the law?" Mr. Lenoir asked.

"Not altogether," Buck replied. "Lawyers have to do a lot of work they don't get paid for—like for those people over in the slums, getting them out of trouble, jail, and all that."

"He means, Daddy"—Jeanette smiled, but she was serious—"he means like the people who live on the east side, maybe along Sixth Street in those flats."

"Yes, that's what I mean." Buck spoke easily, sure of himself. "My dad's just been hired to defend one of them—a fellow lives over there, goes to our school. Jeanette knows him, David Williams. Grand theft he was arrested for, with two other tough guys."

Jeanette stiffened. "Not David!" she said. "Not David Williams!"

"Yeah, David Williams. Some kind of friend you want to be responsible for."

"Why, we know David," Mrs. Lenoir said. "His parents seem to be very nice people."

"I guess I'd better go see Williams," Mr. Lenoir said. "Maybe there's something I can do."

The Lenoir family's reaction was not at all what Buck had expected. They pressed him for details. Mr. Lenoir said he must call the Williams home, and Jeanette gave him the number. They went into the hall to listen while he spoke to Mr. Williams. "Suppose I come over. I'd like to talk with you about it," Buck heard him say.

His wife helped him into his overcoat. "Please tell Mrs. Williams to phone if there is anything I can do," she said.

There was a sudden silence after the front door slammed; then they heard the hum of the car motor. Mrs. Lenoir went to the kitchen to start the dishes, leaving Jeanette and Buck to look questioningly at each other.

"Wouldn't a juvenile delinquency record spoil David's chances for college?" Jeanette asked.

"College! He's not going to college. He'll never see the inside of a college."

"Buck, you talk about David Williams as if you really knew something bad about him. As a matter of fact, I don't believe you've ever taken the time to talk to him. You don't know a thing about him."

"You know, don't you! You've spent plenty of time with him, I bet. Even your folks. I guess you've had him and his family right here in your own home. I can't understand it."

"You don't want to understand it, Buck."

"There's nothing I want to understand about a guy who is as dumb as he is and who goes on the field attacking players just because they're white and who runs with a pack of hoodlums and gets arrested for car theft. He's not my kind and I think too much of myself to get down to his level."

"You wouldn't even ask him about what happened on the field that day. Well, I did. I asked Al Kirinski, too, and some of the others. The only thing David failed to do was speak up for himself. And about his family. My folks invited them over during the holidays. His mother is a very sweet person who used to teach school in the South. She and my mother have a lot in common. They're the same kind of people. They had trouble in the South. My father had trouble, too, and that was why we left down there."

"Then why don't they get out of the slums? Why do they stay there?"

"It takes money to buy a house. You should know that. They don't have enough money for a down payment on the kind of house they want. They're trying to make out. They're doing the best they can for now, and they know that people like you—yes, people like us on the west side—look down on them. Well, there isn't much difference. My father says we're all newcomers, only some are newer then others. And he says all of America is made up of newcomers. Somebody wrote a book showing that the United States is just one mass of minorities, only the Negroes are especially marked because of their color."

"I've heard all that before. All about the race problem, and I'm sick of it."

"Yes, I know you are. But there's David Williams. And he's our problem now."

"Not mine. You can have him and his problems!"

"You're selfish, Buck. You really don't care what happens to David, do you?"

"Why should I? What are you all getting so worked up about? Your dad going running over there to the east side? My dad talking about remembering the ghetto?"

Jeanette's sister, passing through the hall on her way upstairs, laughingly suggested they go sit in the living room and finish their argument. Jeanette claimed they weren't arguing, but Buck knew that they were.

He followed her into the living room and, still standing, turned and asked, "You like David Williams, don't you?"

Jeanette's eyebrows rose even higher than usual. "I hadn't thought about it." She paused. "About liking him, that is, but I guess I do think he's a very nice person." She looked defiantly at Buck. "Yes, I like David, and I like his folks."

When Buck left Jeanette's house it was after nine o'clock. The winter wind was sharp, but even though he was coatless, he walked home with slow steps, his mind deep in thought.

T E N

*T*he Thursday morning that David was to appear in court started almost like a Sunday in the Williams home. It was like a Sunday, but it was also very different. The evening before, David's mother had ironed a clean white shirt for him and checked to see if his best suit needed pressing. She had also decided that he needed a haircut and sent him to the barbershop.

On Thursday morning, they all got up very early and, after breakfast, David and his parents dressed in their Sunday clothes. Mr. Williams was taking the day off from his job. Betty Jane had to go to school like any other day, and she complained loudly. Otherwise, they had little to say. Mr. Taylor had told them to be in court by nine thirty, but Mr. Williams planned to be there before nine.

Throughout the long night David had slept fitfully. He tossed from side to side, his mind refusing to let him rest.

He knew his father wanted him not only to deny he had stolen the car but also to say that he was different from Head and Hap, that really they were not his friends—in short, that he was a "good" boy. David felt that such talk would be disloyal. They were three colored boys in trouble together, and he must not betray them.

The court would be like the situation on the school football field. The white judge would inevitably say, "You might as well go, too!" But David was determined he would not say that he did not know the car was stolen. He would not "chicken out."

He had been puzzled by Mr. Cooper, the probation officer, when he came to visit him at home. Mr. Cooper was colored, and if Head had not warned him David would have thought he was a good guy.

He had asked David all sorts of questions about himself and his family, and David had answered freely until he was queried about the night he was arrested. But then when he refused to talk, the probation officer surprised him.

"Look, David," he said. "You don't have to talk

about it. You don't have to tell me a thing. I'm not trying to get a confession out of you."

His parents thought the probation officer was a fine young man who really wanted to help. David could not be sure.

He wasn't sure about Mr. Taylor, either.

Mr. Taylor wasn't like any of the lawyers David had seen in the movies or on television or read about in books. He was just like someone you knew. He talked just as David's own father talked about the other fellows. They were no good, he said. They were bad company. Well, David told himself, bad company is no excuse. Sure, he had suspected, even before that night, that Head had some kind of a record. So he was bad company. So Billy Atkinson was good company, and Atkinson was on the team, but he had said that night he was going the other way, while Head had at least been friendly enough to extend an invitation. . . . If it had been Head driving his father's car that night, he would have called all the players together and taken them home.

David had left South Town with such high hopes. He had believed that someday he'd have a medical degree and that he'd return to the hills of Pocohantas County and set up his office in a house like the one his father had owned there beside Route One. Only it would be a bigger house with waiting rooms and an operating room and one or two other rooms, like a small hospital, where some of his patients could remain for treatment and care.

Maybe now it would never happen.

He was sick, almost physically sick as he thought of it, but he could not turn his back on Head. He could not "chicken out."

It was bad, but there was nothing else he could do.

This was the decision he reached in the dark.

With the coming of morning, however, he wasn't so sure.

By nine o'clock that morning David and his parents were seated in the waiting room on the second floor of the county building. The county employees came in noisy groups up the stairs and exchanged greetings as they opened the doors to their offices and began their work for the day. At nine fifteen Mr. Williams spoke to a clerk who told him to wait until his son's case was called.

The waiting room filled rapidly with parents and their children. Just before nine thirty a uniformed officer appeared in the doorway. Behind him a line of boys filed slowly past the door. David recognized Head who turned to search the faces in the crowded waiting room. When he saw David, he smiled and lifted a circled thumb and forefinger.

How do you do what's right? How do you really know right from wrong? Should you tell the whole truth or hold back part? Do you save yourself by letting all the blame fall on the other fellow? And if you can't help him anyway, is there any harm in helping yourself?

Right and wrong! He had always thought they were easy to tell apart, like black and white. Right and wrong, they were supposed to be opposites. But were they so different? Weren't right and wrong very close to each other? And black and white? Fellows like Alonzo Wells and Jimmy Hines seemed very sure that white people were bad and hateful, that all of them were trying somehow to league together to make it hard for colored people. Head was like that, too. But Head thought everyone was against him because nobody, white or colored, cared about him.

At last, Mr. Taylor and Mr. Cooper appeared and beckoned to the Williamses. They crossed the waiting room and stepped into the wide corridor to talk.

"We've been talking about the case," Mr. Taylor said, without wasting any time in formal greetings. "The probation officer is not willing to recommend dismissal. However, I'm prepared to argue the matter in court."

David's mother was holding his arm. He felt her hand tighten.

"It's not a matter of what I'm willing to do," Mr. Cooper explained. "It is what the situation calls for. We're trying to think of what is best for David Williams. It looks like he needs the court's help."

Mr. Taylor spoke of the lack of evidence, of David's good grades in school, and of the damaging effects of a court record. The probation officer spoke of the need for guidance and of the difficulties in adjusting to urban living. David felt as though they were discussing someone who wasn't there.

"After all, you know," the probation officer concluded, "I only offer my recommendation. The court, the judge himself, will make the decision."

They waited for more than an hour before their turn came. As they entered the courtroom, David looked about him with awe. The walls were paneled in dark walnut, and the judges' bench, a high platform of polished wood, loomed imposingly at the front of the chamber. Above the platform, on the wall, hung an American flag; beneath it and separated from the rest of the room by a railing, there was a long table.

A uniformed guard led David down the aisle and stationed him inside the railing. Mr. Taylor stood at his side, and his parents stood behind him. Seated at the table facing them was a gray-haired man. He was talking earnestly to Mr. Cooper. At the other end of the table sat the sergeant David had seen in the police station, another man in uniform, and two women. The seats in the main part of the room were all empty.

A side door opened, and a guard brought in Head. He directed him to stand next to David.

"Does this boy have any people here?" the gray-haired man asked.

"Your Honor, I called the case in the waiting room, but no one answered," the attendant replied.

"His mother was cited, your Honor," Mr. Cooper said. "I served her myself."

"Perhaps she's been delayed," the judge said, looking about him. "Let's see now. Who is present? You are David Williams, I take it, and Mr. and Mrs.

Williams." He paused as Mr. Taylor gave his name.
"Yes, the counsel for the Williams boy. How about
the Healey minor? Are you representing him?"

"No, your Honor, I was not asked to," Mr. Taylor replied. The judge turned to Head.

"You are John Henry Healey?" Head nodded.
"Well, John, what about your mother? She knows
where you are, I suppose. Has she been to see you?"

"Yes sir, Judge. She came to see me in detention.
She said she'd be here. She's late, I guess."

"I presume she's on her way. Mr. Bolden," he
addressed one of the guards, "better alert them outside for—let's see—" He glanced at his papers.
"Mrs. Annie Healey. Tell them to send her right
in."

The judge turned back to his audience. "I am
Judge Winston G. Burnett," he said clearly, "and
I believe you know Mr. Cooper, the probation officer,
and perhaps you know Sergeant Delaney of the
Youth Detail. The special court officer is Sergeant
Swanson. Mrs. O'Brian is here, representing the
school board, and Miss Oliphant is our reporter.

"I want you people to be seated now. I don't want
you to be uncomfortable." He waited while they all
took their places. "Not that this isn't serious busi-

ness. It is very serious, and it is important that we act with wisdom. I am not sure what your previous experience has been, or what you may have been told before you came here. There are some basic concepts which I want to make clear. What we do and say later will be within the framework of these concepts.

"First, I want to say that, although we hold our hearings privately and without formality, this is primarily a court of law within the American concept of justice, and there are certain rights which have been handed down through generations. All of those rights are observed here. No one has to give evidence against himself, and every person has the full right to face and question those who bring evidence against him. Any person brought into this court has the right to have counsel, a lawyer to speak and to act in his behalf."

The judge paused and looked at the faces before him as though he wondered whether they understood him. "Yet there are differences between this court and our criminal courts," he went on. "In this court no one is being prosecuted. We do not have a defendant here, because these boys are not charged with any crime. We have no prosecuting attorney. The simple fact is that we have a petition asking this court to assume responsibility for the future of these minors, because allegedly there is grave danger that they will lead lives of crime.

"Since the arrest of the minors and their companion the probation officer has made an investigation and he has submitted a report to the court. . . ."

The judge paused as the door opened and a guard announced Mrs. Healey. She was a tall, plain woman, shabbily dressed.

"Come in, Mrs. Healey," the judge said. "We are just getting started." The attendant led her down to the front row and motioned her toward a seat. She glanced toward the judge, but her attention was on John Henry, who did not look up. She took a seat one removed from his.

"I'm sorry, Judge," she said. "Look like I just couldn't make it so early."

"Well, we're glad you are here. I was just explaining about this court."

"Oh yessir, Judge. I heard all that before. You know me and John Henry, we been here before. I heard all that already."

"Very well then. Mr. Swanson, will you read the petitions?"

The officer stood up to read the formal documents, and David gave them his full attention. He had been surprised to hear the judge say what he did. Now he was even more surprised to hear nothing about grand theft or about any charges really, although the petition said that he and Head had been riding in a stolen car. Earlier the probation officer, too, had said that he was not being charged with a crime, but David had simply not believed him. The two petitions were just alike except for the fact that John Henry Healey was already a ward of the Juvenile Court. The officer sat down, and Judge Burnett thanked him.

"Do you understand the petitions?" the judge then asked the boys.

Mr. Taylor got to his feet.

"Your honor, if it please the court," he said, "I should like to offer a motion."

"Counsel," the judge replied, "if this is to be the usual motion for dismissal, I will suggest that you withhold it. I don't think such a motion would be appropriate at this time. It would be denied."

The lawyer took his seat, but it was clear that he was not pleased.

"John, you have been here before. Do you understand why you are here now?" the judge asked him.

"I understand all right. It's grand theft auto. Only I didn't do it."

"Young man, did you listen while the petition was being read?" Head nodded. "And don't you know that nothing was said about grand theft auto?"

"Yessir. I heard what it said all right. But that's what it means. You know I been here before."

"I suppose you do think you know." The judge frowned and looked down at his papers. When he glanced up again, he said, "You've been on probation nearly a year. Do you think it has done you any good?"

"Yessir. I been doing all right."

"Now in this case, Did you know you were in a car which had been stolen?"

"Oh, no, sir. That's what I was saying. I didn't know anything about it. When they picked me up, this boy told me it was his old man's car."

David thought he must not have heard right.

The judge's face showed no change, but Mr. Cooper's face showed new interest. Behind him, David heard his father stir.

"Would you want to tell us how it happened?" the judge asked.

Head leaned forward in his chair. His words came easily.

"Well, it was like this, see. I was playing basketball, and when I was going home, walking down Sixth Street, I see this boy, David. I already know him from playing basketball with him, and he blows the horn at me and said, Do I want a ride home? And I figured it was cold, but before I get in the car I ask him, and he say it's his daddy's car. So I get in, see, and then he say, Why don't we go out for a ride? And then he asked Hap, that's Percy Johnson, see, Do he want to drive? And Hap say he'll try her, and that's when the patrol come up behind us, and Hap didn't even try to get away 'cause he figured like me that it was his daddy's car, see, so he wasn't worried."

Mr. Taylor had been standing throughout Head's speech. When Head paused, he interrupted, "Your Honor, I object. This witness is making charges; he is giving testimony which is not true. He may in fact be committing perjury, and I respectfully move that the testimony of this witness be stricken from the record."

"Counsel," Judge Burnett replied, "I recognize that after participating in usual court procedure you find this unusual, but I repeat, there are no charges in this court, and the court is privileged to hear whatever the parties wish to say. This minor has not been sworn, so what he says cannot be held as perjury. Objection overruled."

Leaning back in his chair, the judge thoughtfully fixed his gaze upon each member of the group.

"And again I call to your attention the fact that this court exists not to prosecute but to help young people who are in trouble, and it is important that we hear what they have to say, true or false."

Mr. Taylor sat down with a frown.

"Now, back to John," the judge continued, "or do you like to be called John Henry?"

"They mostly call me Head."

It seemed to David that Head was enjoying himself. Under questioning, he explained that David had left the Center early that Monday evening and that they were not really close friends so he did not know what kind of car David's family owned.

The judge turned next to David, but he did not ask him about the stolen car. Instead he asked how David was getting along in school and whether he still wanted to become a physician. Then he turned to David's father and asked him about his job at the

Foundation Iron and Machine Works and about his apartment, whether it was adequate for his family of four. After listening carefully, he said, as though it were the most important matter in the entire discussion, that he hoped Mr. Williams would soon be able to find a better place to live, a place where David could have his own room because every boy needed one.

"John," the judge addressed Head, "I don't know whether you made up your story to try to help your friend Johnson or to save yourself. I only wish I could make you understand that you have been told the truth in this courtroom. We want to help you; you don't have to lie to us. You have been on probation, and apparently you have not learned from the guidance and counseling of your probation officer. So we are going to continue you as a ward of the court, but instead of letting you remain in your mother's home, we are going to place you in a forestry camp where you will work regularly and hard, and live within a regulated order. How long you remain there will depend on your own behavior and development. You will have opportunities to develop some skills, and, if your conduct is good, you'll be granted certain privileges. This is not a correctional institution but a training unit, and we hope you will accept the training and not later have to undergo correction."

The judge cleared his throat. "David Andrew Williams," he pronounced solemnly.

David got to his feet, his knees trembling.

"We have gone thoroughly into your case," the judge said. "The court is inclined to believe that your father and your mother are able to provide you with the right kind of upbringing. The probation officer's report gives quite a full picture of you and your family."

David felt his eyes fill with tears of relief.

"We do, however," the judge went on, "admonish you to follow such a course as your father must have followed. You have many advantages and many opportunities. Your parents are trying to make a good life for you. Make your companions the boys who are struggling for something good. This court is expressing the community's confidence that you can contribute something of value. We hope that confidence is not being misplaced. To the parents of the minor, the court observes that you have brought this boy a long way, through many hazards. This is one more; perhaps it is the most serious.

We hope it will prove to be the last of this type.

"For the record, the allegations are found to be true; the petition is sustained; the minor is admonished; and the case is dismissed."

ELEVEN

On their way home, after the hearing, David's father said very little.

"The judge was very kind. He explained, and you could understand," his mother commented. "I felt sorry for Mrs. Healey. She said she understood, but I don't believe she did. Her son is lost. Maybe she doesn't know it, or if she does, she doesn't know what to do about it."

David was numb with relief that he had not been put on probation. He knew that both his parents felt relieved, but that they were also still unhappy over the whole episode. He was ready to admit that the hearing had been fair and without prejudice. Doubtless, Judge Burnett was an exceptional white man, he decided.

Once home, David decided to go to school. If he hurried, he could make his afternoon classes. While he changed into a pair of khaki pants and a wool shirt, his mother fixed some sandwiches. Mr. Williams shook his head at the suggestion of lunch and went into his bedroom, closing the door behind him. They knew he was having one of his headaches.

When school was over that afternoon, David waited outside the main door, hoping he would not miss Jeanette in the crowd of students that poured out of the building. When he finally caught a glimpse of her, she was with Maybelle and some other girls. Laughing and talking, she started down the wide stairs, without seeing him. A knitted red cap was pulled low over her head, framing her face above the turned-up collar of her white overcoat. She was prettier than any girl he had ever known, David decided.

One of the other girls saw David and spoke to Jeanette who raised a gloved hand in greeting. Then she excused herself and ran down the rest of the steps to meet him.

Her eyes were wide with questions, but her smile was restrained, as if she were afraid of what she might hear.

"I'm glad you waited," she said. "Tell me, How was it?"

He reassured her immediately by saying that his case had been dismissed, and then he told her everything that had happened. At the corner where she usually caught her bus, she announced she wanted to keep on walking.

"What's going to happen to Head?" she asked.

"I don't know," David said. "You know when you think about it, he really hasn't got much of a chance. No father, and his mother can't be much help. In the courtroom he never looked at his mother, but when we were leaving and the guard was taking him away, he waved to me and he was smiling. I can't even be mad at him for the way he tried to put all the weight on me."

"Do you think," Jeanette asked, "that for some reason he was trying to hurt you?"

"No, it couldn't be that."

"Would his story really have helped his other friend?"

"No, but maybe he thought it would. Mr. Taylor told my father that Hap was sure to be convicted in the adult court."

They had walked almost all the way to Jeanette's house. As they crossed the bridge over the parkway, they stopped and looked down at the flow of traffic.

"I'll bet your father's glad it's over," Jeanette said. "My father says that a man looks at his son and wants him to do the things he had hoped to do in life. If anything gets in the way, it makes it hard. Girls, I guess, don't have to be so ambitious."

"But fathers can't understand very well," David said. Then he explained himself. "My dad is real great. I've seen him go through a lot, and I know he left South Town mostly for me—and for Betty Jane. But he can't understand that this was mostly my own fault. He kind of blames himself for me getting in trouble."

"How in the world does he figure that out?"

"Well, mostly because of where we live. You know how it is—east side, slum, tenants. He kind of figures if we had been living in a good part of town, and owning, then I would have had better friends and all."

"Like Buck Taylor, maybe?"

"Well, you know what I mean."

"Like Jeanette Lenoir, hunh?"

"You're twisting me up now. I mean, he means not like Hap and Head. Anyway, he's anxious to move now. When we first came he used to go out, he and my mother, every Saturday, all day long, looking at houses. Always the kind he wanted were too high, or else they weren't for sale to colored. But he keeps looking, him and Ma."

On Saturday when David awoke, it was snowing hard. He had wanted to sleep late, but that was impossible in the living room. Betty Jane was already up, begging him to get dressed and go outside with her.

"A person would think you'd never seen snow before," he said, laughing.

He looked out the window and saw that the snow was piling up fast. He was doubly glad it was Saturday for now maybe he'd have a chance to earn some money by shoveling snow. The weather was certainly different from South Town, he thought.

When he went into the kitchen for breakfast, Betty Jane was already in her ski pants and jacket, determined to build a snowman. His mother and father were also dressed.

"We're supposed to go look at some houses," Mr. Williams said. "We have to be at Mr. Taylor's office at nine o'clock."

As soon as David's case was dismissed, Mr. Taylor had resumed his role of real-estate broker. He knew that the Williams family were more than willing to buy.

"I don't see how anybody can drive in this weather," Mrs. Williams fretted.

"In this part of the country, business doesn't wait on a little snow," Mr. Williams told her. "Besides, today is the one day I can get out, and I guess the sellers will sure be home, and we'll have a good chance to see how well the heating system works. We just have to get an early start."

While they ate breakfast, David announced that he planned to borrow a snow shovel from the man who cleaned the halls and fired the furnace. Then he would go over to Stanton Park, a residential section on the other side of town, and look for work.

"Why don't you buy a shovel?" his father asked. "You can look at it this way—you're going to work, and the snow shovel is your tool. It's like a business; the tools are the investment. Tell you what I'll do." Mr. Williams took out his billfold. "Looks like you want a partner in this business. Let me make an investment. Say I furnish the tools and you pay me. Let's see— You cut me in for one fourth of the profits."

"That's too much, Ed," Mrs. Williams protested.

They finally agreed that David would borrow the money and when he had paid it back, the shovel would be his.

"Looks like," Mr. Williams spoke with an air of injured pride, "if I'm taking all the risk I should get something for a profit."

Betty Jane decided to look at houses, too, so they all left in the car together, Mr. Williams at the wheel. It was cold, and the snow was now more than a foot deep. Already people were out with shovels, and in the streets, plows scraped and clanked as they pushed the snow into neat piles.

David got out of the car on Main Street and watched as it merged with the slow-moving traffic going south. At the first hardware store he stopped and bought a shovel with a stout handle.

He found work long before he reached Stanton Park.

A stout woman, red-faced and unhappy in her efforts to clear her sidewalk, asked him if he wanted to do it. He said he would for a dollar, and he was hired. It took him less than half an hour, and he cleared a front path as wide as the paved sidewalk. He was surprised when the woman answered his ring with a pleased smile and gave him an extra quarter.

The snow shovel on his shoulder, he again started walking. In the next block another woman called to him from her front door. Again he quoted his price, and there was no objection. When he was through, she directed him to her neighbor's. He was kept so busy at a dollar a job, with frequent tips, that he began to wonder what it would be like in more prosperous Stanton Park. By one o'clock he had earned more than ten dollars. In spite of the cold, he was sweating from his exertions, and he had worked up a big appetite. He was not sure how he would be received in a public eating place in a white neighborhood, but he was so hungry that he decided to take a chance and entered an unassuming-looking snack bar.

The place was not full, but there was no empty stool at the counter which was not next to one occupied by a white customer. David figured he had to be careful. He did not want to be told that his "kind" was not welcome, as he knew happened, nor did he want to hear the embarrassing words, "We don't solicit colored trade here."

With his back to the counter, he carefully propped his snow shovel against the wall. Turning, he was soon aware that no one was watching him.

He moved quickly to a stool between two other customers. Out of the corner of his eye, he saw that one was dressed in a Mackinaw and cap, the other in business clothes. Neither of them said a word. Soon the waiter asked him for his order.

"Two hamburgers, with everything on them, and milk to drink," David said. When the steaming sandwiches came, the man in the Mackinaw shoved the catsup bottle closer to David, a gesture more satisfying to David than the food he so hungrily gulped down.

The man finished his lunch and left, and another white customer took his place. When the waiter served him a hamburger, David reached for the catsup bottle and offered it to him.

"Thanks," the new customer said briefly.

David wished he had remembered to thank the man in the Mackinaw.

The wind was blowing when he went out, but the sun was shining. He had decided not to go all the way to Stanton Park. Nearby, not far from the business section, there were still walks to be cleared. In the first block, all but one walk was already shoveled, but in the next were several needing work. No one was home at the first house he tried. At the second an anxious elderly lady told him she guessed her son would come to do the shoveling, but at the third house he was given a job. He had two more jobs in that block, one at the home of a girl from Central High who recognized him. When he was through, the girl's mother generously handed him two dollars and asked him to come back the next time it snowed.

In the next block he was surprised to come upon Mike O'Connor. Mike, bareheaded, was shoveling snow in an old pair of army pants and a blue ski parka. He greeted David with a wide grin. Ever since the first day at Central, in spite of his distrust of white people, David would have been forced to admit that Mike must be placed among the special exceptions: Mike was a "good guy."

"How're you doing, Dave?" he asked. "Making any money?"

"I've been doing well," David replied. "But I've been at it all day. One or two more jobs and I'll be ready to quit." He brushed the snow off his mittens.

"Well, that's just about what I was going to do. Say, why don't we go partners? I just started this job. It'll be a lot easier for both of us, working together, and we'll just go fifty-fifty. O.K.?"

David noticed that Mike was making only a narrow path, not trying to clear the whole sidewalk. He had done the porch steps the same way.

"I don't know if I've been charging as much as I should," Mike said, pausing to lean on his shovel handle. "When I started out, most people kicked at my prices. They want a man to work his heart out for free. I just passed up some of them who wanted to put up an argument. Later I did lower my price some."

David had been wondering about Mike's prices. "What are you getting for a job like this one?" he asked.

"I'm just getting two dollars." Mike seemed apologetic. "That all right with you?"

"That's all right. Sure, it's all right with me." In fact, David was thinking, it was high, especially considering the narrow path Mike made.

"I was asking for three on a job like this, but folks kicked so." Mike was bending again to his work. "Next job we can ask for three if you want."

David did not confess that he had been asking only a dollar. It was not easy to work and talk. Later, they took on several more jobs at two dollars and one corner job for five. By that time, it was getting dark, and they agreed that they had worked enough for one day.

"Hope it snows again tonight," Mike said. "How about us getting together again tomorrow? With a partner you can both do better. Don't you think so?"

He asked David where he lived, and David gave him his address, hoping that Mike would not know it was in a block of shabby flats.

"Say, that's not far from my place!" Mike seemed genuinely pleased. "If it snows, we can get out early. Prices are higher on Sunday—holiday, you know— and lots of men don't want to shovel snow, especially if they did it already on Saturday. They'll be laid up with aching backs. Man, we'll make a killing."

They were walking eastward. Mike did most of the talking, and David laughed at his wisecracks. He was thinking, too.

Today they had worked as partners, and Mike had proposed that they continue to work that way. Mike was white. He was a big football hero, and one of the most popular students at Central High, yet he lived on the east side, not far from where David lived.

David remembered the warnings he had heard. You can't trust them, Alonzo and the others had said. Down South you know white folks are against you and they're honest about it, while here they say everybody's equal, but they don't mean it. They may smile to your face but they'll laugh and knife you behind your back.

Mike was talking about his family.

"You know we always have beans for dinner Saturday night," he said. "I always know what it's to be for Saturday night—beans! My mother says it's her Boston upbringing, but my old man makes cracks about it, says it was her Boston downfall when she met him. But I like beans, you know, the way she cooks them—real old-fashioned, I guess."

David laughed. "I like 'em, too," he admitted. "We eat them with rice."

Along the edges of Main Street, only a little less busy after the storm than in good weather, the snow was in high piles like little mountain ranges. They were soon out of the business district. On Fourth Street the walking became more hazardous, because few paths had been cleared and they moved along in single file.

"Look, I live just around the next corner," Mike said. "Why don't you stop by and have beans with me?"

David hesitated. He was not at all sure why this white boy, friendly as he seemed, would want to invite him to his home to eat with members of his family. He decided against it.

"Oh, your folks wouldn't be expecting me. It wouldn't be right," he demurred.

"It'll be all right," Mike insisted. "We always have plenty. Have to eat up the beans all day Sunday. What a load of beans my mom puts out! Course, we got plenty people there to eat them," Mike ran on. "I guess you never saw a family with so many kids. How many brothers and sisters have you got?"

"Just one sister. She's ten."

"See what I mean? I have three brothers and three sisters. Maybe that's the real reason we eat beans every Saturday night. Here's my corner." He stopped and faced David. "Come on," he urged. "I tell you it'll be O.K. with the folks. They'll be glad to meet you."

David did not want to seem stubborn. "I'll stop by just to see where you live," he said. "If it snows tonight, I'll come by for you in the morning."

Inwardly he wanted very much to see how Mike's family lived.

The houses now were neither large nor well kept, and the neighborhood looked very much like David's. Nondescript buildings stood close to the sidewalk, as though they wished to crowd out any space where, in winter, white snow might blanket city dirt or, in summer, grass or flowers might grow. If Mike O'Connor lived here, David thought, the white students at Central must know it; yet the football team had chosen him captain. Maybe living on the east side was not so bad after all. And somehow David knew that his being colored did not matter to Mike.

In front of Mike's house the sidewalk and the path to the porch steps had been neatly shoveled. Mike said that his younger brothers must have done it, and that he guessed his father had checked to make sure it was cleared properly. On the front porch they stamped the snow off their galoshes; as they bent to remove them, the door opened and a boy rushed out. He was about eight years old and dressed in dungarees.

"Hey, Mike, how much money did you make?"

he demanded loudly. Without waiting for an answer, he ran back into the house, shouting that Mike was home and that he had brought company. The other children hurried to the porch and filled the front hall as Mike led David indoors.

That was the beginning of David's welcome. No one said to him the words, "You are welcome, David Williams," but he knew he was. Mike proved to be the oldest of the children. His younger brothers, ages twelve and fourteen, had been out shoveling snow, too, and had earned enough to make them happy. They had to tell Mike all about their successes and failures and hard work. The sisters, to whom Mike formally introduced David, were less noisy, but they added to the pleasant confusion with their chatter and their laughter.

Mike took David through the house into the kitchen, which was large and brightly lighted. It looked clean, but it needed paint, and the gas range was the same old-fashioned kind that the Williamses had found in the flat they rented.

Mike's mother invited David to sit down and have dinner with her son. "We've plenty to eat, such as it is," she said.

"Thank you. ma'am." David replied quickly.

"Thank you, but I know the folks are looking for me at home. Probably worried. Thank you very much, but I guess I better be getting on home."

He told Mike that if it snowed again that night he would be there at nine the next morning. Then he said good-bye and started home.

When David reached home, full of a new excitement, he found it was quite a while before he had a chance to tell about his day. Betty Jane met him at the door, almost jumping in her eagerness to give him the news. Mr. Taylor had found a house for them! It was hard for her to keep her voice down, and Mrs. Williams kept trying to quiet her because Mr. Williams was lying down with a bad headache.

"Wait till you see that bathroom!" Betty Jane exclaimed as she followed David into the kitchen. "Tile all over just like at school and a shower! And in my own room there's a clothes closet and in your room, too, and all the closets have lights in them. And, you know what? In Ma's and Pa's room the light comes on in the closet as soon as you open the door, and their room is bigger, bigger than two rooms here."

David saw that his mother shared Betty Jane's

enthusiasm but that she was trying to be realistic, too.

"Don't go on so," she said, laughing. "We haven't got the house yet. You don't just look at a house and buy it as if it was a loaf of bread."

While she set David's dinner on the kitchen table, she told him more about the house. It was on the west side, not in Stanton Park, but in a very nice section where all the houses had wide frontyards.

David's plate held beans surrounded by frank-furters and a pile of fried potatoes. As he thanked God for his food, he remembered his own blessing, and when he looked up, he told his mother about his good fortune with the snow shovel.

"I don't even know how much I made," he said. "I'm going to count it after I put this dinner to bed. And, you know, I ran into Mike O'Connor—he's captain of the football team—and we started work-ing partners. I saw his house. He lives not far from here, on the east side, and his folks were real nice. Well, maybe they're not poor, but they don't live so different . . . and for supper tonight they had beans, too, and they invited me to eat."

"They're white people?" Mrs. Williams asked.

"Yes, but—" David did not know how to put it.

"They made me welcome. I figured maybe they didn't really mean it, and if I had sat down there, maybe they wouldn't like it. I don't know."

"Anyway, David"—his mother passed behind his chair and laid a hand on his shoulder—"you knew you had a good dinner waiting for you here, and our house may not be as fine as his, but it's home. And soon we'll be having a better one, and you'll invite him over to have dinner with you."

"No, Ma!" David shook his head. "His house wasn't fine. The things there weren't any better than ours, and the street, Fourth Street, is just about the same as Sixth Street. I don't even know that I'd want to invite him into the kind of house you all are talking about."

"Wait till you see it," Betty Jane interrupted excitedly. "You will then. You wouldn't be ashamed to bring anybody there."

"That's just it. I wouldn't be ashamed, but maybe he would. Maybe Mike—and he's a real nice guy, and we're going to be partners in snow-shoveling—but maybe in a house like that, Mike would think kind of that it would be too good for colored people, or especially newcomers from the South."

"But it will be our home, and I don't think your

friend, especially if he's as decent as you say, would be like that. That would be showing jealousy," Mrs. Williams said.

"Not jealousy—" David was having trouble explaining. He began again. "Now like in shoveling snow today. Do you know the prices he was charging people, and they were paying? His prices were much higher than mine, and he wasn't even giving a good job. He probably made twice as much as I did. He wouldn't have cause to be jealous."

"How much did you make?" Betty Jane demanded. "Why don't you count it?"

David pushed his empty plate aside and counted his earnings. With the bills and the loose silver, he had more than twenty-six dollars. Even after he paid for the shovel, he would have made a profit of more than twenty dollars.

They had forgotten to keep their voices low, and Mrs. Williams was sorry to see her husband coming out of the bedroom in his bathrobe. His tired face showed deep lines. He hadn't slept; the aspirin had done no good, he admitted in response to her questions. He tried to smile his encouragement when David told him about his work and about his hope to earn even more money with Mike as partner.

"That's real good," he said. "It's an ill wind that blows nobody good, and this snow sure gives you a chance to make money. If this keeps up, we will be able to buy that house."

"Are we going to get it?" Betty Jane asked eagerly. "Are you going to buy that house, Pa?"

Mr. Williams did not answer immediately. Silently he watched while his wife poured a stream of hot, fragrant coffee into his cup. He spooned sugar into it and slowly added evaporated milk until the coffee lightened to just the right shade.

"There's a lot to buying a house," he finally said. "It's not as simple here as it was in South Town."

"How about the price?" David asked. "Have you got the money?"

"You don't have to have so much money to start buying. We've got enough for down payment, and the broker figures the monthly payments will be just about the same as a week's wages, and that's supposed to be good. We might have to go into more debt for furniture." He looked around the kitchen. "I don't think your ma would be happy without a modern stove and maybe living-room stuff, and we'd have to buy lots of other things."

"Do you think maybe some other house, maybe

one not quite so fine, would do?" David asked.

"It's on the west side," Betty exclaimed. "That's where we want to live. That's where you said."

"Well," Mr. Williams said, "it's what we can get, and for the money I know it's a bargain. It's just the special way things are right now and in that block."

"What is it?" David half guessed what the answer would be. "What is the special way things are?"

"The neighborhood is changing," his father answered. "One colored family bought in the block, and so white owners there are anxious to sell, even at a loss. The broker says this house is priced about three thousand dollars too low, and the owner will take just about any terms."

David thought a while. He remembered how many times his father had met only disappointment in his efforts to find somewhere for them to live at a price they could afford. He had heard friends say that it was practically impossible for colored people to buy a house at the advertised prices and terms quoted in the paper. He knew that the Taylors and the Lenoirs and many other colored families lived on the west side, and probably most of them had bought their houses from white people who were moving out because the neighborhood was changing.

"I think it's dirty," he said finally.

"You may be right," Mr. Williams said. "But this is one time race prejudice works in our favor."

"I know what you mean, son," Mrs. Williams put in. "And I feel the same way. I'd rather we could just buy with our means the right kind of place at a decent price."

"Isn't there a decent house in one of the neighborhoods where colored people already live?" David asked.

"What few there are for sale are priced too high." His father was shaking his head. "It looks like this is the best way to get out of this neighborhood. I want you and Betty Jane to have better friends than you're finding."

David knew what his father meant. Still he wondered if moving into a big house in a white neighborhood was going to solve anything. He doubted it. Betty Jane was not sure either.

"I like the kids here and in school," she insisted. "They're not so bad. Still I'd like to live in that fine house we saw today." She paused and then asked, "I guess I couldn't keep going to Tenth Street School, could I?"

"No," Mrs. Williams replied. "You'd be going to school on the other side of town. That would be part of it. You'd soon make new friends."

They talked for a long time. At his father's suggestion, David got paper and pencils, and they made a list of the furniture they'd need. They calculated the monthly payments and the interest on the mortgage. While they discussed the prospects, Mrs. Williams put up the ironing board and pressed the dress Betty Jane would wear to Sunday school the next day.

At last they went to bed, David very much hoping that it would have snowed by the next morning. He had written down the address of the house they had talked about, and that, he decided, would be his first call for a snow-shoveling job.

T W E L V E

*I*t had not snowed by the next morning. In fact, there was very little snow that whole winter, and when it came, it was not on weekends. The partnership of Williams and O'Connor did not flourish. The two boys saw each other in the halls at school. Mike was always friendly, but as they had no classes together, they had little in common. Mike, a senior, was to graduate in June, and he complained about the necessity to study.

Mr. and Mrs. Williams, with David and Betty Jane helping, reached their decision. They bought the house, taking title and moving in on the first day of March. David found the two-story brick house every bit as impressive as Betty Jane had claimed, and he was happy to have a room of his own once again.

Mr. Williams, however, found that new furniture

was much more expensive than he had anticipated. The sales people were very persuasive, and they made the credit terms sound easy. When they learned that he was working at the Foundation plant and that he was buying a house, they tried to convince him that real economy lay in purchasing what they called quality merchandise.

"You know there's only two kinds of furniture," one dealer told Mrs. Williams, trying to flatter her. "There's good furniture and then there's cheap furniture. Now we got the cheap stuff, too, but I can see you people know quality, and you probably wouldn't have the junk in your house that ignorant people buy."

"What we'll have to do," Mr. Williams said to his wife, "is try to get settled once and for all. You've got to have a place to invite your friends—the Lenoirs and people like them. And I don't want the kids to be ashamed, and not wanting other kids to see how we live."

Before they came to North Town, his family had lived about as well as any other colored family in the community. A man shouldn't let his standards fall, he felt. But when the bills were totaled, they showed scarcely any margin for living, and he worried. His headaches came more frequently, and they were more intense.

From Sixth Street, David had been close enough to walk to school, or, if he rode, to take only one bus. But now from West Twenty-fourth, after taking one bus downtown, he had to transfer to a second. With the coming of warmer weather, he often walked all the way. In the afternoon he really preferred to walk.

Jeanette lived nearby, and they usually walked together. They found they had many things to talk about. They were both ambitious, for they had grown up with parents who had encouraged them to acquire as much education as possible and thereby to make something of themselves. Jeanette told him about her home in New Orleans, and he told her the story of his family's trouble in the South.

David looked forward to the long walks, and he often went out of his way to take Jeanette to her door. If Mrs. Lenoir saw him, she would invite him in for a glass of milk and some pie or a piece of cake. He always said he shouldn't stop, but he always did.

One afternoon early in May they had walked more slowly than usual and were late, though David knew his mother had expected him earlier to help her set out some flowers. They were arguing, rather giddily,

about the color of flowers, Jeanette insisting that
more often than not they were yellow. David was
trying to prove her wrong, but all they had seen on
the way home were daffodils and bushes of forsythia.

As they approached her house, David was laughing for Jeanette had pointed out that there were
dandelions blooming on her lawn. Then the front
door flew open and Mrs. Lenoir, barely stopping to
smile, called to him. "Your mother phoned, David.
They want you at home right away." His father, she
added, had become sick at the plant and been taken
to the county hospital.

David ran most of the six blocks home. His heart
pounding, he scarcely slowed for the traffic when he
crossed Washington Boulevard. He knew if his
father was so sick that they had taken him to the hospital, it must be serious. If it were not serious, they
would have brought him home. He thought that it
might have something to do with the headaches.
Again he wished that Pa had gone to a doctor.

As he approached home, he felt something like
surprise, surprise to see the house sitting there so
impassively, the white posts of the wide porch still
slim and clean-lined and dignified as though nothing
had happened. He remembered that his father had

said it would be nice to sit on that porch on the warm summer evenings. Fear clutched at David's throat as he turned and crossed the lawn toward the steps. Betty Jane was there on the porch to meet him.

"Where have you been, Dave?" she called, frantic with impatience. "We've been waiting and waiting! Pa's been taken to the hospital. Ma didn't know how to get there, and she had to wait for you. Do you know what bus we take?"

David had his own questions to ask, but Betty Jane did not know the answers. Inside the house, Mrs. Williams, already wearing her hat and coat, was coming down the stairs. She took David's arm.

"Son! We've been waiting for you. Why were you so long? I don't know . . . I don't know . . ." She was clinging to him.

David did not say that everything would be all right. He could not say it. He did not know. When Betty Jane spoke and took her mother's hand, he found a momentary course of action.

"Ma," Betty Jane pleaded, "Ma, we have to go to him."

"I don't think we ought to fool with buses," David said. "We'll have to get a taxi."

He drew away from his mother and went to the telephone. After the Yellow Cab office promised to send a taxi, he announced there was nothing now to do but wait.

"Yes," Mrs. Williams admitted with a sigh, "we'll have to wait. Nothing else we can do now." She picked up her purse from the chair where she had dropped it and reached into it for a handkerchief with which to wipe her eyes.

David, seeing his mother calmer, went to the kitchen. There was nothing there he wanted, but he turned on the water and let it run hard, while he stood leaning against the sink. He covered his mouth with his hand. He was not ashamed to be crying, but he didn't want his sister to hear him. He was afraid. He tried not to think about something serious happening to his father. Instead, he tried to think of some way he could help, but he could find none; rather, he felt it was all his fault. His arrest and all that dirty business had put a terrible extra strain on his father and made his headaches more severe. Then they had moved with too much debt and worry into a better neighborhood. His father had sacrificed too much.

"O God," he prayed. "Please don't let anything happen to him."

He struggled to get control of himself, and when his breathing returned to normal, he splashed water on his face and dried it on a paper towel.

"Got to go," he said to himself resolutely.

While they waited for the taxi to come, Mrs. Williams told David as much as she knew. Two telephone calls had come; the first from Andy Crutchfield who said that Ed had felt sick and gone to the hospital and that she shouldn't be upset if he didn't get home on time. The second call was from a nurse on the staff at the plant. This time she was told that Mr. Williams had been taken to the hospital by ambulance, after collapsing on the job. He was unconscious; his exact condition was not known; but it was suggested that she might want to go to the hospital.

David knew one word for a sudden collapse. He hesitated to use it, and when he did, he tried to have confidence in what he said, "Pa's not old enough to have a stroke."

T H I R T E E N

David was right. It was not a stroke. It was several hours before they knew this, however, and even when they did, the news brought no relief. First, while David and Betty Jane sat patiently in the waiting room, Mrs. Williams had to be interviewed by the admissions office. There she was asked to sign several forms, and when she hesitated, the interviewer told her that someone had to authorize the necessary treatment and, since it was clear that the patient was unable to do so, it was up to his wife, the next of kin. Still hesitating, Mrs. Williams took up the pen. She said she supposed it was all right; only she wished she had someone to advise her.

"It is all right, Mrs. Williams," the interviewer told her, and reaching over, she patted her hand. "It really is. I don't know the details on this case, but I know that you will want the doctors to do whatever is necessary. They will do their best."

"Yes, yes." Mrs. Williams signed quickly without reading the papers. "I know. Whatever is necessary."

"This form"—the woman pointed to it as she spoke—"authorizes diagnosis and treatment including surgery. This one acknowledges financial responsibility, meaning beyond whatever the insurance pays. And this one releases the hospital from liability for personal property and also authorizes us to deal with you as responsible next of kin. You'll be going up to Critical on the second floor. The doctor there may be able to tell you something more, and perhaps he will want to ask about the patient's medical history. I do hope your husband will be better soon."

To David and Betty Jane, their mother's interview seemed endless. Actually they could see by a clock on the wall that it was not long. But the hands moved slowly. It was after five o'clock. The large waiting room was nearly empty. Across the lobby, David could see an arrow labeled "Cafeteria" pointing to the right, and he could hear the clatter of dishes and silverware. He was a little ashamed that he should be thinking of food, but he wondered what would happen if they walked into the cafeteria. Would they be turned away? He thought not, but maybe the colored people there always ate at certain tables.

Here in the county general hospital, as in the schools, there seemed to be no open segregation. He had already noticed other colored visitors and some colored nurses. He wondered if the doctors and nurses—white doctors and nurses, that is—treated colored patients as well as they did white patients. He had heard it said, though he hadn't wanted to believe it, that the doctors experimented on colored people. But Jeanette had told him it was not so, and he believed most of what Jeanette said. Still, he was unsure of many things. He wouldn't always be so unsure, he resolved. Someday he would know the answers. He would learn for himself about hospitals where doctors who were white treated and prescribed for colored men and colored women, and operated on them, laying open their bodies, cutting through the dark skin, and peering into their insides where there were no race problems. He thought of the white veteran who had said, "On the battlefield the black soldiers had guts the same color as mine!"

Finally his mother was through with her interview, and they took the elevator to the second floor. The elevator operator, as though she knew their problem, told them to go down the corridor to the right. There a nurse greeted them. She was stout and past middle age; her cap carried four parallel black stripes. And she was colored. It was easy to talk to her, and after the first few words, some of the fear left Mrs. Williams' face and voice, and David stopped wondering whether his father would be kindly treated.

The nurse reported that Mr. Williams had been in a coma when he was brought in, that his condition hadn't changed, and that there was still uncertainty about the diagnosis. He had been examined by a specialist, who wanted more information about his medical history.

Mrs. Williams quickly described the headaches from which her husband suffered, and the nurse thought that they might be important. But when Mrs. Williams went on to say how sorry she was that she had not made her husband go to a doctor for treatment, the nurse shook her head.

"At a time like this," she said, "whatever happens or however bad it looks, we have to look forward,

not back. There are things to do now. We can't
dwell on the things that we left undone. In this place
we learn that.

"Now!" She became more businesslike. "The
doctor will be seeing you, and you will want to answer all his questions. Tell him all about your husband's health and anything you feel is important.
You just sit down over there, honey. Let the boy go
get you some coffee. There's a machine down the
hall. And don't you worry. Pray, but don't worry."

They did not have long to wait. A doctor in a white
hospital coat was seated beside his mother when
David returned, with a paper cup of hot coffee. He
was a thin-faced man of about sixty with wispy blond
hair. Betty Jane was standing nearby. As David hesitated, the doctor motioned to him and said to Mrs.
Williams, speaking abruptly and with a heavy
European accent, "Drink your coffee. Drink your
coffee."

When he found out about the beating Mr. Williams had undergone in South Town, he wanted to
know exactly how long ago it had occurred and
whether there had been much physical injury at the
time. He asked what medical treatment had been
prescribed, and Mrs. Williams told him that their

doctor, Dr. Anderson, seemed to have done the right things, for recovery had been swift.

"X-rays? What about X-rays?" the doctor asked. "I would see those X-rays from that time. Then with those we make now, maybe we see something."

"Oh, I don't think so." Mrs. Williams shook her head and looked at David for confirmation. "No, I'm sure he didn't take any X-rays. You see that was in the country and in the South. They don't have X-rays there. No hospitals."

"So! So!" The doctor nodded. He was silent for a moment. "So!" he said again. "Now after? When does he have pains before today?"

Mrs. Williams told him everything she could, as accurately as she could. Often she glanced at David when she was not certain, and when she did, the doctor looked at David, too.

Finally, the doctor spoke to him. "What you think, young man?" he asked. "You know something more?"

"Oh, no, sir." David was surprised that he should be asked, but since the doctor had inquired he thought he should tell him what he was thinking. "Only something I did notice. Mostly the pains would come when he was worried about something.

Seems like lately he's had much to worry about."

"So! So!" The doctor seemed to feel it might be important. "Is right!" He stood and looked down at Mrs. Williams, and then at David and Betty Jane.

"To worry is not good," he said. "Now the patient is not worrying. He is waiting. Just waiting. Maybe we will do something. His heart is not bad. His respiration is good. In the pictures we made already, we do not see much. Now you tell me about damage less than one year ago. We will take more pictures and maybe we see more this time. Then maybe we know more of what we must do."

Mrs. Williams had risen. She looked very small beside the tall doctor.

"He will be all right? Won't he, doctor?" she asked.

"Good lady, I wish I could say yes. Now, I do not know. We cannot yet say what is the trouble. In one hour, maybe two, we will know more. His condition, as you know, is serious. He is on critical list. There is nothing for you to do here now. You should go home, maybe give your children some dinner."

"I can't go, doctor!"

"We don't want to eat!" David and Betty Jane said together.

"So! He is a good man. We are going to do everything we can for him." The doctor repeated, "Everything!"

They knew that they could not leave. They would have to wait at the hospital. There was nothing they could do to help. They had told the doctor everything they knew.

If someone had asked what they were waiting for, they could not have said. But really they were waiting for something very important. They were waiting for news—in hope, in desperate hope, that the news would be good; in heartaching fear that it would be bad.

When his mother asked if David and Betty Jane did not want to get something to eat, David told her about the cafeteria on the first floor, but she refused to leave and David would not go without her. Instead, he and Betty Jane walked down the hall to the coffee machine. Feeding two dimes into it and punching a different button, they got paper cups of hot chocolate. From another machine, they bought small packages of cookies and candy bars. With this, they slaked their hunger.

While they were nibbling their cookies, Andy Crutchfield appeared. With him was their pastor,

the Reverend Mr. Hayes, from the First Baptist
Church. Andy Crutchfield offered to help in any way
he could.

"I know it don't sound right to say don't worry,
Mrs. Williams," he said. "But this is what I mean:
don't worry about nothing like money or the job or
getting things done. Ed Williams going to have the
best care they can give. They got some of the best
doctors in the country right here. They know what
to do, and what it costs don't matter 'cause what the
insurance don't pay we going make up, anyway.

"Now," he went on. "I ain't even seen her yet
'cause I came on here only stopping by to pick up
Reverend, so I ain't seen my wife yet, but she's going
cook up some dinner, and when you all are home,
she going run over and do whatever you want as
long as you need her. So that part you don't have to
worry about. Course about Ed, well, we all going
be praying, and I guess I can't say don't worry, but I
say you won't be worrying alone. We with you."

The Reverend Mr. Hayes pledged the assistance
of his church. Then sitting down beside Mrs. Williams, he closed his eyes and, almost inaudibly, he
prayed. Before leaving, he gave Mrs. Williams his
card with his telephone number, and asked her to

let him know about her husband's progress. With the card he handed her a folded five-dollar bill. She might be able to find a use for it, he said, since these things almost always called for more cash than you figured on.

After they had gone, David remembered that Mrs. Lenoir had asked him to telephone her. He had seen a booth on the main floor, and, telling his mother what he wanted to do, he ran down the stairway, rather than wait for the elevator. As he slid into the seat of the telephone booth and pulled the door shut behind him, he heard his name. Jeanette was coming toward him, and behind her was her father.

"We've been trying to see you. They wouldn't let us go upstairs," she explained. "How's your father?"

David told them all he knew, repeating what the nurse and the doctor had said. Then he added that he felt the hospital was doing everything it could and that he trusted the doctor.

"And your mother?" Jeanette asked.

"Ma? Ma is swell. She can really take it," David said. "Betty Jane, she's just a kid. She . . . she . . . she's O.K., I guess."

"Is there anything we can do?" Mr. Lenoir asked.

"Should we notify anybody in South Town? We could send telegrams or telephone, if you liked."

"No. No, sir." David was emphatic. "I don't think we should do that."

In David's native community, telegrams were frightening; too often they brought the sad news of death. Many families in South Town did not have their own telephone, and even now that the Williams family were in North Town, they were not used to making long-distance calls.

There was nothing for the Lenoirs to do, but David thanked them for coming and told them that he knew his mother would feel better for knowing that they had been there. He promised that he would telephone them as soon as he had more news.

When the news did come, it was not good.

At last the doctor returned, accompanied by a tall, young man. A careful examination of a large number of X-rays, he reported, showed that Mr. Williams' skull had previously been fractured. The break had mended, but the thin layer of tissue which lay between the skull and the brain had thickened. In the passing months the thickening had increased, causing more and more pressure. It was this that had caused the intense headaches and finally his collapse. The pressure could be relieved only by an operation.

"Dr. Osborne is a highly competent surgeon," he said with a gesture toward the tall young man beside him. "He is a specialist in brain surgery. He will operate."

"When? When will it be?" Mrs. Williams' voice shook.

"We will not be able to operate until tomorrow morning." Dr. Osborne spoke for the first time. "We're making tests, and he will have to have some treatment." Then he spoke of certain medicines and of intravenous feeding. "Of course, we can't say at this time what the possibilities are, but we will be doing our best."

Mrs. Williams looked at her son and then at her daughter. "We know you will," she said. "We believe you." She put an arm around Betty Jane and added, "We will be praying."

Dr. Osborne suggested that they go home and have supper and try to get some rest. He promised to talk to them again in the morning.

It was past midnight when they wearily took the elevator downstairs. There they found Andy

Crutchfield waiting for news and to help in any way he could. He drove them to his own house where Mrs. Crutchfield had dinner waiting for them. She had prepared fried chicken, hot biscuits, and plenty of vegetables, though she apologized for the meal, saying that she hadn't really had time to fix anything nice.

In spite of their anxiety, they ate. David's well-known appetite was not at all diminished by worry.

After they finished, Mrs. Crutchfield insisted on going home with them. She had an overnight bag already packed, planning to stay as long as she was needed. "Guess Andy be glad enough to get shed of me for a while," she said.

No one believed what she said, and they all laughed. When Mrs. Williams protested that staying overnight was hardly necessary, Mrs. Crutchfield told her, "I know what you would do for me, or for any other one in trouble. Now I ain't saying you need me or I can do so much, but I want to be there anyway for what little I can do. Just don't pay me no mind. I won't be in your way."

She had a ham ready for baking and a shopping bag full of what she called "a few little things," when they got into the car.

After Mr. Crutchfield had taken the others home, he drove David over to the plant to get his father's car.

"I guess you know, son," he said very seriously, "this could be right bad." David nodded.

"Your daddy is a good man," Mr. Crutchfield went on. "He's seen you through to the place where you got good schooling, more than he ever had, lots more than me. Course I know you planned to graduate, and that's what he wanted, too. Well, if you can't stay in school and finish, don't feel too bad. You'll make it. You'll make it good. Same as I got your daddy in out to the plant I can get you in. He made a good record and they'll be glad to put his son to work, and they'll give you a chance to learn, get to be a skilled man. Pretty soon you might have to be the man of the house. You're big and strong. I guess that's what your daddy would want."

David realized the truth of what his family's best friend was saying. He was not unhappy for himself at the prospect. His father wanted him, perhaps even more than David did, to graduate from high school and go on to college. David knew that his father did not know, as David had come to realize, that there were countless hazards to block the precarious way through college, and that only the very smart and the very lucky could hope to enter medical school. He had learned that it was hard for any student, and he knew it was even harder for a colored boy. If it should be too bad for his father, he would indeed have to take his place as the man of the family. He would have to meet his responsibility.

In the parking lot at the plant the guards on the night shift knew Andy Crutchfield. They waved David through on Crutchfield's word, and he drove quickly home.

Mrs. Williams had been told to return to the hospital at nine in the morning. It was scarcely half past eight when she and her children arrived. In contrast to yesterday's quiet, the waiting room on the ground floor seemed a beehive of activity. Every seat was occupied. Mrs. Williams had to wait in line to get passes permitting them to take the elevator to the second floor. The line moved forward slowly.

Many people in the room appeared sick to David. Very few seemed to be visitors. Even the mothers with sick children looked as though they, too, should be under the care of a doctor. If he were a doctor, he thought, he would make a point of looking after the health of the family as well as of the patient confined to bed. If he were a doctor! he thought longingly.

Ahead of him, his mother gave their names and the name of her husband. After checking a card file, the attendant wrote a pass for three.

At the desk on the second floor, a uniformed attendant told them that Mr. Williams was resting comfortably in the post-operative room. She said she would check and let them know when he might be seen.

"Post-operative?" Mrs. Williams asked. "That means . . ."

"Yes. The patient went to surgery at 6:00 A.M." She looked at a chart. "He was there," she said, watching Mrs. Williams' reaction, "he was there more than two hours. You are his wife?" Mrs. Williams nodded. "Perhaps you'll be allowed to see him, but it will probably be some time before they know much about his condition. If you will be seated, I'll locate the doctor. He's expecting you."

They felt cheated. No one had said that the operation would take place so early. Yet, now that it was over, David realized that all of them, especially his mother, had been spared the pain of knowing that for two hours his father had been lying helpless, though unconscious surely and without pain, while surgeons cut into his head. Fearful visions suggested by scenes in movies and pictures in magazines and books swam before David's eyes. They had been just pictures then, but now as he connected them with his own father, active, strong, and close, they were horrible.

He put his arm around his mother and led her to a seat. She was weeping softly. Tears filled his own eyes, and he could not stop them.

It was here that the doctor with foreign accent came to them. He brought a chair and sat down, not to explain what had been done, but to express frank admiration for Dr. Osborne and those who had assisted him. He said with some hesitation that so far the operation had been successful. Mr. Williams' condition was satisfactory. The next several hours would tell—maybe twelve, maybe twenty-four. His reactions when the effects of anaesthesia wore off would be significant.

"Doctor," David asked, "could you tell us what the chances are for full recovery?"

"So! Young man, you want a percentage." The doctor shook his head. "We have no statistics. Never are two cases exactly the same. If you make me say figures, suppose we call it fifty per centum for physical recovery. Then we have something else again for that damage which the operation does not relieve. Sometimes— Must I say this?—sometimes there is left some paralysis or loss of function that cripples, and sometimes it is the mind.

"Only so much we can do," he said, hurrying on, knowing that his words were painful. "Some things we can do, and some he will do."

"You mean," Mrs. Williams asked, "you mean he will have to help himself?"

"More, lady, more. I mean more than that. It is not what he has to do, but what he can do. Is he a man of hope? That is not the same as being a man of strong will. And I think it is more. In my country, in the land I came from, I have seen good men destroyed, thousands of them. Men with strong will, I have seen them broken. In the pogroms, and in ghettos, and in concentration camp. But I have seen other people, who were weak and had no skill and nothing to fight back with but only hope. And somehow, I do not understand it, with hope some people will live when all we know of science and matter will say they should die.

"I am not sure," the doctor said. "Maybe hope is not the word I mean."

"I think I know." Mrs. Williams herself seemed to have gained courage from what the doctor had said. "I believe you mean faith."

"No. It is not faith, not faith like the Christians talk about. Hope is the word most near what I mean."

It was late that morning when they saw Mr. Williams. They were not prepared and the picture shocked them. David had gone downstairs to the cafeteria to bring up sandwiches. They were tired and uncomfortable. Other visitors had come and gone. They had seen a number of patients wheeled by in chairs or lying flat on tables with large rubber-tired wheels. So it was with David's father. An elevator door opened, and a male orderly in a white uniform called out for clearance as he pushed a table before him. A nurse walked close beside the patient, holding high a jar of amber-colored liquid from which a tube hung down and lost itself under the covers. As the group moved closer, Mrs. Williams sprang up with a little cry. Her husband's face—that part of it which showed beneath the bandages swathing his head—was very still. His skin, usually darker than David's, was ashy gray as though it were heavily dusted with white powder.

"Keep clear, please!" the orderly called again.

At four o'clock the kindly colored nurse, whom they had met the day before, returned to duty. She checked the charts and told them that the anesthetic had worn off, but that the patient was being kept asleep under heavy sedation. He was being fed intravenously, and his condition showed no change. In her opinion it was too early to expect any change. She presumed that he would be kept asleep under drugs until the following day. She suggested that the family go home, and Mrs. Williams surprised David by agreeing.

Just before they left, the nurse led Mrs. Williams into the critical ward to stand beside her husband's bed. David and Betty Jane followed them to the door but they did not enter. The nurse was very casual, exchanging greetings in her normal voice with those patients who were able to talk. Going to Mr. Williams' bed, she straightened the covers and smoothed the sheet; then smiling broadly, she took the hand of Mrs. Williams and laid it gently across the lips of the sleeping man.

"You know," she said, "I think he's going to be

all right. Seeing you and his kids, I figure he's got what it takes. Um-huhm! He's probably got it."

Mrs. Williams did not ask whether she meant hope or faith. Whichever it was, she too thought that her husband had it.

F O U R T E E N

Dr. Meyer, the doctor who had lived in ghettos, suffered in pogroms, and survived in concentration camps, decided that his patient was a man who
had hope. It took only a few days of observation and
and tests to determine that he had come through the
operation without loss of physical function.

The question of his mental and emotional condition was less easy to answer. The nurses observed
that he always seemed brighter when his wife was
present, and while he was in a critical condition, they
did not discourage her visits. When he was moved
upstairs to the regular ward, his wife became subject
to the limited visiting hours prescribed by hospital
regulation.

David was out of school three days, Wednesday
through Friday, and on Sunday he discussed with
his mother the advisability of his staying out to work

for the rest of the term. Mr. Crutchfield had already spoken to someone at the plant who had offered to hire the son of Ed Williams.

"Oh, no, David," Mrs. Williams protested. "We don't have to take you out of school. Not yet. I believe things will work out, and anyway we can make it somehow to the end of the semester."

Back in school on Monday, his homeroom teacher asked how his father was. When he told her that his father was still in the hospital and his condition still critical, she expressed her sympathy and promised him any help she could give. His other teachers remarked that they hoped he would be able to catch up on the work he had missed. In biology Miss Nichols told him to make up his experiments whenever he could in the lab. It would not have been difficult to copy someone's lab notes without doing the experiments, but she knew he would not take this easy way out.

At lunchtime he went to the cafeteria with Jeanette. When he told her that he must consider making changes in his plans, that he might have to go to work, she answered almost as his mother had. "Oh, David! Not now!" she said. "You're just getting adjusted. Why, this is no time to stop."

"But you don't understand," he said. "We really need the money."

All their savings had been put into the house, he explained, and they were still heavily in debt for the mortgage and the furniture, and now probably there'd be hospital and medical expenses. He wasn't sure, but he guessed that these last would be much more than any insurance payments would take care of. Jeanette listened closely but said nothing. Then he told her what Andy Crutchfield had suggested. She had been frowning, not so much in annoyance as in thought. Now she smiled.

David had thought for a long time that Jeanette's smile was something wonderful. Now, to his surprise she seemed delighted, and he did not understand why.

"Of course," she exclaimed. "That's wonderful. Why, you could stay on the night shift until the end of the semester and then go on days—or maybe you wouldn't even want to. I didn't know you meant working like that. I thought you were talking about dropping out altogether."

"But I was," David started to say. Then he stopped for he realized she had offered a solution. "That is, at first I was thinking about it the other way. I know

Mr. Crutchfield was figuring for a day job. He wouldn't know that my folks want me to go on through school as much as I do."

"No, he wouldn't, and the people at the plant wouldn't either, but that's all right."

"Every place my father has worked he's made good," David said proudly. "Last summer I worked in a shop where he used to work. It was rough, and the boss made trouble, but just the same, thinking about it now, they had a good feeling for my dad, and in their way they respected him."

"Everybody who knows Mr. Williams has to respect him," Jeanette agreed.

It was one week later that David started working at the Foundation plant. He was on the night shift, from four to midnight, and his starting pay was more than he had expected.

Mr. Crutchfield had not thoroughly approved of David's plan to remain in school. He thought that David already had more education than a man needed. He could not encompass David's dream of going to college and becoming a doctor. He thought that such ideas were for white people, or for very rich colored people, certainly not for anyone within his own circle of friends.

On the job David was classified as a laborer. This he had anticipated. His duties were those of a janitor. He worked with a clean-up crew, all of whom were colored. The lead man, Smith, was settled, past middle age, of the same general outlook as Andy Crutchfield. Steady, reliable, and hard-working, he sought the same qualities in his crew and complained that they were hard to find. He said his men were lazy and inefficient, and he was tired of having to run behind them. He was suspicious of David until he learned he was Ed Williams' boy. After that, he was kinder to him. He gave David more work, but he "ran behind him" less. "Running behind a man," David learned, was Smith's concept of supervision.

If David did not like some of the details of his job, he did enjoy the chance to work and to bring home a man's pay. His daily schedule was soon readjusted. To save time he usually drove to school and then to the plant. His seventh period, the last in the school day, was free on three days, and on the other two, he was in biology lab for the sixth and seventh periods. His homeroom teacher helped him to get excused for the three free days and released "when necessary" from the lab, but he was expected to keep up with his schoolwork.

It was not too hard to do. He found that if he paid closer attention in class and spent more of his study time in the library and less in the noisy study hall, or worse in the halls, he could still turn in his written work and make fairly good recitations.

Friday night at the end of his first week of work, he came home to find his mother waiting for him as usual. During the week she had been sleeping in the early part of the evening and then getting up at midnight to prepare her son's supper.

"I don't see how you're going to stand it, son," she said. "You're not getting your rest, and eating sandwiches and cold food all day!"

"Never mind, Mother." David tried to reassure her. "It's not so bad, and look at this!" He drew a check from his shirt pocket and proudly displayed it. "That's just for a couple of days. More than I made in three weeks at home. Guess I can lose a little sleep for money like that."

"But your health! No amount of money would be worth breaking down your health."

"It's only for a few weeks, Ma. Then school is out." He scrubbed his hands at the kitchen sink while his mother explained that she hadn't had time to make hot biscuits. She had overslept, she said; he would have store-bought bread tonight for supper.

"How's Pa?" David asked, taking his place at the chrome kitchen table.

"He says he's fine. Wants to come home. Really, he's looking better, and the nurses tell me they've never seen such a good recovery." From a container, she poured milk into a glass for David.

"How about the other?" David deliberately busied himself with the liver and onions before him.

"They say it's too early to know really." Mrs. Williams sat down opposite her son. She sighed heavily. "They say that even after he comes home we might not know for a long time."

David had not seen his father since Sunday. At that time he had been fully conscious, awake, and apparently not in pain, but he was clearly not right mentally. He had not recognized either his son or his daughter.

It had been hardest on Betty Jane. She had cried, and David had had to take her out of the room. He had tried to comfort her, telling her that Pa was improving and that they should be thankful he was even alive after all he had gone through. He repeated to her the encouraging words of the doctors and nurses, yet, even while he said them, his arm tightly around his sister, he was trying desperately to believe them himself.

Now as he asked about "the other," Mrs. Williams knew full well what he meant.

She went to the stove and turned up the burner under the coffee pot. She waited there, not speaking, and when the coffee was percolating, she poured herself a cup and started back to the table.

David's plate was nearly empty. He drank the last of the milk in his glass.

"I think I'll have some coffee," he said.

"It might keep you awake," she objected, but she poured him out a cup.

"I'll sleep tonight," David said, smiling.

Seated again, she went on as though she had not been interrupted. "He's just like a little child, maybe five or six or maybe seven years old. It's hard to see him like that. It's like you would have been about the time you were starting school. If only I had gotten him to go to the doctor when we first came to North Town!"

"Ma, you can't blame yourself."

"I'm not blaming myself, but if I had only known!"

"It might not have been any different."

"Just like a little boy! He's glad to see me. He frets when I have to leave him. He calls me 'Maummy,' and when he talks about going home, I can tell it's not this house he means. It's home down South, the farm he grew up on."

"Have you heard from any of the folks?"

"Oh! I forgot." She left the table and got a letter off a table in the front hall. "There's a letter from your Aunt Mattie. She's coming."

The letter from his father's only sister was post-marked Richmond, Virginia, where she lived with her family. Ed Williams was the youngest of six children. After growing up on a farm in Pocohantas County, the members of the family had scattered. Only one brother remained at home. All the others had moved farther north.

When David finished reading the letter, he checked the dates of Aunt Mattie's visit.

"Why, this means Aunt Mattie will be here Sunday," he said. "That's just day after tomorrow."

"Tomorrow, really." Mrs. Williams smiled at the prospect. "It's already Saturday."

"She'll be able to visit Pa Sunday afternoon." He glanced at the letter again. "Of course, she doesn't know," he added. "Will you tell her?"

"Mattie's always been so understanding. I'll tell her. I think she'll be able to help. She and your father were very close."

David yawned and stretched. It was time to go to bed. He knew he would have to mow the lawn in the morning. He usually washed the car on Saturday, too, and did other chores around the house.

"Sleep late tomorrow," his mother said, reading his mind. "You need the rest. Betty Jane and I can manage. You get to bed now."

David said good night. His mother kissed him, standing on tiptoe because he never seemed to bend down quite enough. He went to bed, thinking that tomorrow, after cutting the grass, he would drive over to see Jeanette.

At seven thirty in the morning Mrs. Williams heard her son get up. She met him in the hall with his eyes half open.

"Why didn't somebody call me?" he asked sleepily.

His mother led him back to his room, and when he lay down, she pulled the covers over him. Then she went to the kitchen to warm some milk for him, but when she returned with it, he was sound asleep. He slept until six in the evening.

The school year drew to a close. The week of final examinations was quickly upon David, who prepared for it as best he could. The seniors were getting ready for their graduation. David caught a glimpse of Mike O'Connor hurrying in his cap and gown to the auditorium, where the senior class was rehearsing for commencement exercises. Later that afternoon as he was leaving the building, Mike hailed him. The two girls he had been talking to looked crestfallen as he left them to catch up with David. He fell in step beside him, and they walked toward the high school parking lot where David had the car.

"I bet you're glad this is your last week," David said, "and when you get out of here you'll be gladder still."

"It might not be as rosy as you think," Mike replied. "I'm beginning to see why they call it commencement."

To David's question about which college he planned to go to, Mike shook his head.

"I don't think I'll be going. I can't be hanging around any longer. I'm going to work. Anyway, I can't afford to go to college."

"But you're an athlete, Mike," David protested. "There's always talk about athletic scholarships. What about help like that?"

"I guess I really could swing it, if I wanted to. It's the folks. I've got my basic education now, and my dad's been plugging along, but we're a big family, you know. I think I ought to help. I'll just get me a job."

David was surprised, but he did not indicate it. "Guess I know what you mean. I'm working now. Night shift at Foundation."

"You are? Say, I was thinking about coming out there. Maybe you can get me on. I'll do anything. You know I can work," Mike said earnestly.

"Sure, but . . ." David was about to say that he had only started and had no way to get anybody a job, especially a white boy.

"Look," Mike said, "what I need now is work. They say the best way to get a job is to know somebody, right? So I know you, Dave Williams, and we're already partners, remember?"

David remembered. He wished there were something more he could do to help Mike. Getting his own job had been perilous enough. Andy Crutchfield had been able to swing it only because of David's father.

Mike left him at the parking lot, calling as David drove away, "See what you can do for me!"

At the plant the day shift's time overlapped the night shift by an hour. In that hour David looked up Andy Crutchfield. Just maybe, he thought, the old man would use his influence because Mike was David's friend.

After assuring him that he was getting along fine at the plant and that his father was improving and would soon be home, David told him that a friend of his from Central was looking for a job. He asked whether Mr. Crutchfield would help him get placed.

"Good man, is he? High school graduate?" When David nodded, Andy Crutchfield seemed pleased. "I could use a man like that, might use him on my own crew, if he is willing and respectful."

That wasn't what David had intended. He wished that he had come right out and said it plainly at first. Then he wished that he had said nothing at all and that Mike had not asked him to help. All the men on Crutchfield's gang were colored. They were janitors. Their hopes for advancement were limited to chances for the job of lead man, like Crutchfield or Smith.

"Mr. Crutchfield," David explained, "I didn't mean on your crew. My friend is a white boy, but he's all right."

Mr. Crutchfield seemed to swell up with anger. "A white boy? A white boy? How come you got to look out for a white boy? Ain't you got troubles enough of your own? What he trying to do, get your job? I don't work no mixed crew. Don't want no white man with me. Besides any white boy can get his own job. Let him shift for hisself, I say. If he so poor he got to get you to help him, he trash anyway. I got nothing for a poor white man to do. Not nothing at all."

David started to back away.

"I say No!" Mr. Crutchfield was more and more vociferous. "I got nothing for him. I wouldn't give a poor white man a crust a bread if he starving or a drink of water if he burning in hell. I say No!" He moved suddenly toward David. "And I tell you another thing, you better get some sense and just cause you up North don't think you going look out for the white boys and they going look out for you. They ain't. I say No!"

David, shocked and embarrassed, hurried out of the room. He could hear Mr. Crutchfield scolding when he could no longer see him, and through the night he seemed to hear the echo of his storm as he swept shop floors and dusted offices and sloshed soapy water over the tile of toilet rooms, "I say No!"

On a bulletin board near the main gate was an announcement headed APPRENTICES. David had not read it before, but that night he looked it over carefully and made a note of what it said for Mike: "High school graduate or equivalent. Ages 17 to 24. Testing for aptitudes. Good character. Career-minded."

F I F T E E N

*E*d Williams was discharged from the hospital on June fifteenth. It was a Tuesday, the day of biology finals. David missed the examination, but he knew Miss Nichols would let him take the exam later.

His father had done well. He was no longer confined to bed, and his incisions had healed so clearly that only small scars would be left. But he still thought as a child, and the things he remembered were of his boyhood. His questions showed he was puzzled. So many things had to be repeated. He had been delighted when his sister Mattie appeared, but he talked with her about their brothers as children, and the school they had attended. The Crutchfields had visited him each Sunday, but he remembered Andy only from his life in Pocohantas County. He recalled nothing of his job at the Foundation.

If anyone tried to make him remember, he was hurt. At times he spoke in anger. More often he was silent.

So they brought him home. He rode in the front seat beside David, enjoying the bounce of the soft seat, watching David's movements, at one time reaching out his own hand to rest on the steering wheel and smiling as David turned the wheel and the car responded. Nothing he said showed that he had a hidden impulse to take the wheel. He had nothing to say to his wife or his sister or Betty Jane, who were riding in back.

When they turned into their driveway, he asked where they were. When told it was his home he would not believe it, and although he got out of the car, he did not want to go inside the house. His sister took one arm and David the other while Mrs. Williams went ahead to unlock the door.

He stumbled as he went up the steps. David could feel him trembling and see that his face was wet with perspiration. They talked to him, easing his fears. He was coming home, to his own house to live with his own family. He would have good home-cooking. He would sleep in his own bed. Soon he would be feeling fit as a fiddle.

They went through the motions, and they said the words, but they were not sure. They wanted very much to believe that within a matter of days or weeks or, even, months they would see him well again. They wanted to believe, but they were prepared to care for him if necessary for the rest of his life, and they were determined that no one should hurt or shame him.

After a few days they could tell that he was happy. He enjoyed his house. He would go through the rooms, sliding his slippered feet along the hardwood floors. On the warm summer days and in the evenings, he sat contentedly on the porch. Often he would look about him as he leaned on the porch rail or put out his hand to open the door, and would smile and say softly, "This my house."

He had no idea of the financial problems with which his family was struggling. The total of the insurance benefits and David's earnings fell far short of meeting their bills.

Mr. Taylor went over the accounts with Mrs. Williams. She wanted to return some of the furniture, for it showed little wear, but Mr. Taylor explained that this was no solution.

David often feared that Andy Crutchfield had

been right about his having to become the man of the house. He thought he might have to find a second job instead of going back to school in September. A promotion at the plant would increase his pay, but he had no chance of getting one.

Mike O'Connor had landed a job in the apprentice program, after David told him about it. In his interview and on his application, he had given David's name as reference. He refused to believe that David had not opened the way for him and used his influence in the personnel office. His expressions of thanks were effusive.

Now that school was out, Andy Crutchfield took steps to bring the son of his friend under his own supervision. David was transferred to the day-shift housekeeping crew.

"I want to help you really learn how to work," Andy Crutchfield told him. "That night-shift crowd is mostly no good—they don't even halfway do what little they supposed to do. I don't blame the lead man 'cause he got nothing to work with. We got good men on my staff, and you can learn. By 'n' by, you develop, learn how to handle yourself on the job, we look for a chance to slip you in on a shop job. You be a helper and learning your skills. You might make a first-rate machinist, same as your daddy was. He'll be proud of you."

There was no point in David's trying to explain what his father had wanted for him. He settled for the time being on making good on the day shift. His own hopes for the future were set aside for the hope of a miracle that would restore his father to full health. Nothing else was as important.

He saw Mike often. They ate together at noon and talked about school, about big league baseball, and about high school football. As Mike talked about football, the plays he had made, the coaching and the team organization at Central, David asked questions. He had not dreamed there were so many things about which he knew so little.

In South Town he and his friends had played football without any professional coaching. His school had not sponsored the team. The principal always said the game was too dangerous. The boys had played hard with substandard equipment and inadequate uniforms. Local merchants were solicited for help, and hats were passed at the games for contributions from the spectators. Broken bones were not infrequent, and though no one David knew had been fatally injured in a game, the threat had always been present.

Mike spoke of the strict rules enforced at Central. No player was allowed on the field, even for practice, without full equipment. That was for safety.

He showed with penciled diagrams how complicated patterns of strategy were established. Scrimmage, David learned, was not a hit-and-miss scramble but rather carefully planned drills when each player tried over and over again to perform his own special tasks in order that the team might function properly.

Mike proved to be a good instructor, and David was an eager and willing pupil. Mike brought him books and a football from home. David was fascinated to find that so much information about the game had been reduced to writing. Mike showed him things about handling a ball that he had never heard of. He had never even learned to kick a ball as Mike showed him it should be kicked.

Maybe it was all to the good, he decided, that he had been put off the field before he had had a chance to play that first day at Central. They would have only laughed him off later with his awkward movements and his ignorance of the standard rules. He thought of how ridiculous he must have looked without shoulder guards or a proper-fitting helmet. If the chance should come again— Well, at least he would know more than he had known before.

The hours were long at the plant and the weather was hot, but Mike and David were seldom too tired after work to meet at a playground near the plant for practice.

Some of the men at the plant, Andy Crutchfield among them, thought they were crazy. At the playground the baseball and tennis players stopped to watch the white boy and the colored boy working so earnestly at football. Often they were on the field until dark.

At home David's family settled into an uneasy routine. Mr. Williams seemed to have accepted his role of a sick person. He was passive, rather than cooperative. He spoke slowly; the pitch of his voice was high. There was in everything he said the plaint of a lonesome child. He did what he was told and ate what was put before him. When his sister Mattie returned reluctantly to her home in Richmond, Mr. Williams turned to Betty Jane to fill the place of her aunt. She had always loved her father and admired his strength. She loved him no less in his weakness.

"Pa's kind of asleep," she told her mother, "but I can see he's getting better."

He never seemed to understand about David, and often looked with wonder at this tall young man who called him Pa. He addressed him as David, never calling him son or boy as he had before, and although he watched him, going to work, driving the car, assuming the family responsibilities, he never questioned David. He showed little interest in anything outside his home.

Mrs. Williams was never to forget the way the change came.

One Saturday night when David was out on a date with Jeanette and Betty Jane was upstairs getting ready for bed, Mrs. Williams left her husband looking at television in the living room. Earlier in the evening she had baked a cake, and now she was ready to start icing it.

"Dear!" She heard him suddenly call in his natural voice. It frightened her. She started toward the door and saw him coming toward her. His face wore a puzzled frown.

"Dear!" he said again, speaking as he had not for months. "Have I been asleep?"

She went to him. She must not be excited, she told herself, but something inside of her said, "This **is your** husband."

"Darling!" The word burst from her lips, and then she cried "Oh, thank God!"

He put out his hand, and she took it, lifting it to her face, hardly daring to take him in her arms, fearful that something might happen, that she might be dreaming.

"What is it?" he asked. "What time is it?" He looked around the kitchen as she led him to a chair at the table.

"It's all right, dear. It's all right!" she said.

"But I feel funny. I must have been asleep. I don't remember going to sleep."

Mrs. Williams slipped to her knees beside her husband. "Darling! Ed dear! You've been sick. You've been away. Now you're back—I'm so glad! I'm so thankful!"

He started asking questions, a flood of questions about what had happened.

She was kneeling, trying to answer him and at the same time gasping her thanks. He stood suddenly and spoke. "Hi there, Betty Jane!"

His daughter in her nightgown came running toward him from the hall. She screamed her delight and jumped into his embrace. Mrs. Williams got to her feet. This was the miracle for which they had prayed. This was, at last, the time for which they had waited.

After the first realization of what had happened, Mr. Williams sat as if stunned. His wife was eager to telephone her friends. She knew she should try to locate David, but for a while she could not turn away. There was so much to say, so many things to explain. She told him how long he'd been sick, about the kind doctor, Mattie's visit, David's job, the medical expenses. She soon saw that of his recent experience he could only speak as though he had been dreaming.

Finally she went to the telephone. She did not reach David at the Lenoirs', but she excitedly told Mrs. Lenoir the news; then she called others. They came quickly—the Lenoirs, the Crutchfields, the Taylors, the Reverend Mr. Hayes with his wife, and other friends from the church. When at last David arrived with Jeanette, the house was full.

SIXTEEN

Mr. Williams had been home three and a half weeks when the fog lifted. He was told all that had happened since his collapse two months earlier. With his wife, he went back to the hospital and thanked the doctors and the nurses who had attended him, begging them to forgive him for having been so much trouble. Dr. Meyer was especially delighted and told Mrs. Williams that this case once again supported his theory about the power of certain people to survive.

The doctors examined Mr. Williams at the hospital and found no reason for him to be especially careful. They said he could go back to work and sent a full report to his employers. At the plant, however, it was not easy to convince the medical staff that his recovery was complete. Mr. Williams had to take intelligence tests, psychological tests, and manual dexterity tests. The process took days, but in the end he was allowed to return to his old job, handling the machines he understood so well.

He was very proud of David.

He showed his pride by the way he spoke of his son and by the way he looked at him. He showed it by the way he talked to him, man to man, recognizing that in the family's emergency David had not shirked.

They rode to and from the plant together, with David driving. Some afternoons Mr. Williams came over to the playground and watched Mike put David through his workouts. Other boys had joined them, and a squad was shaping up with Mike as its coach. They did not tackle or block, but they did run signals and practice passing. Mike, who had played at quarterback, was considered especially good at passing. He and David worked hard on pass plays.

"You've got the speed and the ranginess of a good end," he told David. "I never saw anybody at Central who had better hands for receiving. You've really got it, old man."

Although Ed Williams knew very little about football, he felt it would be exciting to see his son play for Central. He did not even consider the thought of David's not going back to school. In fact, he wanted David to leave his job early enough to have a few weeks of vacation before school opened. David thought it might be better for him to stay on as long as possible, for his weekly pay checks were helping to reduce the pile of bills. He was glad, however, when his father insisted that he stop work.

"You know, it's not that I want a vacation," he said, "but football practice starts the twentieth of August. I want to go out for the team. Mike sure has helped me and besides— I see a lot of things different now."

When it was known that David was leaving the plant to go back to school, most of his friends were pleased. The one person who was not was Andy Crutchfield. He thought that David should be grateful for the help his father had given him and that now, with plenty of book-learning in his head, he should turn about and help his father. He had already mentioned David to some of the shop bosses as a good prospect for special training. He told David he was foolish to give up a good job, and he blamed the white boy who was David's friend.

No one was happier than Jeanette. During the

summer she and David had not seen much of each other. His football practice had taken up most of his free time, and during the month of August, Jeanette and her sister had gone to visit relatives in New York. David had written to her, and she had responded that despite all the excitement of New York she was anxious to get back to North Town.

The first day of football practice, David sat with the crowd of prospective players which filled the first three or four rows of the stands. The coach told them what he expected of them.

"Some of you men played varsity last year," he said, "and some of you freshmen maybe never had on a football suit before. This you've got to understand. Nobody's got his job with the team sewed up. The men who play will be the ones we—the coaching staff, that is—think are the best, the best players and the best combinations for the time. This means —get it, now—this means if there's a fifteen-year-old freshie who can give more than a letter man in the position, the freshie will play it."

David liked that. He was not sure that he would be as good as Mike said he would, but he was determined to do his best. Now he could believe what the coach was saying. As he looked about him, he did not have his old, uneasy feeling. He no longer felt that the white boys were threatening him.

The coach complained that the turnout was small, though David estimated about a hundred were present. Some of last year's players, like Mike and Buck Taylor, had graduated. Others were still away on their vacations. Alonzo Wells was there, and when they left the stands, David hailed him, and they ran together to the gym.

"I hope some guy doesn't try to play me dirty," Alonzo said in the dressing room.

The remark dampened David's spirits. "This time I think I'll play it different," he told Alonzo. "I've been getting some coaching on the side. I've learned that whatever happens you don't just quit. You keep going forward, pushing, driving."

Alonzo nodded. "That's right," he said. "And you don't lose your head. That's something I ought to remember. Only I just can't stand nobody handing me no stuff. Looks like I always want to get even."

This time David got the correct equipment. The shoes they gave him were too small, but he exchanged them for another player's. He completed his laps easily, and as he circled the field, he thought

about the things he had learned which might be help-
ful the first day.

That evening when Mike phoned him, David
could report that the summer coaching had been a
big help. The first workout had gone well.

Practice became more strenuous in the days that
followed. The coach balanced verbal instruction
with demonstration and drill. David was carefully
watched. His mistakes were corrected, and occasionally he was complimented.

"Good! Good!" the coach would say. "Only you
don't have to drive your man down so hard. This is
just for practice."

The coaching staff recognized David's possibilities
as an end, and put him with others who were being
drilled in broken-field running, pass-receiving, and
the running of patterns. He had worked on patterns
with Mike, learning to run a planned course, counting the steps, changing directions, holding back until the right instant, and then putting on a burst of
speed.

Just before school started, the squads were organized. The "first thirty-three" was the squad of
experienced players. David was on the "second
thirty-three," with Alonzo who played halfback. He

called David's attention to the fact that Kirinski was a quarterback on the first squad.

"You remember Kirinski," Alonzo said. "That guy we had trouble with last year. Wouldn't pass the ball."

David had almost forgotten Kirinski's name and he was sorry that Alonzo had mentioned it. Here on the field in body-shocking contact he was finding himself thinking less and less about the color and race of those he played with. Alonzo insisted once again that the white boys played dirty against the colored.

"Maybe it just looks that way to you, Al," David said impatiently. "It's a rough game. I guess sometimes they think I'm trying to hurt them. You can't help being hurt sometimes, or hurting the other guy."

"Just watch it," Alonzo warned. "That's all I say. Just watch it!"

David was not looking for trouble. There were times when he recognized unnecessary roughness in a player, but he could not blame the roughness on race prejudice. He himself played a hard game of football.

With the opening of school David was even busier

than he had been at the end of the previous semester. Classes and football practice and homework left little time for anything else. He had still not been re-classified as college preparatory, but he had a good selection of classes. Occasionally he went to Jeanette's house to get help with his French, although they found many other things to talk about, too. At home his mother was anxious about his getting hurt in football, but his father was eager for David to make the team, and he promised to come to a game.

By the end of October, Central had played four games and won the first three. The fourth, against a high school in the state capital, they lost by a wide margin.

The next was to be Central's homecoming game against Eastlake, the conference champions of the year before. Eastlake always had heavy teams, and its players were known to be rough.

That week the coach talked to the first and second squads.

"We are not crying over spilt milk," he said, referring to the lost game. "And we're not making excuses. I don't blame anybody more than I do myself, but by the same measure I don't want it to happen again any more than anybody else does.

"Now we're going into high gear to get ready for Eastlake. Nobody's going to be spared. We're going to make changes and use some new plays to meet power with power and make up in skill whatever we may lack in weight."

It was the hardest-driving week of work David had ever known. Taken from the second squad and put with the first, he lined up at left end, ran plays, worked in scrimmage, and sat through hours after dark in skull practice sessions.

The team already had two good ends—the right end better than the left. At right was Fleming, a junior, six feet two and a hundred eighty pounds, fast and good at defense as well as offense. The left end was Anderson, a two hundred pounder, reliable and experienced but without the ability to shift quickly and change course to get out of trouble. The two made a good combination as alternate receivers.

As the coach had them practice, David would not be used for defense. On offense he would be a decoy, a lively threat as alternate pass receiver.

The first day that David worked with the first team Anderson called him aside to show him how to execute a cut. Mike had taught David during the summer, and he knew that the coach liked the way he did it. He watched as Anderson ran through it in a sort of slow motion.

"Try it now," Anderson said. "Just run through it beside me. You'll get it."

"But you're starting your pattern on the wrong foot," David tried to explain. "Look, if I go down here—"

Anderson drew back, his face twisted with scorn. "Wise guy, huh! Now you're showing me! Look, boy! I was playing football when you were down on the plantation picking cotton. You can't tell me how to do anything."

He had not spoken loud, but Fleming and one or two others heard him and frowned. "Take it easy, Anderson," one said.

David tried to put the incident out of his mind. After a while, he decided that Anderson was trying to help. The crack about the cotton fields was ugly, but, after all, it was not far from the truth.

On Friday they ran through their plays in signals without scrimmage and listened to a rundown on Eastlake's formations. An assistant coach read the names of the squad, and David was told to be ready to play. He drew a clean uniform, number 86, reminding himself that it still did not mean he would get in the game.

It was dark when he left the gym. Alonzo was leaving at the same time, and he walked with David to the bus stop.

"It's swell you're with the first string tomorrow," he said.

"Wish me luck," David replied. "I'll probably need it!"

The bus was crowded, and they stood close together as they rode. David was describing a play he had made during scrimmage when he had tackled and actually brought his man down, when he realized Alonzo was hardly listening.

"I guess you know," Alonzo said, " the quarterback won't be throwing anything good to you."

"Yeah, I guess you're right," David said. "I'll only be in there as a decoy drawing off the Eastlake defense. Maybe they won't throw to me at all."

Alonzo shook his head. "I didn't think you were that dumb," he said. "You know it's that Polack, Kirinski, playing quarter. Man, he'll be throwing the passes and he won't be about to let you get your hands on the ball."

David was annoyed. "Oh, Wells," he said. "You

always hang on to that old feeling that Kirinski has something against you. Maybe he did do you dirty one time but you sure squared that with him personally. Besides that was a year ago," he added.

The bus stopped to let off and take on passengers. Alonzo waited until it started again and the sound of the roaring motor muffled his words.

"It's not only Kirinski," he persisted. "It's just about all of them. What about Anderson? Didn't you have trouble with him?"

"That wasn't trouble," David said. "He was trying to show me how to execute. I guess he got hot because I wouldn't listen to him."

"Yeah," Alonzo muttered, "that's about the way I heard it. So you got the regular first-string men down on you, and you think you're going to get a chance? Look man, let's face it. Maybe the coach gives out with all that color-don't-make-no-difference business. Maybe he wants to bring you along, but the regulars don't feel the same way. You're new on the team, the quarterback don't like you, and you're black. That's three strikes, anyway you count it. You'll see."

Once home, David was feeling so depressed after his talk with Lonzo that he wanted to call Jeanette. But instead, he called Mike who assured him that he'd get a chance to play and wished him good luck. He said he'd be on the bench, watching.

David did not call Jeanette, for she called him. Happy to know that he would be in uniform, she asked his number. She recognized the concern in his voice and advised him to relax, saying that if he got into the game he would know what to do and if they did not play him this time there would be other chances.

"It's not that exactly," he said. Then he told her about the conversation with Alonzo.

For a while she scolded him. Alonzo, she said, carried a chip on his shoulder. He was suspicious and mean. It was really Alonzo who was prejudiced; with his twisted thinking, he looked for evil.

"Why, I know some of the boys on the team," she said, "and I know they wouldn't be so stupid and vicious as to fail to use a good player simply because of color prejudice. David, you just forget what Alonzo Wells says. Nobody's working against you or Alonzo."

After he left the phone, David told his mother that Jeanette really had a lot of sense.

The game between Central and Eastlake was described in the local newspaper as the classic contest between a good heavy team with power and a good light team with speed.

Saturday the weather was perfect for football, cold with a promise of snow in the air. It was bright and clear in the morning, but shortly after midday, clouds shut out the sun. The game was to be played in the city's Memorial Park, and at the kickoff, all twelve thousand seats were filled. Station WNOR carried the broadcast.

Choosing to receive, Eastlake made four first downs without losing the ball. Shifting the line first to right and then to left and keeping Central off balance, they went over the goal line after four minutes of play. They missed the place kick, and the score held at 6-0 at the end of the quarter, with Eastlake on Central's eight-yard line. At the beginning of the second quarter, Eastlake threw a pass into the end zone, scoring their second touchdown of the game. This time they made their conversion with a place kick, and the score stood 13-0 for the rest of the half. Eastlake tried passing again, but Central was ready for them.

In the locker room between halves, the coach made the men know that the game was by no means lost. Central had plenty of stuff left, he insisted, and when the team ran out on the field at the sound of the horn for the second half, David had no doubt that his big chance would be coming up soon. He was in perfect physical condition, but he was tense. In the pit of his stomach, he felt empty. The coach motioned him to take a place near him on the bench. He moved over and waited. Watching with the others, his own body moving with the plays, he forgot his tenseness and his emptiness. He felt as if he were already in the game.

Five minutes of the third quarter had gone by when Central recovered the ball, following a fumble by Eastlake on its own forty-yard line. It was then that Coach Henderson pulled six men off the field, and David was sent in to replace Anderson at left end. Fleming was at right end; Kirinski was at quarterback. In the huddle, Kirinski called the play. David was to run his pattern, Kirinski to pass, Fleming to receive. The signals were called; the ball was snapped. David ran straight ahead, then left three steps and right three steps, and then down the field with only a glance back to see the ball sailing toward Fleming. Another glance, and he saw the safety man on top of Fleming bat the ball from his outstretched hands. David had done his part as a decoy. Two of Eastlake's men had gone for him.

"This we got to make good," Kirinski said in the huddle. He called for a short pass, and David knew he was to run a side-line post. At the signal, he ran his pattern and Fleming ran his. The ball never came. Kirinski fumbled, and the ball got away from him. There was a pile up, but when it was cleared, a Central halfback had possession. For the third down, Kirinski called for repetition of the long pass play, the ball to go to Fleming, with David running as decoy and alternate pass receiver.

Again David took his place. Signals were called, and at the snap of the ball he started down the field, running his diagonals at three-quarter speed. He saw Eastlake's safety man close on Fleming's heels. Then he saw the ball arch high in the air and come over his own path, but so far ahead! His eyes fixed on the ball, he increased his speed. He had to be there before it came down. He was gaining, and then his hands went up together, and at last his fingers touched the ball, and he was pulling it in and tucking it into the tight crevice between his arm and his ribs. His speed did not slacken. He had the happy sensation of flying, not knowing that his feet touched ground. He saw the goal posts ahead, and the bar above as though they were moving toward him, and then he was running across diagonal lines and knew he was in the end zone.

When Kirinski reached him, he slapped David enthusiastically on the back. "Good going, Williams!" He grinned. "I knew you could make it!"

Central converted with a neat place kick, making the score 13 to 7 as the timekeeper's gun fired to signal the end of the quarter.

In the fourth quarter when Central got the ball, David was again sent in on offensive. Kirinski kept the game open with passing, double reverses, and all the fancy plays Central had developed to use against the heavier team. They went on to another touchdown, this time with Fleming carrying. They made the conversion, running the score to 14-13, and the stands went wild.

As David ran off the field, after the second touchdown, he saw Mike jumping up and down on the coach's bench with excitement. He grabbed David, hugged him, and pounded his back.

"Baby," he shouted, "you did it! You did it! I saw you making those patterns. It was beautiful. I told you all the time. I told you!"

Buck Taylor was there, too; less noisy, he shook

David's hand. "You're all right, Williams," he said heartily. "They've been telling me about you. You're all right."

Alonzo Wells was waiting with a blanket for David. As he wrapped it around him and led him to a seat on the bench, he said softly, "You know Kirinski never meant you to get that pass. He thought he was throwing the ball away. You fooled him, but good!"

Sitting shapeless in his blanket on the side lines, in the final minutes of the game, David for the first time thought about the people in the stands. Now he heard their cheers. He turned and looked up at the crowd. The playing field was in shadow but the late afternoon sun had broken through the clouds, lighting a row of American flags silhouetted against the sky. David knew that his father was there, and Jeanette. Principal Hart would be in the crowd, and his teachers. Yes, and Jimmy Hines and his unhappy friends. He could not pick out the faces, white or black or brown, but he knew they were all there. This, he thought, was like America.

As he turned back toward the playing field, a great joy came over him. He knew he was part of Central's team. He did not think of himself as a Negro but as a student of North Central High School who had shared with others in gaining a hard-fought victory.

He was never to forget that scene.

SEVENTEEN

After the excitement of the game, the wild cheering of the spectators, the victorious rush of the team, and the noisy confusion of the showers and the locker room, David's ride homeward with his father was very quiet.

Mr. Williams had brought the car from the parking lot to the exit nearest the team's quarters under the stands. He watched as the players came out in bursts of twos and threes, calling final farewells before going their several ways.

David came out with such a group. He opened the car door and called back, "See you Monday, Kirinski!" But Mr. Williams was already in the passenger's seat, so David went around to the other side.

"Hi, Dad!" he said. "So you saw a real football game!"

"I sure did," his father said, reaching over to

slap David on the knee. "Boy, your ma should've been here. Or maybe it was better she wasn't here. I guess she would have busted wide open with her pride. I 'most did myself."

David maneuvered the car through the heavy traffic, content to let his father talk.

"I knew when you first ran out there something was going to happen."

"But, Pa," David objected, "you got to remember it was all the team, not just me."

"Yeah, I know that," Mr. Williams agreed. "But man alive! Look like I knew you'd make good—and when you was splitting down there and the ball was going over your head—I knew you'd make it, but I prayed anyway. Yes, sir! I jumped up and hollered, 'God help him!' I said it right out loud—'God help him!' "

David laughed. "Well, I guess that was what gave me that extra boost—'cause I mighty near didn't get there."

"But you know when I was praying I wasn't worried," his father insisted. "I just knew you'd make it!"

"You can't always be sure, Pa," David replied. "There's so much more goes into it—all the other players and then you have the other team, too."

"But irregardless to all that, some things you know—" Pa stopped for a minute. "It's like seeing you grow up and taking your place on your school team—and like even taking over the driving while your pa just sits up and rides."

"I like to drive, Pa. Hope I don't scare you too much."

"You don't," Mr. Williams said emphatically. "You're a good driver, but just the same I feel like I got to help you. Sometimes I most shove my foot through the floor helping you put on brakes. When you get your own home and you have a son nearly grown and driving for you, you'll see what I mean." Then he added, "Or maybe it will be your private plane, and your boy will be piloting you to visit the old folks at home."

"Wait, Pa! Me with a plane of my own?"

"Why not? When I was your age I guess my pa didn't imagine me having my own car, and I guess there are as many planes now as there were cars in those days. Down around our section, folks were still using wagons and plowing with mules almost altogether. Why, I can remember the first car I ever rode in.

"First time I ever rode in one I was going to the old Boydton Institute. It was a church school where they used to have nothing but missionary teachers. It was while I was going there they had the first colored principal, man named Dr. Morris. I was on my way to school one morning when his son came along, driving the principal's car. His name was Satchel. He already had a load of boys on board, but he stopped and I got on, too. I remember Andy Crutchfield's brother was one of them."

David tried to imagine the thrill for a country boy of riding in a car for the first time.

"That day in chapel," Mr. Williams went on, "the principal, this Dr. Morris, talked about what we could do when we grew up. He was a good man, and all the people thought a lot of him. He said that we could do anything we wanted to, with God's help. He said we could be anything we wanted to be. I'll never forget how I felt. He asked us to decide what we wanted to do with ourselves, and then he called on us to stand up when we'd made up our minds.

"I decided I would be a mechanic, and that I would have my own automobile, and I stood right up and looked at him. I think I was in third grade, though I was about twelve years old. I was way down front when I stood up, and somebody laughed, but I didn't turn around.

"Then Dr. Morris prayed that God would bless our lives, and, say, if ever I felt like a prayer went home, that one did. When it was over, I looked around and I was the only one standing, but I knew from then on, I was going to be a mechanic, and a good one. That Dr. Morris was a fine man."

David slowed down the car for the left turn into Twenty-fourth Street. He waited for the traffic to pass. He knew that his father had achieved his boyhood ambition. Maybe the praying of the principal had helped. He saw a break in the line of cars, and he swiftly crossed the street.

"That's the way I used to feel about being a doctor, Pa," he said.

"What do you mean 'used to'?" Mr. Williams asked.

"Well, I know now that it's terribly expensive, and it's a lot harder and takes a lot more time than I used to figure."

"O.K., so it won't be easy. It wasn't easy for us to leave down South and get started here—and it wasn't easy for you to get on the team and make that touchdown today. It costs more, and it's harder to get, but if God spares you and gives you health, I don't see any reason why you can't make it. I promise you, I'll do my part."

David swung the car in from the street and stopped in the driveway. For a minute Mr. Williams did not move. David cut the motor and waited.

His father spoke again. "Dr. Williams." He was looking at David, not speaking to him really, just thinking out loud. "David Andrew Williams, M.D."

ABOUT THE AUTHOR

Lorenz Graham was born in New Orleans, Louisiana. He was graduated from high school in Seattle, Washington, and studied at the University of Washington. During his third year at the University of California, Los Angeles, he traveled to Africa to teach in a mission school.

Mr. Graham was graduated from the Virginia Union University and worked as an education officer with the Civilian Conservation Corps. He has studied at the New York School of Social Work and at Columbia University. He now lives in Los Angeles where he is a probation officer.

The Thomas Alva Edison Foundation awarded Mr. Graham a special citation for his adaptation of *The Ten Commandments*. He has also received the Follett Award and the Child Study Association of America Award for his novel *South Town*.